My thanks go to all the people at FASA who work so hard to keep the Sixth World going. Mike Mulvihill and Rob Boyle for keeping me in the Shadowrun® game, and Donna Ippolito for reminding me to do things like write my acknowledgments *before* I turn in the book.

The process of telling a story isn't really complete until the story interacts with an audience, who take it and make it their own. I've been privileged to tell stories to a great audience—the fans of Shadowrun®—in three previous novels and much game product. I appreciate all the encouragement and feedback they have given me. Without them, the world of Shadowrun® wouldn't be half as interesting as it is. This one's for them.

NORTH

CIRCA 2061

TSIMSHIAN
ATHABASKAN COUNCIL
ALGONKIAN-MANITOO COUNCIL

Edmonton

Saskatoon

Vancouver
Calgary

SALISH-SHIDHE COUNCIL

Regina

Seattle
Winnipeg

Pacific Ocean

Spokane

Helena
SIOUX NATION

Bismarck
Fargo
Duluth

Butte

Portland
Salem

Billings

St. Paul
Minneapolis

TIR TAIRNGIRE

Boise

Sheridan

Rapid City

Idaho Falls

Sioux Falls

Eureka

Salt Lake City

Cheyenne

Des Moines

Reno
Provo

Boulder
Denver

Omaha

San Francisco

Colorado Springs

Kansas City

CALIFORNIA FREE STATE
UTE NATION

Las Vegas

Pueblo

Topeka

Wichita

Bakersfield

PUEBLO CORPORATE COUNCIL

Santa Barbara
Los Angeles

Santa Fe

Amarillo

Tulsa

Albuquerque

Oklahoma City

San Diego

Little Rock

Tijuana
Phoenix

Tucson
Roswell

Ft. Worth
Dallas

El Paso
San Angelo

Shreveport

Pacific Ocean

Austin
Houston

Chihuahua
San Antonio

AZTLAN
Corpus Christi

Monterrey

La Paz
Culiacan

Durango
Ciudad Victoria

AMERICA

CIRCA 2061

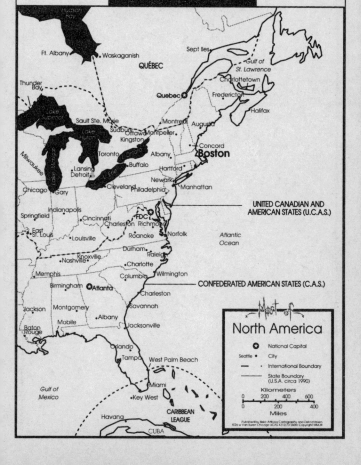

Ft. Albany • Waskaganish

QUÉBEC

Sept Iles

Hudson Bay

Gulf of St. Lawrence

Thunder Bay

Lake Superior

Quebec ○

Charlottetown

Fredericton

Sault Ste. Marie

Sudbury Ottawa Montpelier Augusta

Kingston

Concord

Milwaukee

Lake Michigan

Lake Huron

Toronto Orillia Albany **Boston**

Halifax

Lansing

Detroit

Lake Erie

Buffalo

Hartford

Chicago Gary

Cleveland Philadelphia

Newark

Manhattan

Springfield

Indianapolis

Cincinnati

FDC

Richmond

UNITED CANADIAN AND
AMERICAN STATES (U.C.A.S.)

East St. Louis

Louisville

Charleston

Roanoke

Norfolk

Atlantic Ocean

Memphis

Knoxville

Nashville

Durham

Raleigh

Birmingham ◎ Atlanta

Charlotte

Columbia

Wilmington

CONFEDERATED AMERICAN STATES (C.A.S.)

Jackson Montgomery

Charleston

Albany

Savannah

Baton Rouge

Mobile

Jacksonville

Orlando

Gulf of Mexico

Tampa

West Palm Beach

Miami

• Key West

Havana

CARIBBEAN LEAGUE

CUBA

North America

✪	National Capital
Seattle •	City
▬ ·	International Boundary
___	State Boundary (U.S.A. circa 1990)

Kilometers
0 — 200 — 400 — 600
Miles
0 — 200 — 400

Published by Belo Artizans Cartography and Geocarissen
RQEs w Van Buren Chicago ùCAS K312173 56000 Copyright MM.III

1

Racing through the blackness of cyberspace. Dodging IC programs of glowing neon, digital nightmares from the hellish depths of some programmer's psyche that could rip out his forebrain. Feeling the rush of adrenaline and heat in his meat body while his cyberself stayed cool and smooth as glass and chrome.

That's what Roy Kilaro thought he should be doing.

Using his superior programming and decking skills to break into the heavily guarded data-fortresses of rival corporations, stealing away their secrets while thumbing his nose at the other deckers who tried to stop him. The megacorps were waging a secret war in the hidden recesses of virtual reality, and Roy Kilaro should be out there on the front lines.

He should be a Seraphim, a member of Cross Applied Technologies' elite black ops team—not sitting in the Québec office sifting through data-traffic reports and system logs for CATco's New England facilities. He should be running the Matrix, where he belonged, instead of trapped in a maze of cubicles that seemed to go on forever.

If there is a hell, it probably has a lot of cubicles in it, Roy thought glumly as he watched the data scrolling past. This was such mindless work. He could just as easily have written a program to scan through the activity logs for unusual data or variations in the normal patterns. In fact, he'd recommended it to his boss, and got assigned more fact-checking for his trouble. Cross Technologies was a leader in software development, but it still wanted the "human touch"—which Roy translated as having some human to blame if anything went wrong.

To keep his mind focused, he imagined that the data had been purloined from some other corporate system, that he was sifting it for information with street value, something that would profit the company. It helped to take the edge off the boredom, but just barely.

The thought made him realize how stiff he felt, and he sat back in his ergonomic chair to stretch. He tended to work deep when online, sometimes forgetting about the needs of the flesh. He arched his back to relieve the strain, then put the data-stream on pause while he massaged his neck and rolled his head from side to side. When he settled back to work, the chair's temprafoam cushioning adjusted automatically to the contours of his body.

Roy checked to make sure he hadn't disturbed the fiber-optic cable snugged into the socket behind his right ear. The cable had caught on the arm of the chair, and he adjusted it. The cable was his lifeline, feeding data directly into his brain.

Resume, he thought silently to the terminal he was jacked into. The data began to stream past once more, and his brain sifted through it like sand trickling through his fingers or someone panning for gold in a muddy river. On and on and on until he thought he would scream with boredom. Then he hit a bump. It was like finding a hard object in the soft sand or catching a gleam of gold in the mud.

Wait a minute, he thought. What was *that*?

He zoomed in on the activity log from the corp's Merrimack Valley research facility in southern New Hampshire. With a flicker of thought, he cross-checked the reference, bringing up a data-window before his field of vision. It gave him a view of the building's exterior and other pertinent information.

Roy remembered the buy-out in which Cross had acquired the small biotech facility two years ago. The deal had turned into a fierce bidding war with Novatech before the rival corp mysteriously bowed out. The panicked owners lowered the price, and Cross bought them out for a song. Roy wasn't the only one who'd suspected that shadow operations had made that happen.

The MV facility was under the direction of the company's Bio-Medical Division out of Boston, so the data would already have passed their inspection. Someone who wasn't too sharp must have missed the anomaly.

Roy checked the log entries again. There it was— just a slight deviation, nothing too significant. It was like one of those occasional glitches in the telecom system, where the worst that happened was some voice and vidmail getting lost. This looked more deliberate, more precise. Someone had intentionally deleted and altered parts of the outgoing message log.

More than likely someone having an affair, Roy thought. Or maybe some lonely cubicle rat logging on to one of those virtual sex hosts where you could play with "digital dolls" that looked and felt like the real thing but acted like something out of an adolescent programmer's wet dreams. He should simply flag the file and pass it on to the higher-ups in Information Systems, who would send a routine notice to the employee involved. But something told Roy to keep looking. If nothing else, it was a break in the monotony, an excuse not to dive back into the endless sea of data that threatened to drown him.

He checked the logs again, and this time noticed that some sections were missing. With a thought to his terminal, he ran some pattern-matching algorithms.

Nothing.

It still looked like merely a random glitch in the system, but Roy wondered if whoever had made the changes was extra careful to make it *look* random. Flashing a command across the network at light-speed, he called up some additional data about the Merrimack Valley facility. Scanning through it, he noticed that the place was slated to get some extra security personnel. When he checked the facility's maintenance schedule, he sat back and smiled.

It was Christmastime, and he had some vacation days coming. Maybe he could get away for a few days, check things out down at the MV facility, and see something of the Boston metroplex while he was at it. He knew all the right channels to send his request through, which managers were likely to simply rubber-stamp routine documents that passed through their systems. Within the hour, his request to cross-train with the Information Systems Department by handling routine maintenance and systems checks of the corp's Boston-area facilities was approved.

He copied the relevant data from the logs and downloaded it onto the optical chips nestled in the back of his skull near his brainstem, where he could access the information at will. Then he returned to scanning through the logs, his mood considerably lightened. It would probably all turn out to be smoke and no fire, but he could make an adventure of it, pretend he was involved in some fantastic intrigue like they showed on the trideo. If there were time, he'd try to hit one or two Boston nightspots.

He'd heard that Boston had some good ones.

2

It was a typical busy night at the Avalon, one of Boston's hottest dance clubs. The floor was packed to the max with people writhing to the primal beat blasting from the speakers. Pulsating lights flashed from the ceiling, and a haze of smoke hovered over the dance floor like an artificial fog. A curved bar was set above the dance floor along one side of the room, and it too was crowded with people. There were also several tiers filled with small tables and booths where people could sit, drink, and watch the dance floor below.

Dan Otabi looked around nervously as his eyes adjusted to the dark. It was too bad he couldn't afford Zeiss replacements, the deep emerald-green ones with gold flecks and light amplification powerful enough to see by night as well as by day. Eyes like Derek Hunt had in *Shadowbreakers*. Eyes that could stare down any man and melt the heart of any woman. Eyes like Dan had when he *was* Derek Hunt, fearless corporate operative working in the deepest shadows of the metroplex. He touched the jack behind his ear, wishing he were Derek Hunt right then, or anyone else for that matter—the very wish that had brought him to the Avalon.

He'd dressed for the occasion, trying to imitate the kind of outfits people wore in the sims, but he still felt woefully out of place. People took him in from his short-cropped dark hair to his synthleather boots and dismissed him with a shrug—or less—before turning back to their own pursuits. He glanced around, anxiously looking for the man he'd come to meet, and saw him seated in a booth two tiers above the sunken dance floor. There was an electric moment of recognition, but Dan tried to stay as cool and calm as his contact.

He picked his way through the crowd toward the stairs, apologizing once when he bumped into an ork. Barrel-chested and bulging with muscle, the big meta-human towered half a meter over Dan's head and didn't even bother to stop. His violet-haired companion, dressed in nothing but a strategically applied spattering of body-latex and glitter, hurried to keep up with him.

Dan pushed his way to the stairs, never taking his eyes off the man in the booth as he climbed. The man, on the other hand, seemed oblivious to Dan's presence as he gazed down idly at the dance floor. It was only when Dan finally stood in front of the booth that the man acknowledged him. Once again, Dan wished for Derek Hunt's steel-hard eyes.

The man was human, an Anglo. His greasy brown hair was drawn back from his face into a stubby little ponytail at the nape of his neck. It looked like he hadn't shaved for several days, but the stubble couldn't hide the puckered, reddish line of a scar on his chin. Dan thought it looked like a slash from a knife or a broken bottle. He also figured the man's muddy brown eyes had to be natural because no one would have eyes like that if he could help it. The man wore a battered leather jacket over a heavy black T-shirt and a couple of silver rings on each hand. He looked Dan over with studied disinterest, and Dan didn't quite know whether to bow or extend his hand, so he just stood there.

"You must be Mr. Johnson," the man said, just loud enough to be heard over the blaring music. He gave a faint smile to say that he didn't believe that Johnson was Dan's real name. "Have a seat."

Dan slid gingerly into the booth, suddenly torn between getting what he'd come for and the urge to get the hell out of there. He still hadn't taken his eyes off his contact.

"Did you bring the money?" the man asked abruptly, and Dan nodded.

"Let's see it."

Dan fished a slim plastic rod from his pocket and held it up. The man reached for it, but Dan snatched his hand away, surprised at his own boldness.

"First I want to see . . . the merchandise," he said, thinking about how Derek Hunt handled himself in the *Shadows of Seattle* sim. He continued to stare the man down, no matter how much he wanted to look away. His contact reached into his jacket and pulled out a black plastic case, which he set on the table. Dan could see a flat optical chip through the transparent lid. He bent closer to read some tiny print.

"That's it," the man said, "the Cal-hot edition of *Shadowbreakers VII*. Complete and uncut."

Dan read the title etched onto the chip and looked

up in awe. "You mean with Winona Flying-Horse and, and . . . everything? The sauna scenes and . . ."

"Everything," the chip dealer said with a slow, wolfish smile.

Dan almost laughed out loud at the thought. He had to have it. He started to reach for the case, but the man grabbed his wrist. He picked up the chip-case with his free hand.

"Uh-uh, not until I get the money," he said. "Oh, and the price has gone up."

"Wh-what?" Dan protested. They'd already negotiated the price.

The man shrugged. "Supply and demand. This baby is a hot property." He shook the chip-case for emphasis. "Especially since those explicit pics of Winnie 'mysteriously' hit the Matrix. You want a taste of the real thing—better than the real thing—then you gotta pay. You got a problem with that, take it up with the complaint department."

He nodded toward the top of the stairs. Dan glanced over and saw the same ork he'd bumped into earlier. He was leaning casually against the wall, his dusky skin almost blending into the shadows. His bald head was scarred, and two small tusks protruded over his upper lip. He slowly cracked his knuckles, a reminder that he could snap Dan in two like a twig.

Dan turned back to the dealer. "How much?" he asked.

"Five hundred nuyen."

"But you said three hundred fifty," Dan burst out.

"You want the goods, it's five hundred. Of course, if all you want is regular simsense, you can rent this one at Sim-Station for twenty nuyen. They're all kid-safe and everything."

The man sat back with a mocking smile. Like Dan was going to waste his time with that drek. He'd run those kinds of sims. They were like trideo compared to the simsense that came out of California Free State. The Cal sims didn't leave anything out; you got to feel it all. It was like living out your greatest fantasies in the safety of your own head. He'd heard that the producers and programmers even tweaked the chip's signals to "enhance" the experience and make them seem even realer than real life. Once Dan had gotten a taste of them, he couldn't get enough. Unfortunately, so-called "California-hot" chips were illegal in the United Canadian American States. They couldn't be imported or sold, which was why he was here trying to score.

"It's not BTL, right?" he asked.

"No way, chummer. This is quality merchandise. We're not talking about brain-burners here. This is just entertainment. The best."

BTL chips—short for "better than life"—went even further than Cal-hots. Dan knew about them, of course, but he was honestly afraid of them. BTLs messed with a chip's sim-signals to give users an experience simply not possible in real life. You didn't even have to put up with some flimsy storyline—the BTLs offered pure sensation.

Dan had heard that jacking a BTL was pure bliss, direct stimulation of the brain's pleasure centers. The experience was so intense that most BTL junkies didn't last very long. They stopped caring about anything except chipping until it got so bad they wouldn't jack out even to eat or use the drekker. Of course, the vendors didn't want to lose their customers too quickly, so the chips were tweaked to burn out after a time, keeping the buyers coming back for more.

Sooner or later, though, the chipheads would figure out how to override the cut-out on the chip. They would jack in and never come back. They'd starve to death, lying in their own filth, until somebody found them and called the police. That was if the organ-leggers and ghouls didn't get there first and turn the bodies into spare parts for the illegal organ-banks or, worse yet, a quick meal.

Dan shuddered at the thought, but told himself this wasn't BTL. He wasn't a junkie. It was just some harmless fun, a way to relieve the stress of work. It wasn't his fault the UCAS had declared California simchips illegal. He wasn't hurting anyone.

"All right," he said, tearing his eyes away from the chip-case for a moment. "I guess I . . ." He stopped in mid-sentence when he noticed that the man wasn't looking at him anymore. He was staring down onto the dance floor with an expression like horrified fascination. He glanced at Dan, back at the dance floor, then back at Dan.

"Stay here," he said, standing up and slipping the case into his jacket. He strode toward the stairs as Dan watched in amazement. The man brushed past the big ork, who called out after him as he raced down the stairs. The music was too loud for Dan to hear what the ork said. He looked down at the dance floor, wondering what the man had seen that made him jump up so suddenly. To Dan, it was just a mass of mostly human people, with a sprinkling of elves, orks, and trolls.

Then he had a terrible thought. The police! What if the man had spotted an undercover cop or something downstairs? Or maybe he'd decided to sell the chip to someone who wouldn't object to the price. When Dan glanced at the stairs, the ork was still there. He looked torn, like he wasn't sure whether to go after the other guy or walk over to Dan.

Dan didn't plan to wait around to find out which. He jumped up and headed for the stairs on the other side of the tier, weaving around the people who blocked his path.

He bumped into a dark-haired woman in a synthleather jumpsuit that clung to her curves like Vita Revak's in the classic *Rambo XX* sim. The open neck showed off an expanse of creamy flesh and a sprinkling of freckles. She had long dark hair, a lovely face, and a dazzling smile.

"Hey, honey, what's your hurry?" she asked. Dan looked over his shoulder and saw the ork coming closer as he pushed through the crowd.

"Can I get you a drink or something?" she asked.

Any other night, that would have been a fantasy come true, but tonight Dan's only thought was getting away. He stammered an apology and bolted past her down the stairs. When he reached the floor, he began to shoulder his way through the crowd, ignoring the angry protests and shoves. The only thing that mattered was getting out the front door.

Hammer stood at the top of the stairs and watched Dan Otabi get away.

"Frag," he said under his breath as Trouble came up to him. She was upset that their mark had gotten away.

"What the hell happened?" Trouble asked.

"I dunno," Boom said. "Talon saw something."

She scanned the dance floor, looking for Talon, then spotted him on the other side of the room. "Over there," she said, already starting down the stairs to find out what was going on.

The man who'd been talking to Dan Otabi had vanished. In his place was someone who was younger, cleaner, and better-looking. He was standing on the edge of the dance floor, staring out into the mass of people, his eyes slightly unfocused. Most of the club-goers probably thought he was drunk or stoned out, neither of which was a rarity in the Avalon. His chummers knew better, of course. Talon was a mage, with perceptions beyond those of mundanes.

When they reached his side, Trouble saw that he was crying, the tears running unheeded down his cheeks as his eyes searched the room.

She had worked the shadows long enough to know you didn't interfere with a mage doing his thing, but the look on his face had her worried. She grabbed Talon's shoulder and shook him.

"Talon! What is it? Did you see something?"

He turned his tear-streaked face toward her. "It was Jase," he said over the din. "I saw him. Out there on the dance floor."

His words sent a shiver through her body, but Trouble shook it off. "Jase is dead," she said, as gently as possible amid the uproar. "He's been dead for fifteen years."

Talon nodded. "I know, but I saw him, Trouble. He was here. I'm sure of it."

3

"Let me get this straight," Boom said. "Are you telling me we fragged up a meet that took weeks to set up and maybe lost our only real window on the target site because you thought you saw somebody who looked like Jason Vale in the club tonight?"

"I don't *think* I saw him, Boom," Talon said. "I did see him. He was right there, across the dance floor, as plain to me as you are right now."

Trouble smiled to herself. Boom was a troll, a mass of muscle nearly three meters tall. With his lumpy, greenish skin, ram-like horns, protruding tusks, and the garish Hawai'ian shirts he favored, he stood out in a crowd a lot more than any human ever could.

Despite appearances, he was actually a big part of the "brains" behind their outfit. Everyone acknowledged Talon's natural leadership abilities, but Boom was the best when it came to planning. He also had the connections and knew all the right people for getting them to work in the shadows. Anything that threatened the team's reputation, or his, was a concern.

"I told Otabi to stay where he was," Talon said, somewhat lamely. "I didn't think he would bolt like a jackrabbit."

"You didn't think, period," Boom said. "Taking off in the middle of a meet like that—what did you expect him to do?"

"It doesn't really matter," Trouble said, giving Boom's massive arm a reassuring pat. "What's done is done. What matters is what are we going to do about it?"

Boom glanced down at Trouble, and his anger seemed to deflate. He gave a heavy sigh and scratched behind one horn with a blunt finger. He turned back to Talon. "Sorry I blew up at you, chummer. I guess the stress of this run is getting to me."

"To all of us," Talon said, smiling wanly. His eyes held the same haunted look Trouble had noticed earlier, but he got down to business in spite of it. "I think we can still salvage something from this mess. It's just going to take a little more work."

"Well, the cred's good," Hammer said from his seat near the door of Boom's office. The big ork casually cradled a submachine gun across his lap, ready for anything.

A knock at the door froze the conversation in its tracks. Boom glanced at the monitors built into the surface of his broad desk. He looked up and nodded slightly at Hammer, who went to open the door to Valkyrie, the team's remaining member.

She was dressed as usual: a T-shirt, worn jeans tucked into a pair of heavy leather boots, and a battered leather jacket layered with ballistic armor. Her dark hair was clipped "short and simple," as she put it, revealing the chrome of the datajack behind her left ear. She carried a slim, flat control deck under one arm and a flat-profile pistol in a holster at her waist. Val sauntered in and flopped down on the couch against one wall.

"What's the word?" Boom asked.

"I tracked our boy by remote," she said. "He took the T, so I lost him when he went underground, but I staked out his apartment. He showed up there a few minutes ago. He couldn't have gotten home that fast if he'd made any stops along the way."

"So he didn't talk to anyone else or try to make another score," Talon said.

Val shook her head. "Not unless he met somebody on the train. 'Sides, we've checked this guy out. He doesn't have any street connections. He's a lily-white, sheltered corp-baby. We're the only connections he's got."

"Which is something we can turn to our advantage," Boom rumbled. "We just need to turn up the heat a little, so he'll have to come back for the bait. And I think I know how we can do that."

Boom looked at Talon, who seemed lost in thought. "Tal, what's this about Jase? What did you see?"

"I don't know." Talon gave a baffled shake of his head. "I'm not sure anymore. Maybe it was just a trick of the light or the smoke or something. But I could have sworn . . . " He trailed off and threw up his hands in a gesture of helplessness. It hurt Trouble to see Talon, always so sure of himself, look so lost and confused.

"Are you sure you're up to handling this?" Boom said. "'Cause if not . . ."

"No, no, I'm fine," Talon said. "I'll deal. Let's figure out what we're going to do and get down to it, okay?"

Boom nodded curtly. "Okay, here's what I'm thinking." He laid out the plan, and they discussed it, working through potential problems. When everyone had their assignments, the team broke up to get some rest. It was already quite late.

The club was closing for the night as they emerged from Boom's office. The Avalon belonged to Boom, and it was a good front for his shadow business. The last of the club-goers were trickling out the door onto the streets of Boston, and the cleanup crews had already begun repairing the mess their festivities had left behind.

Talon was down the stairs and almost out the door as Trouble hurried to catch up. He had that lost look again, walking with his head down and one hand jammed into the pocket of his jacket. His motorcycle helmet dangled by its chin-strap from his other hand.

"Hey," she said. "Want to grab a cup of soykaf before calling it a night? I mean, if you want to talk . . ."

Talon gave her a sorrowful smile that made Trouble's heart ache. He shook his head. "No, thanks. I think I need to be alone for a while."

"Okay, chummer," she said gently. "Are you sure?"

"Yeah, but thanks anyway," Talon said. "Talk to you tomorrow." He tucked his helmet into the crook of his arm and walked off toward the alley.

Trouble watched him go, wanting to run after him but knowing she had to respect Talon's wishes. *If only you would let somebody inside, Talon,* she thought. *If only you'd let me in.*

The alley was filled with overflowing dumpsters and garbage cans, the shapes ominous in the barely lit

darkness. Talon had just entered when he heard the
sound of muffled laughter coming from the darkness
ahead. He paused, suddenly alert, one hand hovering
over the pistol holstered under his jacket.

A trio of figures, two humans and an ork, stepped
out from behind a dumpster. All wore beat-up leathers
covered with chrome studs and chains, and their hair
was shaved into patterns, gelled into spikes, and colored a bizarre rainbow. They looked like teenagers.
The ork stood head and shoulders above his friends,
but one of the humans was the obvious leader. He had
pale green eyes—implants of some kind—that glowed
faintly, with no iris or pupil visible. The three of them
were giggling, probably high on something.

"Hey, man," the lead human said, snickering like
he'd just heard the funniest joke in the world, "where
do you think you're going?" The three instantly broke
up into raucous laughter. Talon noticed that the two
humans had closed switchblades in their hands, while
the ork held a heavy length of steel chain in his enor-
mous paws.

He sighed deeply. "Kid, I'm in no mood for this.
You have exactly five seconds to get out of my way
before I accept this as a gift from the gods and take
out my frustration by kicking all of your sorry,
fragged-up asses."

"Just you, old man?" the lead ganger said with a
guffaw.

Talon smiled wickedly. "Naw, wouldn't want to take
on all you wired tough guys myself. I'll probably get
a little help from him," he said, nodding toward the
space behind the gangers.

"What are you . . ." the leader began, then trailed

off as a deep growl came from behind him. The giggling stopped as the gangers turned as one to see a large, silver-furred wolf with glowing green eyes emerge from the shadows. A faint, silvery halo surrounded its body, eerie in the darkness. The leader turned back toward Talon, who was surrounded in a similar aura of violet light.

"Holy drek!" the kid said. "He's a mage! Slot and run!" They turned almost as one and tore down the alley past the wolf, knocking over garbage cans and tripping over themselves in their frantic flight. The wolf started to go after them, but Talon stopped him with a word.

"Let 'em go, Aracos. They're not worth the bother."

The wolf stopped and looked back at him. "Humph," he said, speaking directly into Talon's mind. "I could take a bite or two out of them to teach them a lesson, but they probably wouldn't taste very good."

The wolf loped over to Talon, his astral aura fading back to invisibility. He looked up at Talon with a lupine expression of concern.

"Are you all right, boss?" Aracos thought to him.

Talon knew he could never hide his inner turmoil from his ally spirit. Aracos could read Talon's emotions with his astral senses as well as through the psychic connection the two shared. Besides, Talon hadn't really bothered to mask his feelings.

"Well, I've been better," Talon thought to Aracos, "but I don't want to talk about it now. Let's just get out of here, okay?"

For a moment, he thought Aracos might say something more, but the spirit gave a distinctively unwolf-like shrug and began to shimmer.

"You're the boss," he thought to Talon. The silvery wolf-form melted first into an opalescent mist swirling in the air, then solidified again as a slick red, black, and chrome motorcycle of Japanese make. Chrome traceries in the form of a Celtic knot were etched on one side of the chassis, with the name "Aracos" tricked out in graceful chrome letters beside it.

The bike's motor was already humming as Talon swung one leg over and mounted up. He pulled on his helmet, and the electronics in its visor lit up the alleyway as bright as day. He revved the bike's engine and headed into Landsdown Street. Within minutes, he was speeding toward South Boston, as if he could go fast enough to leave his troubling visions behind.

4

Alone in his bed later that night, Talon dreamed.

He was sixteen again, having run away from the Catholic mission in Southie where he grew up. He'd run because of the things he was seeing and feeling, things that weren't compatible with what the nuns and brothers of the mission taught him. He couldn't block out the strange haloes of light he saw around people or prevent the bombardment by impressions of the emotions of everyone on the street. It was as if the pain, misery, and unhappiness of twenty generations of people had seeped into the concrete and brick of South Boston, permanently staining it and wrapping everything in a dark pall.

He'd ended up in the Rox, which was even worse. The emotional fog there was so thick you could cut it with a knife. He was too poor to get a datajack even at one of the sleazy chop shops operating in the back alleys, but he somehow managed to scrape together enough money to buy relief from his misery in the form of little blue tablets called bliss. Nothing else mattered when he was on bliss, but when he stopped, the sensations and the visions got harder and harder to block out.

One day he was huddled in an abandoned building somewhere in the Rox, coming down off his last bliss high and with no money to buy more. It was only a matter of time before he'd be forced to sell his body on the street. It was the only thing of any value he had left. The colors and feelings were already starting to come back, and he could feel his sanity starting to slip away. He didn't know how much longer he could stand it.

That was when he heard the faint scratching and shuffling sounds of something moving downstairs. He froze, holding his breath and straining to hear as his sweat turned ice cold. Everyone knew the stories about the ghouls that haunted the abandoned sections of the Rox looking for food. They were said to feed on human corpses, sometimes coming out of the shadows to hunt for fresh meat.

He tried to reach for the switchblade in the pocket of his ragged jeans, but his fingers wouldn't obey him properly. He couldn't even get himself to crawl away and hide somewhere. All he could do was lie there, waiting for the inevitable, a small part of him thinking that maybe it would be best if the ghouls found him and put an end to it all. The shuffling drew closer and closer, with the creak of the old stairs heralding their approach.

There were two of them, their gray and hairless flesh stretched tight over their bones. They wore the ragged remains of clothing, probably taken from the bodies of their victims. Their long, bony fingers were tipped with nails like sharp claws. Their faces were long and gaunt, their thin-lipped mouths filled with sharp, tearing teeth. Their white, blind eyes looked out into nothing. They sniffed the air like animals, smelling Talon's fear, the scent of prey. As they came closer, stalking him, Talon felt a whimper rise in his throat. One of the ghouls licked his lips with a grayish tongue.

Then light spilled into the room, light even the blind ghouls could see somehow. They recoiled from it as a shining figure appeared, stepping straight through the wall as if it wasn't there. The figure was tall and handsome, clad in robes of light and holding a long wooden staff in one hand. He raised the other in a gesture of warding and spoke in a voice like thunder.

"STOP!" he commanded. "Leave him alone! He is under my protection."

Talon looked up at the glowing figure and thought of the angels the nuns at the orphanage were always talking about. This being was so beautiful, the light he gave off so protective and kind, although the ghouls didn't seem to think so.

Recovering from their initial shock, they charged forward, hissing at the light that threatened them. The being was unmoved by their attack. He swung his staff in an arc and struck one of the ghouls a solid blow, sending the thing stumbling back, squealing in pain. The staff flashed again and again, tracing glowing arcs around the man of light, driving the ghouls back until they finally fled from the room. Talon could hear them retreating quickly down the stairs. The figure of light moved closer, bending down to touch him gently on the shoulder. Talon's vision began to swim and his head to pound like something was threatening to burst out of it.

"Don't worry," the man of light said. "It's all right.

You're safe now." Then he began to sing a strange, soothing song, and Talon found himself drifting off to sleep . . .

Then he was in a Stuffer Shack, looking through the racks for some munchies. The magical practice Jase was teaching him always made him hungry. Jase just laughed and said that everything made Talon hungry, but that it was only natural for a young man his age. Still, Talon was coming along well, according to his teacher. In something like a year, he had learned so much from the man who'd rescued him from the ghouls, who'd taught him that the strange sights and feelings weren't madness but the awakening of Talon's magical gifts. Jase taught him to control and use those gifts, and so much more. Their relationship deepened, and Talon realized that what he felt for Jase was more than a student's affection for his teacher or gratitude for Jase saving his life. He loved Jase, and Jase loved him. They lived together on the edge of the Rox in a cramped little apartment, but Talon couldn't remember a time when he'd felt happier or more hopeful. For him, it was like a dream come true.

Now, engrossed in choosing a snack, Talon merely grunted when Jase said he was going outside to use the public telecom. A few minutes later, Talon heard the roar of motorcycle engines, followed by the chatter of bullets. He instinctively ducked down as gunfire splintered the Stuffer Shack's front windows, and the cashier and the few other customers also dropped to the floor. When he heard the bikes roaring off, he rushed outside. The ground was covered with broken plastiglass and smashed food containers.

What he saw made him cry out in pain. Jase was

lying on the asphalt in a pool of blood. Talon rushed over and lifted Jase's head off the ground, cradling his blood-spattered body and calling his name again and again, but Jase didn't answer. Talon looked up as the gangers zoomed away on their motorcycles, laughing. He cried for help, then collapsed, sobbing over the body of the man he loved more than life itself . . .

Then Talon was in the apartment they'd shared. The furniture was pushed back against the wall, and he was on his hands and knees, drawing on the floor with chalk and paint. He slowly built a mandala from lines and geometric shapes. He drew one large circle, and a smaller circle with a triangle inside it. Inscribed around it were runes and symbols of power. He took a small brass brazier and a sharp silver knife from his and Jase's shared collection of magical tools and lit candles at the four quarters of the circle. Soon, a bed of coals simmered in the brazier, and he sprinkled incense over them. A sweet, heady scent began to fill the room.

Talon made a quick, sharp cut across his palm with the knife. Blood welled up from it, dark and red. Three drops fell and sizzled on the hot coals, followed by three more, and three more after that. Then he bound the cut with a silken cloth and began his chant. He gathered all his anger and grief inside of him as the blood burned with a sharp, metallic tang that made his eyes water. He looked into the fire and thought of Jase's funeral pyre, then he looked at the blood and thought of Jase's blood on his hands and clothes. He thought of the Asphalt Rats, the gangers responsible for Jase's death, and the flames roared in response.

Talon found the Asphalt Rats later that night, partying in a dead-end alleyway deep inside their turf in the Rox. From the amount of booze and discarded chip-cases scattered around, they must have recently come into some nuyen. Talon stood watching them celebrating, drinking, and laughing after killing the best person he had ever known. A haze of red rage obscured everything he saw and felt. He hated them. More than anything, he wanted them dead. One of the gangers noticed Talon then, but he never got the chance to call out a warning.

Talon raised his arms and shouted his grief to the heavens, a cry of rage that erupted into an inferno whose flames poured into the alley like the fires of hell itself. Some of the gangers tried to run, some reached for their weapons. Most hadn't even looked up before they were engulfed in a blast that charred their skin black and set their hair aflame. The gas tanks of the bikes exploded like a series of bombs, sending a black and orange fireball boiling into the sky and covering the sides of the nearby buildings with soot and ash.

Talon stood there at the mouth of the alley and watched it all happen. He didn't flinch or turn away from the horror of it. His only thought was to see the ones responsible for his pain pay for what they did. The heat of the inferno was cool compared to his rage as he watched the gangers writhe, burn, and die in the flames.

It was over in a matter of seconds. The blackened and twisted remains of the bikes continued to burn, and a stream of acrid smoke billowed up from the alley. The charred corpses lay where they had fallen.

Most of them never knew what hit them, or why. Tears ran down Talon's face as he stared at the ruins.

"Forgive me," he whispered, then turned and walked away without looking back. The cut on his hand throbbed and ached, and he felt drained, empty, like he'd lost a piece of his soul . . .

Then he was lying on a cold concrete floor deep in the catacombs beneath Boston. The floor was covered with arcane diagrams drawn in paint and blood, while dark figures chanted in the shadows at the edge of the room. Above him, a dry, withered corpse dressed in tattered old clothes hung from a rusty pipe by a rope knotted around its neck. The skull-face looked down on him, its eyes burning with fire and its yellowed teeth spread in a macabre grin. A crackling voice whispered in his mind.

Hello, Father, it said. *It's been a very long time.*

Talon bolted awake with a gasp and sat up in bed, his heart thudding in his chest. Drenched in a cold sweat, he threw off the sheets and sat up on the edge of the bed. He leaned forward slightly as he rubbed at his throbbing temples, letting some of the horror of the nightmare fade. It was so real.

He hadn't dreamed it for over a year. Now it was back, as bad as ever. Most disturbing of all was knowing that he'd called down a raging spirit to kill the Asphalt Rats. The spirit that was still out there, somewhere.

Maybe the dream had returned because Talon thought he'd seen Jase tonight. Or maybe he thought he'd seen Jase because of the mana waves and fluctuations that had recently begun to surge. Talon didn't share the general hysteria about the return of Halley's Comet, but no one could deny that magic had been acting strange of late.

No, he told himself. I'm sure I saw him, but why had Jase appeared? Was he trying to warn Talon of something? The only problem with being a mage was that it didn't necessarily guarantee you could interpret everything you saw.

He fell back against the pillows and stared up at the ceiling. He checked the timekeeping function of his headware, and cool blue numbers appeared at the corner of his vision: 04:45:15. He'd only slept for a few hours. He canceled the clock and rolled over, but sleep eluded him. When it did come, Talon did not dream, but he could not escape the ominous sense that something terrible was about to happen.

5

For Bridget O'Rourke, consciousness returned slowly. She struggled against the dark fog wrapping her brain, trying to recall what happened. The last thing she recalled was the get-together at Kelly's. She'd had quite a bit to drink and was on her way to visit the ladies' room. She dimly remembered powerful arms grabbing her from behind and the slap of the drug patch against her neck, over the carotid artery. She remembered the sensation of the powerful sedative spreading through her body, robbing the last bit of her strength. Then she slipped down into darkness as more strong hands dragged her away from the light and the noise of the pub.

The memories jerked her awake as she felt the same powerful arms holding her shoulders and feet, carrying her along. She opened her eyes, and in the dim light, she saw a hideous creature holding her bound ankles. It was an ork, but the ugliest ork she'd ever seen. His skin was gray, almost dead white, and his exposed flesh was covered with lumpy deposits of bony armor. Two long, yellow tusks curled over his upper lip, and his eyes were beady under a massive beetle brow. He could have easily held both her legs in one of his huge hands. Together, his hands gripped like a vice.

She tipped her head back toward whoever was holding her shoulders, and saw a troll who matched the ork ugly for ugly. His face was a hideous mass of warts and twisted bone, with three curly horns of different lengths emerging from the top of his head.

She began to struggle and tried to cry out for help, but she was bound hand and foot with silvery-gray duct tape. More tape covered her mouth, preventing her from screaming. She thrashed about, but the goblins only tightened their grip on her.

" 'Ey, she's awake," the ork said to his companion, glancing down at Bridget with a look that made her shudder. She could tell that he hated her, but that another part of him also wanted her. Terror was turning her insides to water. She was gripped with a panicked need to get away from these monsters, but her struggles were feeble compared to their strength.

"You think we should put her out again?" the troll asked.

The ork shook his head. "Naw, we're almost there anyway."

Bridget looked around and saw that they were moving down an obviously abandoned tunnel with ancient cracked walls and scattered with rubble. Dark moisture leaked in through the cracks, and moss and fungus grew around the water. Rusting pieces of metal protruded from the floor and walls in spots, their original function unknown. The phosphorescent lamps set into the walls gave off a dull green glow that was barely enough light to see by. Bridget was sure she could hear things chittering and scuttling in the shadows, just out of sight.

She'd heard stories about the underground, that

there was a virtual maze of old tunnels and catacombs down under Boston. The tunnels were supposed to be inhabited by street people, squatters, and even ghouls that came out at night to hunt for human flesh. But she had never really believed it—until now.

The ork and the troll came to a stop before a heavy, rusting metal door set into the tunnel wall. The ork handed Bridget over to the troll, who took her as easily as if she were no more than a baby. The ork went to the door and turned the wheel set into its center with a loud squeaking that echoed strangely in the tunnel, followed by a dull clunk. He swung the door open, and the troll bent down to step through, still carrying Bridget.

Beyond the door was a brick-lined tunnel lit with electric lights that cast a yellow glow into the tunnel beyond. The troll's bulk barely fit between the walls as he carried Bridget toward a heavy velvet curtain closing off the other end of the tunnel. He pushed the curtain aside and went through. The room they entered made her eyes go wide.

The brick walls of the chamber were hung with heavy draperies of black and deep purple edged in gold fringe and braiding, making it seem more like a giant tent of sorts. The concrete floor was carpeted almost wall to wall by an Oriental rug woven in rich jewel tones. An antique couch and two chairs with clawed feet were of the same heavy fabric of the drapery.

The only light came from a fire crackling in the marble hearth. The flames glimmered off small objects of crystal and brass scattered over the shelves and side-tables. The air was warm and smelled spicy, like drying herbs, but the dank smell of the underground overpowered it. Despite the warmth, Bridget shivered as the troll set her down on the couch. Where was she?

As the troll bent to remove the tape binding her wrists and ankles, she considered bolting for the door even as it clanged shut and locked with a heavy clunk. She could never hope to outrun the massive troll anyway. And where could she go if she didn't know where she was?

The troll peeled the tape from her mouth, and Bridget let out a yelp of pain. The sting seemed to spark her courage to confront the figure towering over her.

"Who the hell are you?" she demanded angrily. "Where are we?"

"You are in my home, child," a crooning voice said. "Welcome."

The troll immediately straightened up like a schoolboy when an adult enters the room. Looking past him, Bridget saw the heavy draperies part to reveal an old woman dressed in a floor-length robe of black velvet. The long, wide sleeves covered her bony arms to the wrists, leaving only her thin, gaunt hands visible. Draped over her head and shoulders was a darkly colorful shawl held in place by what looked like a cameo pin. She leaned on a gnarled wooden cane that thumped softly against the carpet as she came closer.

As the old woman approached in the firelight, Bridget got a good look at her. She was hideous, a withered hag like a witch from a fairy tale. Her prominent nose was a hooked beak, and she had a sharp, bony chin. Her skin was as wrinkled as a prune, and her small black eyes seemed to take in everything. She chuckled quietly to herself, her lipless mouth curled in a tight smile.

"Yes, welcome to my humble home," the old woman said again, looking Bridget over. "I've been expecting you."

"Who . . . who are you?" Bridget managed to mumble. The old hag's smile chilled her to the bone. Her teeth were small and sharp, like a predator's.

"You can call me Mama, my dear," the woman said. "Everyone does."

"We brought her, like you said, Mama," the troll murmured, sounding like he really was addressing his mother.

Could that be? Bridget wondered briefly. She could hardly imagine it, though the creature in front of her looked old enough to be someone's great-grandmother, at least.

Mama reached up as far as her arm would reach to pat the troll's cheek. "You've done very well, my sweetling," she said. "Very well indeed."

The troll beamed with pleasure. He stood near the entrance to the room, while Mama settled into a chair opposite Bridget on the couch. Bridget looked around the room, searching for a way out of the madness she'd been dragged into.

"Now, let's have a look at you, my dear," Mama said, narrowing her eyes and leaning forward with both hands on her cane. Bridget could feel the force of her stare practically drilling into her. It was as if this crazy old woman was seeing directly into her soul.

Bridget tried to shrink back away from that stare, but she couldn't move. Oh, Lord, help me, she thought. The instant seemed like an eternity before the old crone blinked, breaking the spell that had seemed to paralyze Bridget.

"Very nice," Mama said, more to herself than anyone else. "Yes, you'll do nicely."

"Do for what?" Bridget said. "What do you want with me?"

"Why, you're very special, dear, particularly because of your new friends and their cause."

"I don't know what you're talking about," Bridget lied desperately.

"Of course you do. You're one of them, one of the Knights, and I need someone close to them, but not too close. You're new. They still don't know much about you, and you're young and strong . . ." The hag reached out a bony hand to squeeze Bridget's upper arm.

"Please, let me go," Bridget pleaded. "I haven't done anything! Please, please don't hurt me . . ." Her voice trailed off as Mama smiled again.

"Hurt you? Oh no, my child, you misunderstand. I have no intention of hurting you, not at all!" She shook her head like an indulgent grandma dealing with a grandchild's naive questions, as if the very idea was absurd.

"Then why . . ." Bridget said.

"I need you intact, my dear." The stress the old woman put on the word "need" made Bridget feel like she'd just been invited to dinner as the main course. The stories about ghouls and vampires in the underground came flooding back, and she quailed under the old woman's gaze. Mama seemed to sense her terror, leaning closer as though she could smell it in the air like a tantalizing aroma.

"Yes," Mama crooned. "You'll suit us well enough. Won't she, my pet?"

Us? Bridget wondered.

Mama supported herself on her cane and stood up. She beckoned with one bony finger for Bridget to come closer to the fire. "Come and look," Mama said.

Suddenly the fire roared, and a gout of flames shot from the hearth. Bridget screamed and scrambled along the couch away from the flames until she bumped against the far end. She huddled there, trembling. But the flames didn't burn anything. They gathered into a cloud of fire that hovered in midair in front of the hearth, casting a reddish-orange glow over the room. Bridget almost thought she could see a pair of white-hot eyes deep within the flames, looking at her with an intensity—and a hunger—that exceeded Mama's.

"Yes," whispered a voice like the crackling of flames, "yes, this one will do nicely. Her fear is the key and the gate for me." Bridget shivered as the thing spoke, and Mama smiled.

"Good, then she is yours, Gallow, my pet."

Bridget looked frantically from the old crone to the hovering ball of fire. She tried to get up, tried to struggle, but the flames surged toward her. Fire washed over her body even before she could move a muscle. Bridget screamed and thrashed, rolling onto the floor trying to put out the flames.

The fire didn't burn her flesh, though. She could feel it searing into her mind, into her very soul. She could feel the touch of the fire spirit, and her soul shrank back in terror as the flames seemed to fill her whole being, making her feverish with heat.

"Who are you?" her mind cried out at the presence she felt.

"I am fear," it said. "I am terror. I am rage. I am vengeance."

As it spoke, Bridget felt thoughts and memories welling up within her, things she had tried not to remember: how her mother was raped and murdered by a gang of young elves out for a "wild hunt." The look on her father's face at the funeral afterward. The night she killed her first elf at the age of fifteen. The look of shock and surprise on the elven gang-member's face that such a wee girl knew how to fight so well. How much she hated them, how much she wanted to see them all dead. Hated them all.

"They will suffer," a voice whispered in her thoughts. "They will all suffer."

Bridget O'Rourke's mind fell into a dark place, and the flames shrouding her body flickered and died. The woman that rose from the floor was not her in anything but appearance. She ran her hands over her body, luxuriating in the feeling of flesh and solidity.

"So long," Gallow whispered with Bridget's voice. "It's been so long . . ."

"Yes," Mama said. "Are you pleased with this little gift, my pet?"

Gallow turned toward the old woman, fire flashing in Bridget's blue eyes. It regarded Mama for a long moment before replying.

"Yes," it said finally.

"Good. Now there is something you can do for your Mama. A little errand, but I think you will enjoy it. I know how much you have missed your dear, dear father."

Bridget's eyebrows rose slightly, and her pretty mouth twisted in a grimace.

"Talon," Gallow whispered, then smiled wickedly.

"That's right," Mama said. "It will be a chance to see him again and to feed well along the way. You'll need to keep up your strength, my pet. The time is approaching, and events are already set into motion. Listen carefully, and I will explain what you need to do . . ."

Rory MacInnis hated guard duty more than he hated almost anything else in his young life. It was mind-numbingly dull, and besides, it wasn't like anyone was going to come and find them. The Knights of the Red Branch had escaped the authorities in Boston for decades. Living here in the Rox, they could continue to hide for another thirty years before Knight Errant or the Feds would bother coming in after them.

Rory knew they wouldn't be hiding much longer, though, because everything would soon change. The Knights were going to win back their homeland and overthrow the fragging elves who thought they could just barge in and take over a whole country as easy as you please. Well, the elves obviously didn't understand the Irish at all or they'd know the people wouldn't give up their land without a fight.

Truth to tell, Rory would have liked to see a lot more fighting than he had since joining up. There was a lot of planning, skulking around, and hiding out in places like this abandoned factory building in the Rox. There were meetings with people and deals to be made. Rory knew it was because the Knights weren't strong enough to confront the elves head-on, and so they had to seek out other means. But he'd still rather be out busting heads and collecting a few pointy elven ears than waiting around on guard duty.

He was so lost in thought that he almost missed the movement on the monitor in front of him. He glanced at the grainy LCD display, which was wired up to tiny cameras placed outside the factory. There was definitely someone coming. A woman was making a beeline from the rusted fence toward the door that Rory guarded, like she knew exactly where she was going. He picked up his Ingram and checked its read-out, making sure the gun was fully loaded and ready. Then he picked up the commlink next to the display screen and spoke into it.

"Nils, this is Rory. We've got company coming up to the front."

"Roger that, lad. We're on our way over. Lie low."

Rory went to the door, but kept his eye on the monitor. The woman walked up to the door, bold as brass, and rapped on it three times. Rory checked the spy hole in the door and breathed a sigh of relief when he saw who was waiting outside. He quickly threw back the bolt and cracked open the door to peek around it.

"Geez, Bridget!" he said. "What are you thinkin' coming here out in the open like that, woman? Get in here!"

Bridget stumbled in through the door, and Rory could smell the stench of liquor on her. Phew! She must be drunk as a skunk, he thought as she almost fell against him.

"Sorry," Bridget said, slurring her words slightly. "Got a little lost."

"I'll say." Rory grinned knowingly. "Lost inside a bottle, eh?"

"Jus' a few drinks to celebrate," she said, bleary-eyed, like she couldn't quite focus on his face.

"Well, a couple people were wonderin' where you nicked off to," Rory told her. He figured that a lass as good-looking as Bridget must have some fellow on the side. He wouldn't have minded spending the evening at some pub himself.

"C'mon," he said, taking her by the arm. "Let's get you to bed before the commander sees you. I swear, lass, one day somebody's going to mess up, and there's going to be hell to pay."

6

Dan Otabi slotted his credstick into the reader at the gate, confirming his authorized access to Cross Applied Technologies property, then drove to his designated parking space in the lot. He killed the engine and rested his hands on the steering wheel, letting his head fall back. He still hadn't recovered from his meeting with the chip dealer last night. It had really shaken him up.

After leaving the Avalon, he'd gone by subway to where he'd left his car. He kept looking around the train, thinking that any minute an undercover cop would arrest him or that one of the dealer's cronies would jump him. It had taken a couple of hours of simming to calm his nerves when he got home. By the time the chip shut down, it was very late, but Dan still had trouble getting to sleep. His head was filled with images of himself as a sim hero, but he was no Derek Hunt in the encounter with the ork at the Avalon. He'd been nothing more than Dan Otabi, someone who could never take on a powerful, cyber-enhanced metahuman.

He'd had trouble waking up today when his internal alarm clock gently but relentlessly chipped away at his sleep, bringing him back to consciousness and the harsh realities of a cold Monday morning in December. For about the hundredth time, Dan wished there was a chip that would let his body go through the motions of getting up, eating, showering, driving, and working while his mind was off getting some rest and enjoying itself. Maybe that was the kind of chip Novatech or Truman Systems should come out with next. Dan would be first in line to buy one—assuming they weren't outlawed like the California-hot chip he'd tried to score last night. Why was the best stuff always illegal?

He knew he couldn't sit there all day, so he got out of the car. He slung the case he used to carry his chips and other work items over one shoulder. The bag also contained a few chips that weren't work-related, just in case he found a few spare minutes around lunchtime for a short break.

He keyed the alarm system on his car. The company lot was secure enough, but he thought it was a good habit to keep up. He walked toward the entrance, slipping the lanyard of the laminated ID over his head with practiced ease. The imbedded chip in the ID spoke silently with the main computer system of the building, confirming Dan's identity and his authorization to be in the facility at this time of day. Security cross-checks had taken place invisibly before he ever reached the front door, of course. The lobby was decorated for the Christmas season with fake plastic wreaths, holly boughs, blinking Christmas lights, and some red and green ribbon and shiny little ornaments. It all looked so fake to Dan, so flat compared to when he was simming. That looked real.

"Hey, Dan, how's it goin'? Looks like you had a busy weekend!"

"Yeah, you could say that, Lou," Dan said to the security guard on duty. Most days, he liked Lou well enough, but today he wasn't in the mood to chat. The old guy was getting near retirement age, and he liked to talk. Dan had heard all about how Lou had turned ork as a teenager back in the twenties. Apparently, people who'd goblinized into orks and trolls lived a lot longer than the ones who were actually born that way later on.

He knew that Lou had been married for more than thirty years to another ork. He was a great-grandfather already, and his kids were in their thirties, which for orks made them seem at least as old as Lou, if not older. Odds were halfway decent that Lou and his wife would outlive their grandchildren and become great-great-grandparents before they died. Dan wondered how Lou kept his sunny disposition day in and day out. It must be hard enough just being an ork, but the idea of outliving your kids and grandkids really seemed unfair to Dan.

"You kids and yer parties," Lou said. "Well, I hope you had fun."

"Not nearly enough," Dan said with a wan smile. Lou chuckled and shook his head as Dan took the hall down to the "gopher farm."

That was what his co-workers called the maze of cubicles that occupied most of the main floor where he worked. They were standard-issue corporate gray, set off by the slate blue carpeting. The cubes got their nickname from the way the workers would pop their heads up over the walls from time to time to talk or look around, like gophers poking their heads up from their holes.

Dan rounded the corner of the maze that led to his cube, chosen carefully because the location didn't let passersby see in. That small measure of privacy turned out to be a disadvantage that morning, however. He stopped dead in his tracks in the doorway of his cubicle when he saw someone else sitting in his chair.

The man was human, probably about Dan's age or a little younger. He was dressed in "corporate casual," an open-necked polo shirt of dark green and a pair of black synthdenim jeans over what looked like black, steel-toed boots. His red hair was long and carefully combed in front, but clipped short on the sides and in back. A slim fiber-optic cable trailed from the chrome-lipped jack behind his ear, running down over his shoulder to the terminal on Dan's desk.

The stranger glanced up at Dan from whatever he was doing, which Dan took to mean he couldn't have been too deeply immersed in the virtual reality of the Matrix. The red-haired man smiled, revealing perfect white teeth, and reached up to tug the cable from his datajack.

"Oh, hi," he said. "Your boss said it'd be okay to use your terminal for a while before you got here. I'm Roy Kilaro." He held up the ID tag that hung from a lanyard around his neck. "I'm with Information Systems from the main office in Montreal. You're Dan"— he squinted at Dan's ID tag—"Otabi, right?"

Dan nodded. "What are you doing here?" he asked.

If Kilaro took offense at Dan's abruptness, he didn't show it. "Routine maintenance check of the data-traffic systems," he said with a wave of his hand. "Nothing major, just some things the Powers That Be want checked out."

Dan felt a stab of fear, but he forced himself to sound calm. "What sort of things?"

"Sorry. Top secret." Kilaro winked as though the whole thing was some kind of joke, but Dan didn't think so. Kilaro let the data cable reel smoothly back into its slot next to the terminal and pushed back from Dan's desk. "I'm all done here, so you can have your cube back. Sorry to barge in unannounced."

"No problem," Dan murmured as Kilaro stood up and reached for the strap of a flat black case sitting on the floor at his feet. Dan could guess what it contained. Only serious computer systems specialists carried cyberdecks.

As Kilaro looped the strap over his shoulder, Dan noticed the tail end of a tattoo curling down toward his wrist. It looked like some kind of Asian dragon.

"That's quite a tattoo," he said, trying to keep Kilaro talking to see if he could learn more about what he was looking for.

Kilaro smiled and pulled up his sleeve a little further. "A souvenir of my misspent youth. Tattoos were all the rage back then," he said. "But I don't want to take up any more of your morning, Dan, and I've got a lot more to do so . . ."

"Oh! Of course," Dan said, stepping aside to let Kilaro pass.

"Have a good day," Kilaro said over his shoulder as he sauntered out of the cubicle.

"Yeah, you too," Dan called after him, watching him from the doorway and wondering what had really brought Kilaro down from Montreal. He was afraid he knew what it was.

He walked over to his terminal and sat down. He picked up the optical cable, then sat for a moment trying to calm himself. Then he reached up and slotted the cable into his datajack. He logged into the system and began to run a routine startup, still wondering what Kilaro had been up to.

Roy Kilaro reached the lobby, where he stopped at the security desk.

"All set there, Mr. Kilaro?" the ork security guard asked him.

"For now, Lou." Roy slid his ID through the card-reader to log himself out of the system. "I might be back to check up on a few things."

"So you're gonna be in town for a few more days?"

"Maybe. Why?"

The old ork grinned. "There's so much going on these days. People have been celebrating the fiftieth anniversary of the Awakening all year long. Salem's been really busy. That's where my granddaughter lives. Did I tell you she's a witch? Must take after her grandmother there." Lou chuckled at his own joke.

Roy gave a short laugh in return. The anniversary didn't mean that much to him, but he'd been following the mixture of hoopla and panic surrounding Halley's comet with some interest. "Thanks for the tip, Lou. Maybe I'll have some time when I'm done here. For now, there's no rest for the wicked." He hefted his cyberdeck case to say that he had to go back to work.

The ork nodded. "I hear you. Have a good one."

"You too," Roy said, and went out through the

building's sliding doors. The sky had begun to darken over with clouds since he'd arrived this morning, and he wondered if it was going to snow.

He'd spent the morning poking around in the facility's computer systems without turning up anything definite. Dan Otabi's sudden appearance had been interesting, though. Roy could tell he was nervous, maybe even scared, and that was suspicious.

He reached his car and told his headware to send the coded unlocking signal via the tiny radio transmitter in his skull. The alarm system beeped twice, and the headlights flashed him a greeting as he popped open the door and slid behind the wheel of the rented Nissan-Chrysler Spirit. He dropped his case onto the passenger seat beside him.

Yeah, Otabi's sudden appearance had been interesting. Roy had chosen his cubicle on purpose, of course. A talk with Otabi's manager had clued Roy to the man's reclusive, almost antisocial tendencies, which made him a prime candidate for whoever had doctored the facility's telecom records. Plus, Otabi was a data-management specialist, and he had the skills to pull it off. Unfortunately, Otabi or not, the intruder hadn't left any fingerprints behind in the system that Roy could find.

He thought again about the look on Otabi's face when he saw Roy sitting at his terminal. He looked guilty, but nobody would accept that as proof of wrongdoing. If Roy was wrong, or if the guy simply decided to dig in his heels and deny everything, Roy would have problems of his own before this was all over. If he was going to score points with the big bosses in Québec, he needed to deliver the whole thing wrapped up like a present, showing how he'd taken care of a threat to CATco on his own.

He tapped in the ignition sequence onto the steering keypad. Let's find out where Mr. Otabi lives, he thought, pulling out of the company lot. As he drove through the gate and onto the street, Roy called up the personnel files he'd downloaded into his headware.

He tapped Dan Otabi's home address into the car's onboard system, then headed for the highway that would take him there.

7

Talon sipped his rapidly cooling soykaf from a paper cup, willing the bio-chemicals in it to kick-start his body. He was tired and listless after a night of restless sleep, and for once he was grateful even for the watery-gray light of an overcast day. The chill December wind had chased a fair number of people into the Java-Hut for a cup of something warm. Or lukewarm, as the case might be, Talon thought, swirling the soykaf around in his mouth before swallowing. There was something that made soykaf lose heat faster than any other substance known to man.

The door opened, bringing with it a blast of cold air and a new arrival in the form of Trouble, who Talon had been waiting for. Her real name was Ariel Tyson, but the handle suited her. She and Talon had first met over the barrel of an Ares Predator she'd been pointing at him. Someone had hired her to dig into his past, someone who wanted to lure him back to Boston from DeeCee, where he'd been shadowrunning with the team of Assets, Inc. Trouble was the bait, designed to help lure him in. When it was all over, Talon had decided to stay in Boston. Since then, he'd gotten to know Trouble better as both a friend and a teammate.

She was dressed in her usual leather jacket, close-fitting jeans, boots, and a T-shirt. Today, the shirt was dark blue. Her cyberdeck case hung under a strap over one shoulder, but Talon knew she carried a pistol in the shoulder holster concealed under her jacket.

Trouble was all business. She never wore jewelry and hid her green eyes behind dark sunglasses. Her long, dark hair was pulled back with a clasp in the shape of a silver Celtic knot. Silver also gleamed from the datajack behind one ear.

She slid into the seat opposite Talon without stopping to order anything at the counter. He, of course, was sitting with his back to the rear wall of the Java-Hut. That way he could keep his eye on the doors, and be able to make a quick exit out the back if necessary. Trouble knew he was watching her back too.

"I got your message," Trouble said. "How are you doing?"

"Almost awake." He took another sip from his cup. "You want something?" he asked, nodding toward the counter.

She shook her head. "I'm ready when you are."

Talon downed the last of his soykaf and crumpled the cup in his hand.

"Okay, let's go." He tossed the cup into the trash on the way out.

He followed Trouble to her car, a dark green Honda ZX Turbo. They were headed for Dan Otabi's place.

Talon slid into the passenger seat, and was instantly belted in by the safety harness. Sitting behind the wheel, Trouble pulled out a thin cable and jacked into the car's autopilot, which gave her direct control over the Honda's on-board computer. It wasn't the complete control you got from a control rig like Val used, but it was good enough for driving in the Boston area.

They rode in silence for a bit, then Trouble looked at him with concern. "Didn't you sleep last night?"

Talon gave a short laugh. "Shows that much, huh?"

She nodded. "Yeah, some."

"Trouble, I've got a bad feeling."

"About the run?"

"I don't know, about everything. Something's going on."

"You really believe you saw Jase last night, don't you?"

"Don't you?" he asked.

She shrugged. "I don't know. I'm no mage. I work with data, stuff that makes sense. You're the one who tangles with spirits and spells and whatnot. You're sure it was him?"

"Yes, I'm sure."

"Sure it was him—or sure it was something that looked like him?"

Talon thought about that for a moment. "I don't know. It happened so fast. I mean, I'm sure it looked like him, but the whole thing happened so fast . . ."

"Hey, Tal, don't get me wrong," Trouble said, laying one hand over his. "I believe you saw something. All I'm saying is that it might be not be what you think. Maybe somebody is fragging with your head."

"Maybe," Talon said. "And I'm going to find out."

"How?"

"Visit the astral planes to find out if Jase is trying to contact me or if it's something else."

"When?"

"After the run. I want to get biz taken care of first."

"If it's somebody trying to mess with you," Trouble said, "we'll help you out."

"I know. That's not what I'm worried about. What if it is Jase trying to reach out to me somehow?"

Trouble didn't have an answer, and they lapsed back into silence for the rest of the drive to the apartment complex where Dan Otabi lived. They pulled up alongside a keypad at the gate. Trouble put on a pair of black leather gloves as she lowered her window with a mental command.

"Hello, and welcome to Arlington Park Apartments," said a smooth, synthesized voice from the hidden speakers. "Please enter your residential code or the apartment number of the person you are visiting."

Trouble tapped some numbers into the keypad. A tone sounded from the speakers, and the voice said, "Thank you. Mr. Otabi's apartment is number 308, second building on your left. Please enjoy your visit." The gate began to slide open, and Trouble drove directly to a numbered space in front of one of the entrances to the complex.

"Not bad," Talon mused, looking around. Arlington Park wasn't as posh as some corporate condoplexes he'd seen, but it was ritzy enough for a sarariman like Dan Otabi. He lived alone, which suited their purposes.

Trouble parked the car. "Ready?" she asked.

"Yeah, except for one last touch." Talon wove his hands through the air, making mystical passes from his forehead to his feet, then he turned and did the same for Trouble. When finished with that, he closed his eyes in concentration, his fingers interlaced at his chest. Finally, he clapped his hands and blinked a couple of times, like he was coming out of a trance.

"What'd you do?" Trouble asked.

"Masking spell," Talon said. "In case someone sees us."

"Good idea. We shouldn't have any problem with the electronic security. It thinks we're authorized 'guests' of Mr. Otabi. The frame I planted in the building system will erase the records of our little visit before it deletes itself. Let's go."

From the lobby, they took an elevator to the third floor, where Otabi lived. As they were exiting the elevator, they passed a human woman and a younger elf, who saw an ork and a human in their late teens or early twenties. The young elf looked at the "ork"—Talon—with studied distaste and gave them as wide a berth as possible in the hall.

Good, Talon thought. The elf would definitely remember seeing a couple of scruffy metahumans near Otabi's place at this time of day.

"This is it," Trouble said when they reached number 308. She slipped a maglock passkey into the reader in the door-lock. It clicked immediately, and the LED light turned from red to green as the passkey scrambled the maglock's systems. Talon pushed the door open, and they went in.

Otabi's apartment was a slightly neater, more adult version of a college dorm room. There was a small kitchenette with a collection of dishes stacked in and around the sink. Off that was a living room with floor-to-ceiling windows and a balcony overlooking the grounds around the building. An entertainment center holding a trideo unit, stereo, and other modules filled one wall.

Facing it was a large sofa with a low, Japanese-style table in front of it.

Talon bent to examine some items scattered over the table while Trouble quickly checked the other rooms.

"All clear," she said.

Talon gestured to the items on the table. "It's all here." A Novatech Sandman simsense player and a handful of chips and their plastic casings were scattered over the tabletop. The player looked like last year's model, and there were easily a dozen chips.

"There's a lot more chips in the bedroom," Trouble said.

Talon picked up the Sandman and stuffed it into his carrying bag. "Look around for more hardware," he said. A quick search turned up an older chip-player made by Fuchi, Novatech's predecessor. That followed the Sandman into the bag, along with more of Otabi's chips.

"Why don't we just slip our chip in with his other ones," Trouble asked, "or replace his player?"

Talon shook his head. "That'd take too long. We've got to be sure Otabi uses the chip. We have no way of knowing which are his favorites without a lot of legwork we don't have time for. We also don't know if he'd recognize a fake. We've got to make him come to us. Did you get anything else?"

"Yeah, trid chips and drek like that. Nothing major."

"Okay, then let's buzz. Leave the door open slightly. That should get somebody's attention."

As they left the apartment and proceeded down the hall, they passed a different man coming out of the elevator this time. He was a red-haired human who looked like a corporate type on his day off. The man gave Talon and Trouble a long look, and Talon in his ork-form couldn't resist giving him a tusky grin as he and Trouble stepped into the elevator.

Roy Kilaro walked past the two rough-looking metahumans, who got into the elevator he'd taken to the third floor. They certainly had no business in a place like Arlington Park, and he looked at them curiously. He walked down the hall to Dan Otabi's apartment, then stopped short when he saw that the door was ajar. The LEDs above the maglock were flashing back and forth between red and green, indicating that the lock was scrambled, probably by some sort of passkey.

Roy glanced back toward the elevators. It looked like somebody had beat him to it. He'd been planning to talk to the neighbors as well as toss Otabi's flat, but the open door changed his plans. He couldn't risk being implicated in the break-in because it would tip off Otabi. He turned back toward the elevators.

He was leaving without getting the proof he'd hoped to find, yet he was more suspicious than ever. Someone else had wanted to get into Dan Otabi's doss bad enough to break in. Otabi was hiding something, and Roy Kilaro was going to find out what it was.

8

As Trouble and Talon drove away from Dan Otabi's apartment, Trouble noticed that the sky had cleared and was alight with stars and the waxing moon.

"So now we wait and see if Otabi contacts you?" Trouble asked.

Talon nodded. "Um-hmm. Without his simsense toys, he's going to be desperate for a fix, and the only dealer he knows is me. I think his habit will cancel out what happened at the Avalon the other night."

"Maybe he'll just go down to the local Warez, Etc. and pick up a new simdeck."

"I don't think so. He's had a taste of the good stuff. He won't be satisfied with anything less. The regular sims just won't do it for him anymore. Even if he does decide to get another deck and some chips, there are still some things we can do."

"So that leaves the next move up to him," Trouble said. "Val will be keeping an eye on Otabi, but we can't do much more until he takes the bait. Want to go grab a bite?"

Talon shook his head. "I think I'd better go back home and try to catch up on some sleep."

"Want me to drive you back to your place, then?"

Talon shrugged. "I could take Aracos . . ."

"You're dead on your feet, Tal. Let me take you home. It's no big deal."

"Okay," he said, settling back against the seat. There was a moment of silence as Trouble shifted lanes, navigating through the maze of Boston streets with ease.

"Can I ask you something?" she said.

Talon gazed over at her from under hooded eyes. "Sure."

"Has there . . . have you been involved with anyone else since Jase?"

"You mean romantically?"

"Yeah."

Talon took a deep breath and let it out with a long sigh. "Yes. No. Not really—I mean, yes, I've been involved with other guys since Jase died. I hooked up from time to time in college, and there are a lot more available guys in the shadows than most people think." He gave a wry smile. "But it was mostly brief encounters or short flings. I never met anyone like Jase, somebody I was really, truly in love with. I think I managed to convince myself it was love a few times, but those never panned out. I guess when it comes to romance I'm as hopeless as our buddy Otabi. I think I should stay away from simsense, though. I can see how plugging into a perfect fantasy life where you've got everything you ever wanted could be addictive."

"Yeah," Trouble said.

"How about you?" he asked. "Has there been anyone since Ian?"

Trouble glanced over at Talon, then back to the

road. Traffic had slowed through a series of lights, and now they'd came to a stop.

"Not really. I guess we're a lot alike in that respect. Ian was my first real love. Looking back on it, I was pretty naive at the time. I've dated here and there since then, but that's about it."

"Our business doesn't exactly give us many opportunities to meet the right people, does it?" Talon said.

"No. Besides, what are the chances of the right one coming along anyway? You don't run into that kind of person every day."

"Are you sorry you called it quits with Ian?" Talon asked. "For me, there wasn't much choice, but . . ."

"Most of the time, no," Trouble said. "He cared so much about freeing the Irish that it seemed to mean more to him than I did. I guess I didn't really want to share him with a cause, you know?"

"Yeah, I can see that."

The traffic began to move again, and they lapsed back into silence as Trouble cut through the city to South Boston.

Talon began to go over the run with her. They agreed that, if all went as planned with Otabi, they should be able to pull it off with ease.

"The only other thing that bothers me is that we don't have any real information on the Johnson," Talon said. That bothered Trouble as well. Most employers—"Mr. Johnsons," as they were known—valued their anonymity. Shadowrunners, however, liked to know whom they were working for, just in case their Johnson tried to use them for some secret purpose of his own. The team knew very little about their current employer, apart from the fact that his credit was good.

"I'll see if I can dig up something," Trouble said, pulling up to the curb in front of Talon's doss.

He got out of the car. "Good. I'll give you a call when everything's set for the meet."

"Okay." She watched him until he'd climbed the front steps and gone through the door of his apartment house before putting the ZX back into gear. At the stop sign, she glanced back again before driving on.

Don't be stupid, she told herself, but she really didn't have much choice. People in love were always doing stupid things, weren't they? She turned the corner, but didn't head for home to start tracking down information about their Mr. Johnson. She drove toward the Rox, a section of the Boston plex that most people avoided if they could.

She was headed for "Doc's Clinic," as it was known among the locals. It had no official name because most of the places and people in the Rox didn't officially exist. When the metroplex government was formed, they decided to write off southern Roxbury and the Lowell-Lawrence Zone. From then on, the only market in the Rox or Lowell-Lawrence was the black market. That included medical services, and Doc's Clinic was one of several that patched up Rox residents for a reasonable fee and no questions asked.

That same policy made it popular with people who, for various reasons, preferred not to visit the licensed hospitals and doctors. In addition to stitching you up or giving you something for whatever ailed you, Doc's was a place to get certain modifications, if the price was right and what you wanted was available. The mods included anything from a cyber-replacement hand to new eyes to a new face that wouldn't be quite so well known to the authorities.

"Doc" was Dr. Daniel MacArthur, a former combat medic for Ares Macrotechnology. He'd served in the Desert Wars for a while after discharge from the UCAS military. Then he went to work for Ares, with some "consulting" work on the side until his bosses caught on. Ares booted him out and his license to practice medicine was revoked. In the Rox, however, everyone called him Doc, and no one cared about the license because he knew what he was doing. There weren't many street docs better than Doctor Mac.

The first person Trouble saw when she came through the door was Hilda, Doc's combination nurse, receptionist, and bouncer. Hilda knew how to set a broken bone, draw blood, apply a dressing, and dozens of other things Doc needed done around the place. She handled the clinic's computer files, keeping the records straight (and ensuring certain things were never recorded). Being a troll, Hilda was also more than able to handle anything from a punker whacked out on chips to a dissatisfied customer looking to cause trouble.

At the moment she was changing a dressing on the arm of one of the Bane-Sidhe, a local gang. Trouble knew them well, mostly Irish kids, the children of Irish immigrants like her. The ganger Hilda was treating was an ork, and Trouble wondered if his parents were orks, too. A lot of metahumans had felt distinctly unwelcome in the new "paradise" of the Sidhe, and had emigrated to the UCAS. Two of his chummers stood nearby, watching the whole procedure with bored expressions.

"Hey, Trouble," Hilda said, glancing up briefly. "Have a seat and I'll be right with you, honey." She finished up with the kid in a few minutes, accepted the cred he offered, and sent the three gangers on their way.

"Looks like business is good," Trouble said.

"Always is," Hilda replied with a sigh. "We'd be better off if we didn't have to waste time patching up the gangers, but their money lets us help other people who don't have any. You wouldn't believe the strange cases we've been getting lately. I just hope it's not some new disease starting the rounds. Anyway, what can we do for you today, Trouble? Aren't you feeling well?"

"No, it's nothing like that," Trouble said. "I just want to talk to Mac if he's got time."

"Sure thing. You just wait right there." Hilda disappeared into the back of the clinic and returned a few moments later with Dr. MacArthur in tow. With his receding hairline and the deep creases on his face, Doc looked older than his thirty-seven years. He was still quite fit, though, and carried himself like a soldier. He was wearing blood-stained hospital scrubs—apparently "donated" by Boston General, from the stenciling on them—and he gave Trouble a weary smile.

"Why don't we talk in my office," he said, while Hilda went to her desk and began tapping away at the computer.

Trouble followed Dr. Mac into his office, then perched nervously on the edge of a chair. Dr. Mac leaned back against his desk, looking at her with concern.

"So, what can I do for you?" he asked.

Trouble hesitated, not quite sure how to put it. "I've got a medical question for you, hypothetically speaking."

Mac nodded. "Go on."

"How . . . how involved is a sex-change operation?"

Mac's brow furrowed more deeply. "Female to male?" he asked. Trouble nodded, biting her lower lip a bit.

"Well, it can get pretty involved. Female-to-male changes are more difficult because we have to craft an artificial Y-chromosome for the cloning process. Then there's growing all the necessary organs, including skin grafts, followed by several surgical procedures and extensive hormone therapy. The whole process can take several months and costs tens of thousands of nuyen. And, of course, it's still not one hundred percent effective in all cases. I can't say I get a lot of call for that kind of thing in my practice. Cosmetic work, sure, but not gender reassignment type-stuff."

"I see," Trouble said quietly.

"I know it's none of my business," he said, "and I'll understand if you'd rather not say, but can I ask why you want to know?"

"It's personal, not business," Trouble said.

"All right, then. I withdraw the question. But if there's anything you want to talk about . . ."

"No, but thanks for the info, Doc," Trouble said, getting to her feet.

"Anytime," he said, moving to open the door for her. "Take care of yourself."

Trouble smiled feebly. "I'll try."

She said good-bye to Hilda and went back to her car. She sat with her head resting on the steering wheel for a few minutes, thinking about her emotional dilemma. She wasn't ready to go home, and she knew a place where she could actually do something about how she was feeling.

An hour later, Trouble was sitting at a bar in South Boston, downing the last of her scotch on the rocks. She thunked the tumbler back down onto the bar and gestured for the bartender, rattling the ice in her glass.

"One more," she said, sliding a hardcopy note across the bar. The bartender poured another and slipped the cash into his pocket. Trouble took a sip from her drink, savoring the burn of the liquor down her throat and the feeling of numbness that followed. It was numbness she was looking for, a way to smother all her feelings and make her forget about them, at least for a while.

She was still berating herself for being an idiot. Sure, she'd been attracted to Talon from the first time they'd met, very attracted, in fact. But when she found out that nothing could ever come of it, she had tried to put her romantic feelings aside so they could be just friends.

That had turned out to be a lot harder than she'd imagined, especially with the two of them working together all the time. Still, she thought she'd been handling it well enough. Then Talon thought he saw the ghost of the long-dead love of his life. Was that possible?

Hell, she told herself, if the other magical stuff Talon could do was possible, why not that? After all, he was a wizard. Universities taught courses in applied magic, her parents had left an Ireland ruled by elves, and the bartender serving her looked like something out of a fairy story to scare little kids. If she could accept all that, why not ghosts?

The answer was obvious. It was because of the identity of this particular ghost and the feelings it had stirred up in Talon, that's why. He was hurting; anyone could see that. She knew that Talon thought he'd finally laid the pain of his grief to rest, but did you ever really get over losing someone you love so much?

She looked into her glass and swirled the scotch around the ice cubes. Maybe because she never saw Talon get serious with anyone else, she'd let herself indulge the possibility that one day he'd come around and see what was right there in front of him. Now his lover was back from the dead.

God, I'm jealous of a ghost, she thought bitterly. How pitiful is that? She couldn't believe she'd gone to Dr. Mac to inquire about changing into someone Talon could love the way she loved him. The whole thing was insane. She didn't want to be a man, but Talon would never want her as a woman . . .

"Frag him," she muttered, taking a long swig of her scotch. Frag him for being so nice, so oblivious, and so damned unavailable. She set the glass back down on the bar, wishing she had something to hit.

"Ariel?" someone said from behind her, and she immediately recognized both the voice and the accent.

She froze for a second, then turned around slowly. Now she was the one who was seeing ghosts.

"Ian?" she murmured.

Standing there was Ian O'Donnel, looking for all the world almost unchanged since she'd last seen him ten years ago. Though he had to be over forty, he looked as fit as a much younger man. His hair was the same reddish brown, but with a bit more gray than Trouble remembered. He had the same warm smile and neatly trimmed beard, and he still dressed more like he belonged in the Old West than in twenty-first century Boston. Tonight he wore battered jeans, a pullover shirt, military-style boots, and a long duster that showed telltale signs of armor beneath.

"Ariel Tyson, as I live and breathe," he said. He hadn't lost his Irish brogue or the sparkle in his eyes that she'd always found so attractive.

"Ian, what are you doing here?"

"Well, it's a semi-free country," he said, "and I came in for a drink. May I?" He gestured toward the stool next to her and, when Trouble nodded, he sat down, resting his elbows on the bar.

"It looks like you're ahead of me," he said, indicating her empty glass. He turned to the bartender. "Scotch neat, and another for the lady."

When their drinks arrived, Ian raised his glass. "Here's to old times," he said, tapping his glass against hers.

"Funny you should say that," Trouble said. "I was just talking about you to someone."

"A boyfriend?" he asked, arching one eyebrow.

Ariel couldn't help but chuckle. "No." She cast her eyes downward. "Just a friend."

"And did you tell your friend how much it broke my heart to see you go?"

"Ian, I—"

He laid a hand over hers. "I'm sorry. I shouldn't have said that. It's just . . . it's been such a long time and . . . well, I never stopped thinking about you, love."

"Are you saying there's no lady in Ian O'Donnel's life these days?"

Ian shrugged, then took a sip of scotch. He set the glass down and stared into it for a moment.

"There aren't many ladies who can deal with the likes of me, Ariel. In fact, I can only think of one." He looked into Trouble's eyes and smiled.

"Flatterer," she said.

"It's only the truth. Odd, though, us running into each other after all these years. I was just thinking about you earlier today, wondering what you were about, and now here you are."

Trouble set her glass on the bar. "I really should go," she said. This was making her nervous.

Ian didn't let go of her hand. "I wish you wouldn't. Can't you stay a while? I mean, what's so important that you can't spend some time with an old friend?"

She smiled. He was right. Nothing she had to do was urgent. Her research could wait for a few hours, and no one would be missing her tonight.

"All right, Ian," she said. "Why not?" Trouble didn't know whether it was the scotch making her feel so warm and comfortable or Ian's presence and his tender smile.

Right then, she didn't much care.

9

The next day, Talon cruised up to the Avalon on Aracos. Most of Landsdown Street was still asleep. It wouldn't wake up again until nighttime when the club-goers would line the streets, everyone trying to get into the trendiest and most popular clubs. This afternoon, the street was empty except for people on their way to somewhere else and the squatters sleeping in doorways until someone chased them away.

Talon hopped off Aracos, and the sleek motorcycle shimmered and vanished into the air. Aracos was still there, however, invisible and intangible to the physical world, in case Talon should need him.

"This operating by day thing is almost becoming a habit," Aracos said into Talon's mind. "Are you giving up being nocturnal?"

"Not as long as I'm in this business," Talon thought back. "But it's safer for the team to meet when the club is closed, and we've got some planning to do. Besides, you don't sleep."

"True," the spirit said, "but I find this place much more interesting at night."

"Much easier to get a few drinks, you mean."

"That, too."

Talon went in through the Avalon's back door. Most of the staff knew that Talon was a shadowrunner, and a mage, which improved his status in their eyes. The fact that he tended to be somewhat mysterious about his abilities and that he was known to have a familiar spirit following him around didn't hurt, either.

He took the stairs to Boom's office. At the top, Aracos spoke again in his mind. "All clear, boss."

Aracos always went ahead of Talon to make sure everything was safe. Even in a place Talon considered his second home, it was wiser not to take chances, not in his business. Such caution had saved his life on a number of occasions. He rapped twice on the door to Boom's office, then paused and rapped again. A moment later, Val opened the door and let him in.

Boom was sitting behind his massive desk. He was talking to Hammer while giving the occasional glance at the data scrolling across the display built into the translucent desktop. Hammer was sitting in a chair flanking the desk, dressed in loose khaki pants and a close-fitting T-shirt of ballistic cloth. His pistol was tucked under his arm in its shoulder rig, and his leather jacket was draped over the back of the chair. Not visible was the commando knife he kept strapped to one ankle inside the beat-up combat boots he always wore.

Val closed the door and went back to the couch against the wall. She, too, was dressed for action in black jeans, a cropped T-shirt, and boots. Her own beat-up jacket was tossed over one arm of the couch.

Talon glanced around the room. "Where's Trouble?"

Val and Hammer both shrugged as Boom waved Talon to one of the other chairs. "She's not here yet," he said. "She called a little while ago to say she got the message but that she'd be a few minutes late."

Talon nodded and dropped into a chair. He was curious, though. It wasn't like Trouble to be late, but he didn't press Boom for details. If the troll didn't want to say more, then it was none of Talon's business.

"So," he said, not wasting time, "we got a bite?"

Boom grinned and nodded. "Last night."

"Well, that didn't take long," Hammer said.

"What did you expect?" Val asked. "This suit has definitely got it bad. When you're that hooked on sims, you can't go for more than a few hours without one."

Talon knew that Val spoke from personal experience. She'd been heavily into simsense as a kid. It was only the equally addictive rush of rigging that let her overcome her dependence on them. Talon often thought, he might have gotten hooked, too, if he'd had the nuyen for a datajack back when his magic was first developing. Anything could have happened if Jase hadn't found him and taught him that he wasn't going mad and not to be afraid of who and what he was.

"Talon, you still here?" Boom said, bringing Talon's attention back to the conversation at hand.

"What? Oh, yeah, sorry."

"Thought you'd gone out-of-body on us or something."

Talon laughed. "Just thinking. Now, what were you saying?"

The troll raised an eyebrow. "I told him I wasn't

sure I could get in touch with you, but that I'd try my best and get back to him."

"And you left him hanging?" Hammer asked. "What if he decides to go to somebody else?"

Boom shook his head. "He won't. First off, this guy knows zero about getting the hardcore sims. He only found us because we gave him a trail to follow. He's not likely to be thinking real straight without his daily fix, and he's scared. He's afraid of getting caught doing something bad, and the more people he talks to, the more chance of that happening. No, it'll be a while before he gets desperate enough to try to track down another supplier. Waiting will make him that much more eager to get what we've got, and that much more likely to use it once he does get it."

"And then we've got him," Talon said with satisfaction.

Two knocks at the door sounded, followed by a pause, then two more knocks. Talon got up and opened the door.

"Hey," Trouble said.

"Hey," he replied.

"Sorry I'm late." She walked past Talon into the room.

He noticed that Trouble was wearing the same clothes as when they'd gone to Otabi's apartment yesterday. She'd never been a fancy dresser, but he'd never known her to sleep in her clothes unless she had no other choice. More than likely, she hadn't gone home last night. He was more curious than ever, but still didn't ask.

He closed the door while she took a seat next to Val on the couch.

"You didn't miss much," Val said. "Boom was just saying he's heard from Otabi, but that he hasn't gotten back to him yet."

Just then an electronic ringing noise came from the troll's desk. Boom glanced down at the ID code of the incoming call.

"Ah, speak of the devil," he said. "Looks like somebody's getting impatient." Boom tapped the touch-sensitive surface of the desk with one thick finger, transferring the call to the cell-phone built into his skull and wired directly to his speech and hearing centers. He also ran the audio through the tiny speakers in his desk, so the others could hear the whole thing.

"Hello?" The voice sounded both nervous and desperate even in just those two syllables.

"Hello, Mr. Otabi," Boom said to the empty air, his voice relayed over his headphone. "What can I do for you?"

"I, ah, just wanted to know if there was any progress regarding . . . what we talked about earlier."

"As a matter of fact, yes," Boom said, turning an eye toward Talon. "I was just about to call you. I set up another meet for tonight. Eleven o'clock, here at the club. Is that acceptable to you?"

"Can . . . can you make it any sooner?"

"I'll see what I can do," Boom said. "Why don't you come by at ten, and we'll see."

"Okay," Otabi said. "What about the price?"

"Four thousand nuyen, which includes the deck modified to your specifications. Paid on a certified credstick."

There was a long pause on the other end of the line.

"All right. See you at ten."

"You got it," Boom said, and Otabi hung up. Boom rubbed his hands together in anticipation. "That should do it. Our boy is hooked. All we have to do now is reel him in."

"Is all the hardware ready?" Talon asked.

Boom nodded. "We've still got the simchip. I also acquired a few run-of-the-mill chips and a modified deck from a chummer who's got a warehouse full of old Fuchi stuff that got sold off for a song when the corp broke up. He's good at making just the right modifications without asking any questions."

"Wiz," Talon said. "Then all we've got to do is wait for Otabi to show up and make the deal. This time there won't be any problems." No one rubbed it in that he'd fragged up the previous meet.

"Our timetable's a little off," Hammer said. "Maybe we should make sure everything else is still in place so this will go down like we planned it."

"Is that doable?" he asked Trouble.

She started, as though she'd been thinking of something else. "Hmm, oh yeah, no problem there. I can't go too deep into the system without tipping security that something's up, but it shouldn't be a problem to get the kind of data we need."

"Great," Talon said. "I think that covers it."

He called up his time display. They still had hours before the meet with Otabi. "Who wants to grab a bite? I'm starving." Hammer and Boom nodded, both of them known for their larger-than-human appetites. Val also said to count her in.

"I think I'm going to pass," Trouble said, throwing her jacket over her shoulder. "I've got some things to take care of. Will you need me tonight?"

"Um, no, I guess not," Talon said.

"Good, then maybe I'll get a head start on that Matrix overwatch work. Give me a call when we're ready to go." Without further ado, she headed for the door.

"Sure . . ." Talon said as the door opened and closed, ". . . thing." He directed a quizzical look at the others, who just shrugged. At least he wasn't the only one in the dark about what was up with Trouble.

A little while later, the runners were gathered at a restaurant in Chinatown. It was one of their favorite spots, but it was odd for them to be here so early. They usually came late at night after a run. Most Chinatown eateries were open all night.

Talon picked at his lo mein with his chopsticks. "It was kind of weird for Trouble to take off like that," he said. The noise of the restaurant was enough to mask casual conversation, and he had Aracos on the lookout for anything suspicious.

"Not that weird," Hammer said, demolishing another chicken wing. He tossed the bones onto the plate in front of him. "She tends to get kind of caught up in stuff, you know?"

"You mean obsessive," Val said with a smile.

Hammer smiled back. "I wouldn't say that . . . well, not to her face anyway. It's just that when she gets into something, she gets totally into it, you know? Devotes all her attention and energy to it, especially when it's a run. She probably just wants to make sure everything is set for when the run goes down."

"Yeah, but it's not like she has a lot to do on this one," Talon said. "She handled the research and dug up the info on Otabi. There's some overwatch, but the rest of it is pretty much up to us."

"Maybe that's it," Boom said. "She doesn't have a lot to do so that's why she wants to make sure everything is perfect."

"Or she's feeling a little left out," Val speculated, scooping some more rice onto her plate. "I mean, that happens when you haven't got a big part to play."

"Yeah, but that happens to all of us," Talon said. "Is something bothering her?"

"You're the mage," Hammer said around another mouthful of food. "Can't you tell?"

"I suppose I could, if I'd thought to look," Talon said. "But I don't generally go around checking out everyone's aura, and by the time I noticed she was acting funny, she was gone. Besides, I wouldn't feel right about reading my friends' auras without permission."

Hammer nodded. "I appreciate that, chummer." Then he turned to Val. "Remember how Geist used to do that all the time? Look at you like he was looking right through you? Man, that was spooky."

"Oh yeah," she said with a laugh. "And you weren't the one going out with him. Being with someone who knows what you're feeling all the time—sometimes even before you do—can be a real pain in the hoop."

"Really?" Talon said. "I thought most women wanted a guy like that."

"Well, there's sensitive and then there's too sensitive," Val said, running a finger along the rim of her water glass.

She gave Talon a wicked smile. "I guess you're just insensitive enough, Talon."

10

More and more, Roy Kilaro was sure that Dan Otabi was the man he was looking for, and he decided to keep a close eye on him. Sooner or later, Otabi would make a mistake that would give him away, and Roy could triumphantly expose the danger to the company.

There might even be a promotion in it, he thought, maybe to a security job. Or even a chance to work with the Seraphim, the company's famous (or infamous, depending on who you asked) counterintelligence division.

Roy decided to set up some programs that would alert him to any unusual activity at the Cross Bio-Medical Merrimack Valley facility, particularly on the part of Otabi. The whole reason he'd introduced himself to Otabi was in hopes of spooking him enough that he would make a mistake.

Once his monitors were in place, he picked up a radio tracker at the local Warez, Etc. store. It was the kind of spy-gear parents bought to keep track of the whereabouts of their kids when they'd borrowed the family car. It didn't have much range, but it would have to do.

From there, Roy drove to Cross MV facility. He

located Otabi's car in the lot and planted the small magnetic transmitter under the bumper. Then he returned to his own vehicle parked nearby to wait and watch everyone going in and out of the facility.

It was late afternoon before he saw Otabi come out and drive off in his car. Roy activated the tiny tracer and followed at a discreet distance, checking the GPS map on his dash to see where the sarariman was going.

It wasn't far. Maybe a kilometer or so from his office, Otabi stopped to make a call at a public vidphone. Watching from a short distance away, Roy regretted not buying surveillance gear that would have picked up what Otabi was saying or identified whom he was calling, but he hadn't thought of it. Otabi's call was brief. A minute later, he was back in his car and returning to the office. Roy briefly considered trying to crack open the public telecom to access its memory, but decided it would be too difficult and too risky. Better to stay on Otabi and see what he did next.

He followed him to a nearby town, concealing the Chrysler-Nissan Spirit behind a big Titan truck while Otabi went into the bank and then came out again shortly after. His last stop was through the local McHugh's drive-through to pick up some food, then he returned to the Cross facility.

Roy didn't see him again until well after quitting time. Otabi drove home to his apartment, but apparently didn't bother to inform the police about the break-in, because none showed up. Roy thought that was confirmation that Otabi had something to hide. He'd looked edgy and nervous that day, like he was expecting something to happen, maybe something related to the call he'd made from the public vidphone.

Roy waited in his car across the street from Otabi's apartment complex, sipping lukewarm McHugh's soy-kaf from a paper cup.

It was nine-thirty before Otabi appeared again, went to his car, and drove away. Roy waited a few moments before taking after him, just long enough to create some distance. The tracker was still operating, so he wasn't worried about having to stay so close that he'd give himself away. Otabi drove toward the bridge into downtown, and Roy followed.

At the Fenway Park stadium, Otabi pulled into a parking garage. The stadium was dark, so it didn't look like he was planning to attend a game. After circling the block without finding a parking space, Roy also drove into the parking garage. He hoped Otabi hadn't spotted him. Fortunately, someone on the first level was pulling out just as he was coming in, and Roy quickly claimed the space. He killed the engine and the lights, and waited for Otabi to come out.

He must have parked on one of the upper floors because he emerged from the stairwell a few moments later. Roy kept his head down and watched in his rearview mirrors as Otabi shoved his hands into his jacket pockets and left the garage on foot. Roy got out of his car and followed, careful to keep his distance as Otabi continued a short way up the street, then crossed over to Landsdown Street.

The street was lined with nightclubs, and Otabi went up to one whose name was proclaimed the Avalon in big neon letters. Roy waited until Otabi had actually gone in before he went to stand in the short line at the entrance. Within minutes, he'd paid the cover and went in.

He didn't take off his jacket, figuring its armor-cloth lining would come in handy if things got hot. He was painfully aware of how unarmed he was; if things did turn ugly, his only defense was to run. Of course, most of the clubbers around him wore considerably less, though sometimes they wore long coats over their scantily clad bodies.

It was still early and not too crowded, but the music was already going full tilt, with a thudding bass Roy could feel in his bones. Multicolored lights cut through the dark, smoky interior and shimmered on the dance floor. He stayed close to the walls, trying to stay inconspicuous as he wandered into the main room, taking everything in.

He spotted Otabi right away, but not on the dance floor. The sarariman was sitting and talking to someone at a table in one of the tiers that surrounded the main floor. The other guy looked Anglo and he was dressed like most of the other club-goers, but that was about all Roy could tell. He could see something lying on the table between Otabi and his companion, but he couldn't make out what it was. Roy pondered whether to try to get closer, then decided it was wiser to hang back near the entrance, just in case.

He watched as Otabi drew a slim plastic credstick from his jacket pocket—which he'd probably picked up at the bank earlier today—and handed it to his companion. The other man slid the package across the table to Otabi, who quickly snatched it up, then stood to leave.

Roy walked away from the entrance so that Otabi wouldn't make him as he exited the club. After waiting a few moments, he followed Otabi out without another look at the man sitting upstairs or betraying any other interest in the situation.

Otabi went directly home with whatever he had picked up from the man at the Avalon. Roy guessed it was chips rather than drugs. Otabi just wasn't the type to go for the organic stuff. He was probably into sims, maybe beetles. Roy knew that BTL-abuse was all too common in the high-tech, high-pressure corporate sector. The package could have contained something else, of course. Roy had no way of knowing without confronting Otabi directly, and he wasn't ready to do that yet.

He could make an anonymous call to Knight Errant, who might send officers to investigate, but all they could do was question Otabi. Roy didn't think they could get a search warrant based on an anonymous tip.

Thinking he should call it a night, he started up the Spirit and headed back to the hotel, mentally working out what he should do next. He had no idea that he, too, was being followed.

11

As Dan Otabi and then Roy Kilaro left the Avalon, neither one noticed the small object about the size and shape of a trashcan lid hovering near the roof of the building. Painted matte black, it blended into the shadows behind the neolux lights of the club. But to the small lenses clustered on its underside, the night-time street was as bright as day. They picked up everything, from the sweat on Dan Otabi's brow to the nervous glances on the face of the man tailing him from a careful distance.

Valkyrie nudged the Roto-Drone forward slightly, staying near the rooftops as the two men headed down the street, Otabi well in the lead. She kept pace with the man following him, and his profile swelled to fill her field of vision as she zoomed the drone's cameras in. Val was jacked into a remote control deck in Boom's upstairs office. She looked asleep, but her senses and her nerves were linked to the drone's systems, letting her see what it saw, controlling its movements with a thought.

She flitted and hovered above the rooftops, past other nightclubs as the two men headed for the parking garage. Val risked being spotted when she zipped the drone across the road to hover a short distance near the garage. Nobody seemed to notice the dark shape moving quickly overhead.

She saw the second man get into a car, and zoomed in on the license registration. It could be useful later on. As he pulled out of the garage, Val revved up the drone's motor and started following. Traffic was typical for a night in Boston, so she was sure she'd be able to keep up.

"We may have a problem," Boom said as Talon came into his office.

"Yeah, I saw him," Talon said. "Any idea who he is?"

"Val's still tracking him," the troll replied, nodding his head toward Val, who was slumped on the couch against the wall. A small remote control deck was cradled in her lap, and a thin cable snaked up to the chrome jack behind her ear. Her eyes were rolled back in her head while her brain lived in the virtual world of the machine. Talon knew that Val was also recording any other interesting information the drone collected so they could go over it later.

"The run might be compromised," Hammer said.

Talon nodded. It was a concern they all shared. "Maybe, but let's not hit the panic button until we know more about this guy and why he's following Otabi."

"Aren't too many reasons why he would be," Hammer said.

"I can think of a few," Boom put in. "He could be a cop looking into the break-in at Otabi's place, or one who got suspicious about it. Depends on whether

Otabi reported it to Knight Errant. He could be a friend Otabi asked to come along and keep an eye out for trouble . . ."

"Or he could be corp security, watching Otabi because he's a possible risk," Talon concluded.

"Yeah, that's the most likely one," Boom said.

"And since it's Cross we're dealing with, there's one other possibility," Talon said. "He might be a Seraphim." The Seraphim were well known in the shadows for their ruthless efficiency in protecting their employer's interests.

"I don't think so," Boom said. "We caught on to him too easily. From what we saw out there, he's too amateur for Seraphim. If they were running a tail on Otabi, it'd be a lot harder to spot than that."

"You're right," Talon said, "but that doesn't rule out the possibility that he's corporate security of some kind. Have you got the security logs?"

The troll nodded and tapped the surface of his desk as Talon and Hammer came around to look over his shoulder. The dark glass surface of the desktop lit up with four images of the man following Otabi, digital stills taken from the security cameras placed throughout the club. Boom manipulated the controls and zoomed in on the images, refining the resolution. The man was human and Anglo, or so he looked. Probably in his twenties, with a shock of coppery hair. He wore a dark leather jacket over nondescript street clothes.

"I don't recognize him," Talon said. "I don't think he was in any of the personnel files Trouble pulled on the Cross MV facility."

Boom ran a quick image-comparison program.

"Nope, no matches. He's not in the personnel files for the facility at all."

"Could he be wearing some kind of disguise?" Hammer asked. "Not necessarily just makeup, but some kind of spell?"

Talon shrugged. "Maybe. I couldn't risk checking him out in the astral. He might have noticed me if he did have some kind of magic. Aracos might have seen something, though. Aracos?" he said to the empty air. There was a shimmering like heat waves rising off hot asphalt, and a golden-feathered falcon materialized, alighting on Talon's shoulder.

"Aracos, did you notice this guy?" Talon pointed toward the display on Boom's desk.

"Yes," the spirit said, its thought-voice carrying to everyone in the room. "He's a mundane, no magic on him, either, at least not that I could see. He was definitely interested in what was going on between you and Otabi—curious, intrigued, and a little apprehensive."

"What about cyber?" Talon asked. "Any of that?"

"Not much," Aracos said. "Some implants, mostly in his head, like yours."

Boom tapped the glass with one huge finger. "You can see the jack," he said. "Probably just some headware, then."

"Doesn't sound like corporate security," Hammer said. "It also doesn't look like he's packing, although it's hard to tell from these pictures. He might be carrying something concealed under that jacket, but I can usually tell when a guy's carrying, and he doesn't look it."

"So who are we dealing with here?" Talon said. "A

friend? An amateur? Maybe even a private investigator?"

"Dunno," Boom said. "We need more to go on."

"I'm going to give Trouble a call," Talon said. He mentally accessed the menu of his headphone and had it dial Trouble's cell-number. A small bell icon flashed in the corner of his field of vision as it dialed. There was a faint click as it connected, then Trouble's voice sounded in his ear through the subdermal speakers. "Hi, leave me a message . . ." It was the answering function of her phone.

"Hey," he said, "this is Talon. I'm at the club. Call me back." Then he disconnected.

"She didn't pick up? That's not like her," Hammer said, a note of concern in his voice. He'd known Trouble the longest.

"She's got her phone turned off for some reason," Talon said. "We'll just have to wait till she calls back."

They went over some other angles from the security cams, and ran a more thorough check through the personnel files Trouble had lifted from the research facility. They didn't turn up anything useful. Then Val stirred and pulled the cable from her jack, letting it spool back into the control deck. She arched her back and stretched her arms overhead with her fingers laced together.

"Drone's on its way back in," she said. She picked up the deck and went to sit down closer to Boom's desk. "I tracked the guy back to Otabi's apartment complex. He watched Otabi go in, then drove to the Westin Inn out on Route 2. I've got visuals of him and the car, including the plates. Trouble can run them and see if anything comes up.

"Another thing," Val went on. "From the way he followed Otabi here and back, I'd say he's got some sort of tracer on his car. He stayed back a good distance most of the time, being careful not to be seen."

"Sounds like a pro," Hammer said, but Val shook her head.

"Dunno about that," she replied. "I mean, he was careful, but it didn't look like he was operating with back-up or any kind of plan except to follow Otabi to see where he went."

"And that brings us back to not knowing enough about him," Talon said. "Val, let's download the sensor logs from your drone and see if that tells us anything." The drone had returned and landed on the roof of the club, so Val copied the logs onto chips that they slotted into Boom's desktop computer. Unfortunately, the logs didn't reveal much more than they already knew. By the time they were finished going through them, Boom's desk vidphone beeped.

"Maybe that's Trouble," Talon said as Boom tapped the answer button. The voice that came over the desk's speakers wasn't Trouble's, but it was familiar.

"Chummers, it's Derek. I can't talk long, but we're a go. I've nearly got the information we need. It'll be ready on schedule, so proceed as planned. Hunt out."

There was a click as the caller hung up, and the line went dead. Boom shut off the phone with the touch of a button.

"Man," Val said, "he's even more far gone than I thought."

"Yeah, the personafix program worked fast," Talon

said. He turned to Boom. "Any chance he could be faking it? That the guy trailing him tipped him off?"

Boom pondered for a moment before shaking his head. "No, you saw how Otabi reacted to getting that chip. Unless he's the greatest fragging actor in the world, there's no way he's faking it, even if he knew what the chip was for. The guy who sold me the program promised results, and he's good. While slotting that chip, Otabi really believes he's Derek Hunt, corporate shadowbreaker, working undercover to expose a ring of corporate spies, get the girl, and save the day, all in a couple of hours plus commercials. According to Val's flyover, it doesn't look like Otabi's shadow actually talked to him, either."

"So, it looks like we're still a go then," Talon said. "So long as nothing happens to compromise Otabi between now and then. We'll have to keep a close eye on things, but we'll go ahead like we planned tomorrow night. With any kind of luck, maybe we can turn the fact that someone suspects Otabi to our advantage. We set for now?"

Boom nodded.

"I'll see you all tomorrow," Talon said, walking to the door. "Boom, if Trouble calls, fill her in and ask her to track down what she can about our mystery man. I'd at least like to know his name and who he works for before this all goes down. And ask her to call me, okay?"

Trouble rolled over and looked at the cool blue numerals glowing on the face of the clock with a sigh: 11:24 p.m. She really, really didn't want to get up, but her sense of duty was greater than her desire to stay in bed. She picked up her cell phone to retrieve her messages, which scrolled across the tiny screen. As she read them, she sat up and thumbed the phone off.

"Hmmm?" came a voice from the other side of the bed.

"Ian, I have to go," she said softly. Suddenly he was completely awake. He sat up, the sheet falling from his bare chest. His sea blue eyes were filled with concern.

"Go? Why? Is something wrong?"

"No, just work," she said.

"Can't it wait for a while?" He wrapped one arm around her shoulders and playfully pulled her back against him.

Trouble sighed. "I wish it could, but this job will be over soon." She leaned over to plant a lingering kiss on his lips. "When it's done, I'll have a lot more free time."

"Then hurry up and get it done," he said with a smile. He kissed her again and started to get up himself.

"You can stay if you want," Trouble said quickly. "I'm not kicking you out."

"I should be going anyway. I've got some things to do, too."

He didn't say what, but Trouble knew he was talking about the terrorist Knights of the Red Branch. She picked her clothes out of the pile scattered on the floor, intermittently handing Ian the ones belonging to him. In short order, both were fully dressed. Trouble picked up the shoulder bag holding her deck and other essentials while Ian shrugged into the shoulder harness with the heavy Ares Predator pistol he favored. It was the type of gun he'd taught Trouble to use and that she still carried. He threw his long coat over it to conceal it.

"I'll walk you down," he said gallantly at the door. Trouble made sure the maglock engaged before they went down the hall to the elevators.

"So how much longer do you think this job will take?" Ian asked as they stepped onto the elevator.

Trouble hit the buttons for the lobby and the parking garage. "Not long," she said.

"Good." He took an optical chip from his coat pocket and pressed it into her hand. "Call me when it's done?"

She looked into his eyes. "I will."

The elevator pinged, and the doors opened. Ian stepped out with a look of regret. "I'll see you later, then," he said, and the doors closed behind him.

On her way down to the parking garage, Trouble pulled out her cell phone and held it to her ear.

"Avalon," she said into the mike, and the phone automatically dialed the private line to Boom's office. After a couple rings, he answered.

"Boom, it's Trouble. I got a message from Talon. What's up?"

12

In the alley across the street from the apartment building, Gallow waited impatiently. None of the feelings that seethed deep in the spirit's heart showed on the face of Bridget O'Riley, except as a tightness around her mouth. Since joining up with the Knights of the Red Branch as instructed, Gallow had been assigned a number of simple, menial tasks. One of them was maintaining watch for the Knights' leader while he carried out his dalliance with one of Gallow's enemies. How it wanted to simply walk into that building and burn it to the ground, slaughtering the helpless creatures within while they screamed for mercy. How Gallow wanted to take the heart of Talon's friend and present it to him as a gift, right before it tore out Talon's soul and devoured it.

But Gallow could do nothing of the sort. It was bound to Mama Iaga, who knew its true name and forced it to obey her. And for now, her commands were clear. Gallow must infiltrate the Knights of the Red Branch and await the proper moment to act, even though the waiting was likely to drive it mad. It consoled itself with the fact that Mama had promised to give it what it wanted—revenge on Talon before claiming the mage's life and his body as its own. If only there wasn't this interminable waiting.

A flicker of movement from the apartment building caught Gallow's eye. Staying close to the shadows of the alley, it watched Ian O'Donnel come through the front door of the building, hands deep in the pockets of his long coat. It continued to watch as O'Donnel crossed to where his car was parked. The street was virtually deserted, with no sign of any threat. As instructed, Gallow took the small commlink from one pocket and spoke into it.

"Watcher to Base. The Hound is on the path home. Over." The code phases indicated that Ian O'Donnel was heading back to the Knights headquarters.

The tiny mike in Bridget's ear crackled. "Roger that, Watcher. Come back in."

"Understood," Gallow said, switching off the commlink. With O'Donnel finally returning to the Knights HQ, it would have time to see to a few other matters. The spirit walked over to the beat-up motorcycle it had concealed at the end of the alley and kicked the engine to life. It had come to enjoy the roaring power of such machines, so similar to itself in many ways. It would have been greatly angered to know how like Talon it was in that respect. Gallow cruised to the end of the alley and paused for a moment.

A familiar car emerged from the parking garage of the building. It was the woman's car, the one called Trouble. The car pulled out onto the street and headed in the direction of the city, just as O'Donnel had a few minutes before.

Gallow knew that the two of them were involved,

but it had little understanding of human feelings. To it, sex was simply another tool for manipulating people into doing what it wanted, for luring them to their destruction through one of the weakest points of the psyche. It had no idea how deep O'Donnel and Trouble were into each other. But its place was not to question, Gallow thought bitterly, only to obey. It would inform Mama Iaga of what it had seen, and she would react as she always did, acting like she'd known all along what would happen. Gallow didn't care, so long as it ultimately got what it wanted. Then, perhaps, Mama Iaga would find out how dangerous it was to consider such a powerful spirit nothing more than a servant.

The motorcycle roared down the street as Gallow began searching. It had to make a stop before returning to the KRB headquarters. Fortunately, the streets of the metroplex offered what it needed in abundance.

It spotted a small cluster of three women standing together on a street corner, and a smile curled Bridget's lips. It brought the motorcycle to a stop at the corner, pulling closer than the turn required. There was little traffic, most of which simply went around the bike, ignoring the little scene at the corner.

"Ladies," Gallow said with a nod. The three women looked at each other, then one of them shrugged and stepped forward.

"Hi there," she said. "You looking to party?" She was young and wearing a latex body sheath that left little to the imagination. Chrome rings were spaced around her waist like piercings through her second-skin. Her hair was dark, but tinted with blue highlights

that matched her eyes. Gallow doubted either was
natural.

"Yes," it said, drawing a credstick partway from its
wrist-sheath in a provocative manner. The woman's
eyes lit up, and Gallow almost laughed out loud from
the hunger it could taste in her. "Three hundred
enough?" it asked, and the woman's aura flickered
with pleasure and a tinge of resignation.

"Not usually my scene," she said, "but why not?"

"Get on, then," Gallow said, indicating the back of
the bike. The woman walked around the bike, swung
one leg over the saddle and circled Bridget's waist
with her arms. She leaned close as Gallow revved the
motorcycle and pulled away from the curb. In moments, they were speeding away.

They had gone only a short distance before Gallow
picked out a suitable alley and turned into it, slowing
as it passed a dumpster where something squealed and
chittered at the noise. Near the dead end of the alley,
Gallow killed the engine.

"Here?" the woman said, with a look of surprise
and alarm.

Gallow didn't speak. It climbed off the bike, pulling
the girl along with the supernatural strength that
flowed through Bridget's slim form. The spirit pinned
her against the wall and pressed Bridget's body against
hers, feeling the movement of flesh against flesh. What
sensations the physical world had to offer!

It slipped Bridget's fingers into the tight neckline of
the whore's suit and tore it down the front, the latex
ripping almost like skin, exposing the white flesh beneath. The woman moaned, although Gallow saw no
fire, no passion, in her spirit. That would change soon

enough. It pressed Bridget's hand against the exposed flesh.

"Oh, you're so hot," the woman whispered in Bridget's ear. "I . . . owwww!" she cried out, trying to break away from the other hand holding her like a vice. Gallow pulled Bridget's hand away, and the woman looked down in horror at the handprint burned into her flesh like a brand. Her eyes welled with tears from the pain.

"Oh, God," she whispered, looking into Bridget's eyes, and the fear poured from her like a geyser. Gallow gasped and drank it in, the most delicious nectar imaginable. It raised Bridget's free hand, which suddenly burst into flames, earning it a shriek of terror from the woman and another rush of fear. Gallow wanted to savor the moment, but it didn't have much time.

"Please, please, don't kill me!" she begged, sobbing.

The burning hand reached out toward her face. She shrieked and tried to get away before Gallow clapped its hand over her face, muffling her screams and filling the air with the sound of sizzling and the smell of burning flesh. The spirit threw its head back as it drank the woman's life-force to the dregs. Her body withered under its touch, becoming dry, brittle, and oh so flammable. When Gallow released her and stepped back, nothing was left of her face but a blackened skull. The body pitched forward onto the ground, and flames licked across the dry, dead flesh. In moments, the corpse was burning rapidly, and soon there would be nothing but ash and fragments of bone.

Gallow turned and walked back to the motorcycle, starting up the engine and driving out of the alley. It felt the power of its victim's life thrumming through it, and how it savored the feeling. But this was only a pale substitute for what it truly desired—to do the same to Talon's friends, enjoying every morsel of his fear before devouring the mage's soul and taking his body as a new shell to continue the hunt.

Soon, it thought. Soon enough, Father, I will see you again.

13

"Okay, Talon, we're in place," Val said as she killed the van's engine. "In place," as it happened, was a public parking garage just down from the Merrimack Valley Bio-Medical facility on Amherst Street. It had been less than twenty-four hours since they'd placed the personafix chip into Dan Otabi's eager hands, and now the run could begin.

The garage was almost empty. The day commuters were on their way home by now, and most of the remaining cars belonged to those working late or on the second shift. There were even fewer cars or people up here on the top floor.

"All right," Talon said. He keyed open a comm channel with his headware. "Trouble, we're in position and ready to go."

"All set here," came the reply in his head. "Just say the word."

"Stand by. Boom, how's our 'friend' doing?"

"He's still inside the facility," the troll said, "and his shadow Kilaro is still outside."

Trouble had cracked the system files of the car rental agency Kilaro had used and was able to get his name and System Identification Number. From there, it was a simple matter to find out that he was a systems analyst with CATco, living and working in Montreal. They still weren't certain what he was doing in Boston, but they'd decided to risk going forward with the run as planned.

"Make sure they both stay there," Talon said. "The minute Kilaro makes a move, give Trouble a yell. I'm turning coordination over to you, Trouble, and going on radio silence. Let's do it."

He clicked off the commlink and shut down his headware. He didn't want any distractions for this.

"Ready?" he asked Val, who was sitting in the front seat of the van. She turned and gave him a thumb's up.

Talon turned to Hammer, who was at the wheel. "Remember, if anything goes wrong, just give me a good slap, and I'll know to get back here. Otherwise . . ."

"I know, I know, no unnecessary jostling of the body," the big ork said. "I know the drill, Talon. You take care of the magical security, and I'll worry about the rest."

"Well, I'm hoping we won't run into anything major."

Talon had laid out a colorful Indian blanket in the back of the van. Sitting on it was the same Sikorsky-Bell Microskimmer they'd used to trail Kilaro the night before. Constructed from lightweight plastics and alloys, it was the size of a trash can lid and equipped with a powerful, quiet turbine engine.

Val settled the remote control deck into her lap and snapped the cable into the jack behind her ear. A moment later, the Microskimmer powered up with a

hum and rose about ten centimeters off the floor of
the van, creating a stiff breeze.

Talon took a silver ring in the shape of a snake
biting its own tail off the middle finger of his left hand.

"Tape," he said to Hammer, who tore a piece of
silvery duct tape off a roll and handed it over. Talon
took the tape in his left hand while lightly holding the
ring in his right. He looked at the hovering drone
through the circle formed by the ring and began chanting quietly in Latin, focusing his attention on the
Microskimmer.

He knelt down and tapped the ring against the surface of the drone three times, then secured it to the
Microskimmer's hull with the tape. The drone listed
slightly, shimmering and distorted like something seen
through a haze of heat, then vanished from sight.

"Frag," Hammer said softly. "I never get used to
that." Though the drone was now invisible, the hum
of its engine and the breeze from its fan were audible.

"Val?" Talon said.

She spoke slowly, her senses caught up in the experience of merging with the drone.

"All systems still go, Talon. No interference from
the spell. This is wiz." She smiled, her eyes closed and
her hands dancing absently over the remote deck.

"Okay, Hammer," Talon said. "Let it out, and we'll
get going."

Hammer climbed out of the van and made sure the
coast was clear before opening the rear doors. The
invisible Microskimmer hummed its way out. Hammer
shut the doors and got back in the van. Talon was
stretched out as best he could on the blanket in the

rear of the van, a small Japanese pillow under his head.

"Aracos," he said in his mind

"I'm here," Aracos said instantly.

Talon settled easily into a trance, leaving his body and focusing his senses on the astral plane. His heartbeat slowed and his breathing deepened as he loosed his astral form from his physical body, slipping into the astral like an amphibian sliding into water.

The astral plane unfolded around him as he escaped the bonds of physical reality. The van seemed the same as before, but he could see glowing auras of light around Val and Hammer. Their auras revealed to him their emotions—excitement and nervousness combined with the control and restraint of true professionals. He could see Aracos hovering near the roof of the van in the form of a golden eagle, his aura glowing with mystic power. Talon's astral body wore clothes much like his regular street gear, and on his hip was a shimmering dagger. A fire opal gleamed from the pommel of its golden hilt. A silver chain with a dark, silver-wrapped crystal hung around his neck, duplicates of items worn on his meat body.

"Let's go," he said to Aracos. They passed easily through the van's armored doors, for those doors were only shadows of the physical world. To Talon's astral senses, the Microskimmer hovering outside was perfectly visible, surrounded by the telltale glow of his invisibility spell. So long as his enchanted ring remained in contact with the drone, his spell would keep it hidden from the physical world.

As the Microskimmer began to move, Talon and Aracos followed. The drone traveled quickly, but two beings impeded by neither gravity or matter had no problem keeping up. Val piloted the Microskimmer expertly toward the Cross facility, a short distance away.

"Stay with the 'skimmer," Talon told Aracos. Then he shot forward, the world around him becoming a blur as he moved at the speed of thought toward the building, arriving almost instantaneously. The exterior looked the same as when he'd scouted it in astral form for the run. Dull and blocky, it radiated a heavy feeling of apathy built up by the workers who trudged through their jobs day to day. He did not note any magical defenses, but that didn't guarantee none awaited within.

Talon hadn't dared investigate too far inside the building for fear of tipping off security too soon. Security was the main reason he and Aracos were along on the run. Before the Awakening, it used to be possible to penetrate security using just technology, but now that security included magic, you needed magic to counter it.

The Microskimmer and Aracos arrived shortly after Talon did. The drone took up position close to the roof of the facility, hovering over the bulky air-conditioning system. There was a faint pinging sound as a small metal object detached itself from its underside and dropped onto the rooftop. It was domed, oval-shaped, and about ten centimeters long. While the Microskimmer hovered, the small metal object sprouted legs. It was a Shiawase Kanmushi, or "beetle" drone, used primarily for surveillance work, though Val had a slightly different use planned for this run. The Kanmushi scuttled across the roof to the ventilation duct and climbed into it.

"In we go," Talon said to Aracos. "Hope you're not claustrophobic." "Likewise," the spirit shot back with a flicker of mirth. Following the Kanmushi, they passed through the roof as easily as through the doors of the van. The ventilation shaft was dark, of course, but that proved no hindrance to Talon and Aracos's magical senses. The beetle operated through its on-board sensor package, guided by Val. It moved unerringly down the shaft, making its way through the ductwork as the tiny servomotors in its legs whirred faintly. It traveled across the duct and then down, taking the path they had plotted using the building plans Trouble had dug up for the team.

Talon and Aracos trailed the Kanmushi down the vent shaft, and they could see a faint glow coming from the bottom of the shaft. The beetle didn't seem to react to it, so the light must have been invisible to its sensors. Talon felt a faint breeze whistle up the shaft. Even though he was immaterial, the breeze was present on the astral plane as well.

"Air elemental," he muttered. He'd heard that the research facility had "discreet" watcher elementals on site. What better place for an air spirit to hide out than in the ventilation ductwork?

"C'mon, Aracos," he said. They had to take care of the watcher before it could alert someone to their presence or, worse yet, interfere with the Kanmushi. Even Aracos couldn't materialize in the narrow vent shaft, but an air elemental's material form was gaseous. It could fit through any space, but was solid enough that it might damage the drone if they let it.

Talon drew the dagger at his waist as he and Aracos charged forward. The elemental saw them and tried to flee, but too late. It was not a particularly powerful spirit, and the fight was over almost before it began. Aracos's astral form seemed to flow like quicksilver as he became a silvery-colored wolf, and seized the wispy form of the elemental in his jaws. Since they were both spirits, Aracos could hold the elemental, although it struggled and tried to flow out of his grasp.

"Good work," Talon said, rubbing his familiar's head. "Hold it here and keep it from giving an alarm while I follow the drone."

The wolf nodded, and Talon continued after the Kanmushi as it completed its journey into the building. It stopped at a ventilation grate. Two of the drone's spindly legs reached out and tapped gently on the grate. A moment later, a hand reached down and pulled the grate away.

Talon slipped through the wall into a storeroom filled with office supplies. Kneeling on the floor was Dan Otabi, his aura showing the same mix of excitement and control that Talon had come to associate with runners at work. Damn, he thought, he really does think he's Derek Hunt, heroic shadowbreaker, on an undercover mission.

With cool efficiency, Otabi withdrew an optical chip from his pocket as the silvery carapace of the Kanmushi opened with a pop to reveal a tiny storage compartment. Otabi slipped the chip inside and closed the compartment, his aura flashing a measure of satisfaction and concern.

"There's the evidence we need, Vince," he muttered. Vince was one of Derek Hunt's teammates in

*Shadowbreaker*s. To Otabi's mind, the pilot of the tiny drone was another member of "his team," and this was part of a mission. The programming on the personafix chip had done its work as advertised.

The drone backed into the vent opening, and Otabi carefully replaced the grate. Then he straightened up and wiped his hands on his pants before leaving. Talon passed through the wall again to follow the drone back up to the roof. They encountered no further resistance on the way out.

"How're you holding up?" Talon asked Aracos.

"Well enough, although this thing seems too stupid to know when to give up."

"They don't build 'em all like you, chummer," Talon thought with a grin.

"That's for sure," Aracos shot back. "I have to admit that you really know how to summon a spirit."

Talon felt a momentary surge of pride. It was true that he'd done a great job in summoning up Aracos. Then he thought about the spirit he'd called up to avenge Jase's death, and the feeling of satisfaction evaporated. He'd certainly learned a lot about summoning spirits since then. Or so he hoped.

When they reached the roof, the beetle drone exited the vent and crawled under the Microskimmer, which dropped down to pick it up. There was a "plink" sound as the skimmer's magnetic gripper grabbed the Kanmushi. Then its engine whined, and it lifted smoothly off the roof and back toward the garage. Talon and Aracos followed it. When they reached the parking lot, Talon glanced down to see whether Roy Kilaro's car was still there. He saw no sign that the "shadow" had moved from his stakeout, which was good.

Back inside the garage, Talon slipped through the side of the van and back into his body lying on the floor of its rear compartment. He took a moment to reorient himself as his physical senses came rushing back to him. He opened his eyes, blinked a couple times, and sat up while Hammer went around to open the back doors of the vehicle.

The Microskimmer glided in and dropped down to the floor as its motor wound down. Talon willed the invisibility spell to end, and the skimmer emerged into visibility as he bent to remove the tape and recover his ring from its hull.

"Okay, cack the spirit and meet us back here," Talon thought to Aracos. The air elemental's master would sense the spirit's destruction, though he wouldn't know exactly how it had happened. The team couldn't afford to leave the spirit behind to reveal something about its attackers.

Moments later, a golden-feathered falcon appeared and alighted on the seat back as Val jacked out of her remote deck. She and Hammer had changed seats, so she jacked into the van's controls and started the engine.

Talon keyed his commlink and opened a channel to the rest of the team. "Team One to Two and Three," he said. "Mission accomplished. We're heading back. Nice work, everyone. Now all we have to do is wait for the drek to hit the fan."

14

Roy Kilaro was still doggedly tailing Dan Otabi, but he was getting tired of it. For one thing, Otabi showed no further signs of unusual behavior, where before he had seemed furtive and nervous. Like tonight, Roy thought. Dan Otabi had left work late that evening, then went straight to his car and drove home, where he stayed for the rest of the night. Roy was convinced that the change in Otabi's demeanor had something to do with his visit to the Avalon the night before. He guessed that he'd gone there to score chips, or drugs, or something else along those lines.

Roy had been sitting outside Otabi's apartment complex for hours, and had started to think it was time to call it a night. If Otabi was slotting chips, he was probably sprawled out on the couch or the bed running one right now. Roy could try to break in, but he didn't particularly want to get arrested. He decided to call it a night.

Thinking about all that had happened since he'd arrived in the Boston plex, he realized that his hopes of making a big splash with this investigation had just about fizzled out. The fantasy of winning a promotion by exposing a plot that posed a danger to the company was being extinguished by the tedium of following someone as dull as Dan Otabi.

He made up his mind to tell Otabi's supervisor about his suspicions in the morning. Let him sort it all out. That way, Roy could be on the next flight back to Montreal. He shuddered at the thought of the piles of work probably awaiting him back in the office. Still, it couldn't be worse than the fiasco this had turned out to be. Back in his hotel room, he took off his clothes and tossed them on the floor. He was asleep moments after his head hit the pillow.

The insistent prodding of his headware woke him in the morning. He showered and shaved and got dressed. It didn't take long to pack up his small suitcase and his deck in its case, then he checked out of the hotel. With his bags in the trunk of the car, he drove up to the Merrimack Valley research facility one last time.

"Morning, Lou," he said to the security guard on his way in.

"Morning, Mr. Kilaro," the ork returned brightly. "Here to check out some more systems?"

"Something like that," Roy said.

Lou watched his console as the security sensors swept over Roy like invisible hands, searching for signs of contraband, weapons, or dangerous cyberware. Then the ork took out a visitor badge, ran it through an encoder, and handed it to Roy.

"Here you go," he said. "You're all set. Hope you can finish up before Christmas. You wouldn't want to be away from home for the holidays, right?"

"Right," Roy said. "Thanks."

His destination was the office of Rebecca Sloane,

director of the Merrimack Valley facility. He had read her personnel file, along with those of other staff members, on the trip from Québec. She was an efficient, if not brilliant, manager who had worked for Cross Bio-Medical for twelve years. Before that, she'd been an administrative assistant at Fuchi. Her no-nonsense, professional attitude had gotten her promoted several times since joining CATco. She was divorced, with two children.

Sloane's secretary stopped Roy as he approached her office.

"May I help you, sir?" the woman asked, rather nervously, he thought.

"I'm Roy Kilaro, Information Services, from the head office," he said. "I'd like to see Ms. Sloane."

"I'm sorry, Mr. Kilaro. She's in a meeting right now."

"I see. Do you know when she'll be available?"

"I'm afraid not, sir."

"Well, could you at least tell her I'm here?"

The secretary hesitated for a moment, then picked up the phone on her desk.

"Ms. Sloane?" she said. "There's a Mr. Kilaro here from head office Information Systems to see you." She listened for a moment, then looked over at Roy. "You can go right in, Mr. Kilaro. She's expecting you."

Expecting me? Roy thought, but he kept the surprise off his face.

Rebecca Sloane was in her late thirties and wore a dark blazer and matching trousers over a silk blouse. Her long dark hair was tied back tightly at the nape of her neck, and she wore small, diamond-stud earrings. She had a worried expression and dark circles under her eyes. It looked like she hadn't gotten much sleep.

Also in the room was an elf, who sat facing Sloane's desk. Like most of his race, he was tall and thin. His pale, angular features were accentuated by the unrelieved black of his shirt, pants, and boots. His hair was black, too, worn long to the shoulders. The only spot of brightness was a silver pendant around his neck, a small, five-pointed star enclosed within a circle.

Roy figured him for a mage, and wondered what he was doing here.

Sloane walked toward Roy, extending her hand to shake Roy's. "Well, Mr. Kilaro, thank you for getting here so quickly," she said.

Roy stared at her in confusion.

"You were sent by head office, weren't you?" she asked. "In response to my request."

"Request?" He felt like a total idiot.

"The security . . ." she began, then stopped short. "Why are you here, Mr. Kilaro?"

"There seems to be some kind of mix-up," Roy said. "I'm with Information Services. I came down a few days ago to look into some data-traffic and system quirks that turned up in your regular logs. I wanted to report my findings." He looked from Sloane to the elf and back again. "Has something happened?"

Rebecca Sloane also glanced over at the elf. She rubbed at her forehead as though she had the makings of a serious headache.

"Sit down, Mr. Kilaro," she said. "As long as you're here, maybe you can be of some help." Roy took a seat next to the elf.

"Mr. Kilaro, this is Cary Greenleaf. He's with the

Magical Resources department. Last night, Mr. Greenleaf sensed a magical intrusion in the facility."

"What kind of intrusion?" Roy asked, suddenly going cold.

"I can't be sure," Greenleaf said in a pleasant tenor voice. "One of the spirits I bound to watch over the facility was destroyed by an unknown force, a magical intruder who left no other traces."

"Was anything taken?"

"We've got people looking into that now," Sloane said. "We don't know. So far, we've found no other signs of a disturbance or break-in."

"Could it be a false alarm?"

Greenleaf shook his head. "No, impossible. Something destroyed my elemental."

"Shadowrunners," Roy said softly, almost without realizing it.

"That's what we think," Sloane said. "Which is why I called the head office as soon as Mr. Greenleaf reported the security breach late last evening. I assumed you'd been sent to assist in the investigation."

"Actually," came a voice from the doorway, "that's my job." They all turned to see a man dressed in an immaculate black jacket and pants, black leather shoes, and a deep blue shirt with a mandarin collar. His short blond hair was brushed back from a high forehead and cold, blue-green eyes. He carried a slim black briefcase in one hand. Sloane's secretary stood behind him looking helpless, like she wanted to say something but didn't dare. The man came in and closed the door quietly behind him.

"And you are . . . ?" Ms. Sloane asked cautiously.

"Gabriel," he said. He reached into his jacket and

withdrew a slim plastic card. As he pressed his thumb
to the back of it, a holographic image of him appeared
on the front of the card, along with a gold cross.
"Cross Special Security," he added.

Seraphim, Roy thought in awe, as Sloane's eyes widened. The head office must have thought her call was
serious business if they'd sent one of their elite agents.

"I'm here to investigate the security breach you reported, Ms. Sloane," Gabriel continued smoothly, slipping the ID back into his pocket. "Who is this?" He
looked directly at Roy, who wished he was anywhere
else in the world at that moment.

"Roy Kilaro, Information Services," Roy said before Sloane could answer.

"And what is your involvement in this matter, Mr.
Kilaro?"

"I . . . ah, actually may have some information
that's related."

Gabriel looked at him so hard that Roy wondered
if he was reading his mind. A feat like that was probably well within the Seraphim's abilities. Unlike
Greenleaf, however, Gabriel didn't look like a mage.

Gabriel nodded curtly, accepting Roy's explanation,
then turned back to Sloane.

"Please describe what occurred," he said.

She walked around the desk as if she was glad to
have it between her and Gabriel. Then she leaned
forward and put her hands on the desktop, as if to
steady herself.

"Last night at . . . around seven o'clock . . ." She
glanced toward Greenleaf for verification, and he nodded. "Last night at around seven, Mr. Greenleaf here

sensed a magical intrusion—the destruction of one of the guardian spirits for the facility."

"What time exactly?" Gabriel asked Greenleaf.

"Seven-oh-four. I logged the time the instant I felt the elemental vanish, then contacted Ms. Sloane and Mr. Armont."

"My head of security," Sloane supplied helpfully.

"Are there any other signs of intrusion or indications that anything was taken?"

"Not so far," Sloane said. "My security people are looking into that right now."

"And I assume no one else has been informed about this," Gabriel said.

Sloane shook her head. "No one except for my security chief and his staff."

Apparently satisfied with that answer, Gabriel turned his attention back to Roy.

"You said you have related information?"

"Possibly," Roy said. "I was checking some system logs filed with the head office and noticed minor alterations of data coming out of this facility." All eyes in the room focused intently on him as he spoke.

"They were very small, most likely random glitches. I asked to take over the regular maintenance inspections of the systems in this area so I could check them out for myself." He looked from Gabriel to Sloane, both of them obviously waiting for him to say more.

"I traced the data-trail back here, and I suspected Dan Otabi, a computer systems specialist. When I spoke with him, he seemed nervous when he found out I was from Information Services."

"Did you reveal your suspicions to him or anyone else?" Gabriel asked.

"No, I thought that was premature," Roy said. "I didn't have any hard evidence. So I kept an eye on Otabi instead . . ."

Sloane's hand slapped down on her desk. "You were spying on one of my people?" she demanded, incredulous. Roy started to respond, but Gabriel held up his hand for silence.

"I'm not interested in what Mr. Kilaro did, Ms. Sloane. For now, all I want to know is what he saw and heard. Continue, Mr. Kilaro."

Roy swallowed and went on. "Otabi's apartment was apparently broken into, just after I arrived. The next night he went to a nightclub in Boston, where he met with a man and bought something from him." Roy saw a spark of interest in Gabriel's eyes.

"What club?" he asked.

"The Avalon."

"And what did he buy?"

"I don't know," Roy said. "I think it may have been chips or drugs. He went straight home afterward. His activities yesterday and last night seemed normal, although he did leave here rather late."

"What time?" Gabriel asked.

"At seven-twenty," Roy said, "which is not long after Mr. Greenleaf says his spirit was destroyed."

Gabriel pulled up a chair from the far side of the office and sat down. "Mr. Kilaro, I want you to go over everything you've done since you noticed the anomalies at the head office, step by step. Don't leave out anything. But first, Ms. Sloane, please find out if Mr. Otabi reported for work this morning. If so, inform your security people that he is not to leave the building."

Sloane immediately picked up the phone to call security. Gabriel turned his attention back to Roy, who began to recount everything he knew in as much detail as he could remember. Gabriel listened intently, interrupting only to ask for clarification, which sometimes helped Roy remember some little detail or another. He noticed that the Seraphim agent didn't take notes, yet seemed to be absorbing everything Roy said. Roy figured that was thanks to some kind of hardwired recording or data-system.

When Roy was finished, Gabriel sat back in his chair. "Ms. Sloane, is Otabi here?" he asked.

She nodded. "Yes, security said he reported for work this morning at his regular time, and he hasn't left the building."

"Call him in. I'd like to speak with him."

Sloane tapped a button on her desk and exchanged a few words with her secretary before hanging up.

Gabriel stood up and walked slowly to the window. He continued speaking while gazing out at the landscaped grounds surrounding the facility.

"What do you know about Daniel Otabi, Ms. Sloane?"

"Not too much," she said. "He tends to keep to himself. I've really only spoken with him at quarterly reviews and such. I can tell you he's a good employee, does his job, rarely calls in sick."

"But something of a loner?"

"Yes, I guess you could say that. Do you think he's some kind of spy?"

"I'd prefer to meet him before I form an opinion," Gabriel said, then Sloane's phone beeped.

She picked it up, listened for a moment, then said, "Yes, send him in."

The door opened, and Dan Otabi entered, escorted by Sloane's secretary. He looked tired and wore a light windbreaker over his work clothes. Just as Roy was thinking how odd that was, Otabi reached into his jacket and pulled out a flat-black pistol that he leveled at Gabriel. The secretary screamed, and the rest happened so fast that Roy barely saw the Seraphim agent move.

There was a blur of motion as Gabriel's foot connected with Otabi's wrist, sending the gun clattering to the floor. Otabi dropped to his knees, clutching his right hand against his chest, and suddenly there was a gun in Gabriel's hand, aimed at Otabi's head. Gabriel's expression hadn't changed a whit; he wore the same cool, calculating look he'd had since first entering the room.

Recovering from the shock that had momentarily paralyzed him, Roy went to pick up Otabi's fallen pistol. He looked at it in surprise.

"It's fake," he said.

"What?" Gabriel asked, never taking his eyes off Otabi, who didn't move.

"It's fake," Kilaro repeated, hefting the gun. "It's a paint gun, shoots a low-level laser like a laser-sight or a pointer that 'paints' the target. They use them in games where the players wear laser-sensitive jumpsuits and helmets that pick up when a beam strikes them . . ."

"I'm familiar with the game, Mr. Kilaro," Gabriel said dryly. "Well, that explains how he managed to get a gun past security." He extended his free hand palm up, and Roy gave him the gun.

Gabriel looked at the paint gun, then back at Otabi. "Why did you pull this?" he asked.

Otabi raised his head and glared. "I'm not telling you anything," he said through gritted teeth.

Gabriel stepped forward and grabbed Otabi by the back of his jacket, hoisting him to his feet as if he were a rag doll.

"All of you, out," he said, then turned back to Dan Otabi. "We need to have a conversation."

Sloane, Greenleaf, and Roy filed quickly out of the room, and the door locked with a click behind them.

Rebecca Sloane went over to reassure her secretary, who was still in shock over the sudden threat of violence. Greenleaf calmly took a seat behind a low table in the waiting area and turned one of the datapads to face him so he could scroll through the news pages. Roy stood there wondering what he should do, then went to sit down next to Greenleaf.

The minutes seemed to drag like hours while they waited. Finally, the secretary's phone rang. Sloane answered it herself, spoke a few quiet words, and then went back into her office.

Roy stared at the door, wishing he could see through it. He wondered if Greenleaf could do that if he wanted. Mages were supposed to have such powers. The elf didn't look the slightest bit ruffled, however, as if this sort of thing happened all the time. Roy supposed that being a magician and routinely dealing with things like spirits would make you pretty blasé about industrial espionage and shadowrunners.

Several uniformed security guards entered the waiting area. One of them knocked on Sloane's door, which opened to admit him and his companions. Then Gabriel came out of the office, briefcase in hand.

"You two, come with me," he said to Roy and Greenleaf. Two of the security guards reappeared from Sloane's office, carrying the limp body of Dan Otabi between them. Roy wondered if the poor guy was dead, then saw him still breathing. He looked groggy and only semiconscious.

"Where are we going?" Roy asked Gabriel.

"I can't answer that for security reasons," he said. "The less you know at this point, Mr. Kilaro, the better. Now, please come with me."

Although the words were phrased as a request, Roy didn't argue. He took his deck carrying case and got up to follow Gabriel. He knew an order when he heard one.

15

Gabriel led Kilaro, Greenleaf, and the security guards carrying Dan Otabi's limp form to the rear of the research facility, away from the most trafficked areas. Security discreetly cleared the way for them. Except for a uniformed security guard, the loading dock was deserted when they got there.

Gabriel descended a set of ferrocrete steps to a sleek 2060 Eurocar Westwind parked near the entrance. Roy heard a faint click as the car's locks disengaged, thinking it had to be the work of a headware radio or commlink. The security guards bound Otabi's hands with silvery cuff tape before loading him into the backseat.

"Mr. Kilaro," Gabriel said, gesturing for Roy to get in. Roy climbed into the backseat next to Otabi's limp form. The man was still conscious, but he seemed to be in a daze, barely aware of his surroundings. Gabriel took the driver's seat, and Greenleaf got into the passenger side.

Gabriel rolled down the window as an older man in a Cross security uniform approached. Roy recognized him from the personnel files as Roger Armont, head of security for the Merrimack Valley facility.

"Is everything ready?" Gabriel asked.

"They're finishing the loading now, sir," Armont said deferentially.

"Good. Inform me when we're ready to move out," Gabriel said. "I'll follow them to the drop-off point."

"Yes, sir," Armont said, then turned and walked away briskly.

The window slid back into place, cutting off most of the sounds coming from outside the car. The uncomfortable silence inside was broken only by Otabi's unintelligible muttering.

"What did you give him?" Roy asked, reaching out to turn Otabi's face toward him for a better look.

"Leave him be," Gabriel said curtly. "I've already told you that the less you know about this, the better off you are. I suggest you sit back, relax, and keep quiet."

Gabriel's "suggestion" was obviously intended as a threat, and again Roy obeyed. He sat back against the Westwind's plush upholstery and kept his mouth shut. Still, as Otabi's head lolled back, Roy couldn't help noticing a chip inserted into his datajack.

That must be what had put him in this state, Roy thought. Not drugs, but some kind of simchip. Was he right about Otabi being addicted to sims or even to BTL? Or was Gabriel just using the chip to keep Otabi docile?

Gabriel started up the Westwind and pulled smoothly away from the Cross Bio-Medical building. The car doors were locked, and Roy noticed that the controls were located where only the driver could access them. Obviously, the Westwind's passengers weren't going anywhere unless Gabriel wanted them to. If Greenleaf was bothered by the turn of events, he didn't show it. He sat gazing calmly out the window.

As they reached the exit, Roy noticed an unmarked Chevrolet-Nissan van pulling out of the research park just ahead of them. Gabriel fell in smoothly behind the van and kept pace with it as they drove out onto the main road. The mid-morning traffic was light, and they made good time. Gabriel stayed behind the van, glancing periodically into the rearview and side-view mirrors. At one point, Roy started to turn to see if someone was following, but a word from Gabriel stopped him.

They picked up the highway heading north, traveling away from Boston. Roy decided there was only one other place they could be going. Sure enough, about twenty minutes later, they picked up Route 101 East to the airport in Manchester. Although Logan Airport handled most of the air traffic for the Boston metroplex, the Manchester Airport was a major subsidiary hub, particularly for business travelers in the upper New England states. Roy had flown into Manchester on his way to Boston, and now it looked like he was leaving the same way, although not quite in the manner he'd planned.

When they got to the airport, the Westwind continued following the van, which did not stop at the terminal. It drove toward the hangars that corporations leased from the airport for privately owned aircraft. That made sense, Roy thought. It wasn't like they could get Otabi past airport security in his condition.

A Federated-Boeing Whitehorse cargo plane was parked in front of one hangar, its wings tilted up in takeoff and landing position. The CATco logo was emblazoned across the side of the wide-bodied plane, and its cargo bay door had been lowered from the tail of the plane to the tarmac. The passenger entrance was also open, with a wheeled stairway in place. The van pulled around to the tail, while Gabriel stopped the Westwind in front of the hangar and got out.

"Come with me," he commanded Roy and Greenleaf. He gestured to two security guards near the plane, and the two burly metahumans came running, straining at the seams of their uniforms. They picked up Dan Otabi like a rag doll and helped carry him to the plane. Roy noticed the other uniformed Cross personnel unloading items from the back of the van onto the cargo platform. There were seven or eight silvery metal cylinders, each less than a meter tall and topped with a valve cap. Roy glimpsed a bio-hazard symbol and some writing on the side of one of the cylinders before Gabriel ushered him up the stairs to the plane. The passenger compartment was relatively small, yet roomier than the commercial jet he'd taken from Montreal, since there were fewer seats. The two metahumans hauled Otabi over to a seat and strapped him in, while Kilaro and Greenleaf also took seats and fastened their seat belts.

Gabriel stood by the doorway, stepping aside to let the metahumans exit the compartment. Roy looked out and saw the security personnel shutting the doors of the company van. The troll rapped on the back of the vehicle, which immediately began to drive off. The ork security guard climbed back up the stairs, ducking his head to fit his tall frame through the doorway.

"All loaded up," he said to Gabriel, and then smashed his massive fist into the man's solar plexus.

Gabriel's breath went out in a whoosh as he doubled over. The ork followed up immediately with an upper-cut. Gabriel stumbled back against the bulkhead, then slid down to the floor.

Roy tensed in his seat and thought he saw Greenleaf about to try something, but the ork moved quicker than the eye could follow. Suddenly there was a gun in his hand, a very big gun, leveled in their direction.

"Don't move," he said. "Don't even blink."

Roy sat staring into the dark bore of the hand-cannon, not doubting in the least that the ork was dead serious. He heard the muffled sound of gunfire—like air guns, or weapons with silencers—from outside the plane, but he didn't dare turn his head to look. Out of the corner of his eye, he saw Greenleaf, who looked like he was going to faint. Perhaps the elven mage wasn't so unflappable after all.

The ork was reaching for the door to the crew cabin when suddenly the air around him seemed to thicken, becoming a yellow-greenish smoke. The big ork began to cough and choke like he was being hit with tear gas, and Roy glanced around, wondering where it was coming from. Were the security guards using gas to drive them out of the plane?

But the gas didn't expand. It stayed close to the ork's big bulk, swirling around him. He fell back against the door and raised his gun. Roy ducked down as the gun went off with a dull "whump" that echoed through the cabin.

That was when he saw Greenleaf stand up, and Roy realized this must be another of the mage's air spirits, like the one destroyed by intruders. The elf murmured something too softly for Roy to hear as he leveled his hand toward the struggling ork.

Even as he did, a silvery-furred wolf appeared out of nowhere and slammed into Greenleaf, knocking him into the aisle between the seats. Another man, a human this time, came charging into the cabin. He, too, was clad in Cross security coveralls, and he held a pistol in his left hand. In his right was a gleaming dagger that he raked through the noxious mist surrounding the ork. The vapor parted neatly up the middle and began to disperse. It slid off the ork and gathered into a small cloud. Roy thought he could see a pair of glowing eyes in the middle of the cloud, glaring at the man with the knife. The man thrust his dagger into the center of the cloud, and it instantly broke up and began to disperse.

Then the man reached out to help the ork steady himself. "You okay?" he asked. When the ork nodded and waved him away, the human turned back to the passenger cabin.

Roy glanced over and saw Greenleaf pinned under the wolf, which was standing on his chest. The man went over to the mage and, without a word, raised his pistol and shot him in the chest. Roy flinched at his cold efficiency as the man turned toward him. He wore a small silver loop through his right ear, and Roy saw the telltale gleam of a datajack behind it.

"Unless you want the same, stay down and stay quiet," the man said.

Roy slumped into his seat and offered no resistance. He glanced again at Greenleaf, expecting to see a bloody wound, but instead he saw a tiny dart sticking out of the elf's skinny chest. A tranq-dart, Roy thought. So, these shadowrunners weren't quite as ruthless as they seemed. Either that, or they wanted their captives alive for some reason. Roy didn't find that particularly comforting.

The ork opened the door to the flight deck and dragged the pilot and co-pilot out. As he brought them into the passenger cabin, the troll "security guard" and a human woman entered. The woman moved quickly to the flight deck, and then the troll pulled the door shut.

"Get going, Val!" the man with the dagger said, then turned back to the ork and the troll. "Take care of them," he ordered, indicating Kilaro and then the troll came into the passenger compartment, shutting the door behind him.

The two metahumans picked up Gabriel and Greenleaf and put them into their seats, fastening seat belts around them, then indicated that Roy and the flight crew do the same. From outside, Roy heard the sound of the Whitehorse's turbo-props firing up. He looked and saw a CATco van approaching along the perimeter road, possibly the same van they'd followed here. It was about a hundred meters away as the Whitehorse began lifting off the tarmac and rising straight up into the air.

The plane climbed to well over a hundred meters before the tilt-wings rotated, turning the turbo-props. They shot forward and continued to climb up and away from the airport. The two metahumans kept their weapons trained on their captives, while the human who seemed to be their leader stood at the head of the cabin. He seemed to be lost in thought or listening to something no one else could hear, probably talking to a confederate via a headware radio or comm system. Roy saw his lips move slightly, as if he was sub-vocalizing into an internal pick-up.

The terrain passed quickly beneath them, then the pilot took the Whitehorse up to a mid-range cruising altitude, and the landscape below turned into a collection of children's toys. There were no signs of pursuit or interference that Roy could see or hear.

"Trouble says we're clear at the moment," the leader said to the two metahumans. "She's working on masking our approach through metroplex airspace so we don't run into any problems."

"What . . . what do you want with us?" Roy asked. Suddenly the eyes of all three shadowrunners were on him, and he swallowed hard.

"We don't want anything with you, chummer," the leader said. "We've got what we want. I wanted to leave all of you back at the airport, but circumstances forced us to alter our plans slightly. If you'll just cooperate and don't give us any grief, you get to walk away from this in one piece. You have my word on that."

His eyes narrowed, and his voice hardened. "On the other hand . . . well, let's just say it'll be better if you play nice, *so ka*?"

He holstered his pistol and sheathed his dagger, then stripped off the Cross uniform and tossed it aside. He wore regular street clothes underneath.

The leader turned to the ork and the troll and said, "Keep an eye on them." Then he spoke to the silvery wolf, which stood patiently in the aisle. "Make sure he doesn't try anything else, Aracos."

Roy watched in amazement as the wolf nodded knowingly and flashed a wolfish grin before settling on its haunches next to Greenleaf's seat. After the leader disappeared into the forward cabin, a dead silence fell over the passenger cabin.

After a bit, Roy could see the skyline of downtown Boston in the distance. It looked to him like the plane was banking to the west in an arc around the outskirts of the plex. Traffic below thinned out as they crossed over the Roxbury district, which he knew the locals referred to as "the Rox." Most of it had been abandoned by the city around the turn of the century, when the earthquake that leveled New York City also did some damage to the Boston area. He'd heard that the Rox was still inhabited by society's castoffs: gangs, the SINless, the poor, the homeless, and criminals like shadowrunners.

The plane began to descend over the area, coming in so steeply that Roy thought the pilot might have lost control or was planning to crash-land the Whitehorse for some reason.

Gabriel recovered consciousness as they began to descend, a livid bruise already purpling along the side of his jaw. He stayed quiet, keeping his eyes on the armed shadowrunners as the ground drew closer. Roy knew that looking to him for help was pointless. Even if Gabriel did have the power to act against a group of armed shadowrunners, Roy suspected he was smart enough to protect his own skin.

About a hundred meters above an empty lot left behind by some demolished buildings, the plane's wings tilted. It hovered over the ground, almost at a complete stop, then slowly descended into a cleared area just large enough to accommodate the cargo-lifter. The turbo-fans whined down from their full power, but kept running as the leader emerged from the flight cabin.

He opened the outer door of the passenger compartment and lowered the stairs to the ground. The ork immediately went out and descended the stairs while the leader turned back to his captives.

"All of you, out," he said, gesturing toward the door. Slowly, they unfastened their safety belts and stood up. The shadowrunners directed Gabriel and Roy to help move the unconscious Greenleaf, while the captain and co-pilot helped move Otabi under the watchful eyes of the shadowrunners. When they were on the ground again, Roy saw a dark van waiting, concealed behind a half-demolished wall. The woman who'd piloted the Whitehorse opened the van's back door, and the ork and troll got everyone loaded into it.

As the three drew slim pistols, Roy was seized with the urge to bolt and run. The pistols chuffed once, then twice. He felt a slight sting where the tranq-dart struck him in the chest before he slumped to the floor, his world fading to black.

16

Three people, two men and a woman, emerged from the rubble of the demolished buildings around the clearing where the Whitehorse had landed. Talon kept his hands near his weapons as he approached from around the wings, but not too close to startle the newcomers. He was certain that the surrounding rubble concealed more than the three he saw, and that they would try to ambush the shadowrunners if things didn't go their way. It was what he would have done if the situation were reversed.

The cargo door of the Whitehorse was down, and the silvery metal cylinders stacked on it were in plain sight. Anyone could see that gunshots from Talon's position stood a good chance of puncturing one or more of them. He hoped that would help to keep things civil.

He stepped forward while the rest of the team loaded their unwanted captives into the van, which was concealed behind a half-collapsed wall. He kept his hands in plain view and relaxed as the two men and the woman approached.

The man in the lead was young. Hell, they all were, Talon thought. Not one looked over twenty-five—and probably not likely to see thirty. The shadows were a dangerous business, considered a young person's game. At thirty-one, Talon was an old man to many other runners. Some shadowrunners were older than he was, but not many.

The lead man had curly dark brown hair and a boyish, freckled face, but his cold eyes must have seen a lifetime of hardship. He wore a brick-red leather jacket that showed the stiffness of armor plating in spots.

Talon didn't recognize any gang colors. Johnsons—corporate and otherwise—often used gangs as go-betweens or messengers. He figured this was one of those times.

"You've got the data?" the young man asked, without bothering to introduce himself or his companions. Any names he gave would be a lie anyway.

Talon reached slowly into his pocket and produced a small clear-plastic case. In it was an optical chip containing the data they'd liberated from the Cross Bio-Med facility last night. He held it up so the man could see, but he didn't hold it out to him.

"The payment?" Talon countered, and the young man took a slim, plastic wand from his jacket pocket.

After the two items changed hands, Talon slotted the credstick into his portable data-reader, where the numbers glowed on the screen. His counterpart did the same with the chip, though Talon couldn't imagine how he would know whether or not the data was genuine. He'd looked it over himself as a matter of course, and it was all complex chemical diagrams and equations. Still, the guy seemed satisfied, as was Talon. The proper amount was on the stick, along with the confirmation codes their Johnson had given for the run. These were the legit "couriers" for the goods.

"All yours," Talon said, stepping aside to let them at the canisters on the cargo pad. "But make it quick. We can't afford to stay here much longer."

That was no lie. As it was, Talon wasn't crazy about conducting this part of the run in daylight. Standing around in the open, even in the Rox, was an invitation to trouble. The sooner they got everything wrapped up, the better he would feel.

The lead man gave a low whistle, and more people emerged from concealment to assist in moving the canisters. Talon saw that he'd guessed most of their locations, although one or two surprised him. He assumed a few more still hid within the rubble. They quickly began to unload the canisters from the cargo pad and carried them off.

There was probably an entrance to the catacombs around here, Talon thought. Numerous abandoned subway and maintenance tunnels ran under parts of the metroplex, particularly the Rox. They were home to all manner of people, and all manner of things, as Talon knew from experience.

As the men finished their work, the woman walked up to Talon. She had long red hair, deep blue eyes, and a curvy, athletic figure barely concealed by her rough clothes. She produced another credstick from the pocket of her short jacket and held it out to Talon.

"A small bonus," she said, "for a job well done."

Talon took the stick and got a better look at her. A chill shuddered through him as she turned and walked away without another word.

Man, she's a creepy one, he thought. He wasn't usually affected by the attitudes of the people he encountered in the course of a shadowrun. They tended to be unpleasant and, like this crew, pretty hardened. But the feeling of sheer contempt that radiated off the woman was so strong that Talon could feel it even without the use of his mystical senses. Still, he was used to being looked down upon as an "alley runner" and "street scum" by people a lot loftier than some ganger slitch with a chip on her shoulder. He shrugged and slotted the second credstick, which showed a tidy little bonus on it, as promised. It made the hassle of the run well worth it.

Talon pocketed the credsticks and the data-reader as the gangers began to leave. Boom came up as the last of them disappeared from sight.

"Ready to hit the road, term?" he asked. "We're all packed up."

Talon nodded. "We set with the Whitehorse?"

"Val's taken care of it," Boom said. "Look." They both turned as the cargo-plane's turbo-fans began to rev up with a loud whine, kicking up a cloud of dust and sand as it lifted off. It rose above the tops of the buildings, then the wings tilted into flight mode. The Whitehorse turned east, still climbing into the overcast sky. There was no one onboard, of course, but Val had programmed the plane's dog-brain to fly across the metroplex, then out over the ocean. Either someone would manage to intercept it or override the dog-brain (which would be difficult, at best), or it would run out of fuel and crash hundreds of kilometers out to sea, where nobody would ever find it. Either way, it wasn't anything the runners had to worry about.

They'd only been on the ground a few minutes, but

even with Trouble running interference with metroplex air-traffic control, they might have been detected. Fortunately, Knight Errant Security handled police duties for the Boston plex. Though they were known as a hoop-kicking paramilitary outfit, Knight Errant was also a subsidiary of Ares Macrotechnology out of Detroit. And their number one corporate rival was none other than Cross Applied Technologies.

CATco would be reluctant to trust the local authorities to handle the matter of a missing cargo plane, preferring to keep it "in the family." They would more than likely invoke corporate extraterritoriality as a member of the Corporate Court. Since the Rox was technically a zero-zone outside the plex's jurisdiction, and Cross property was like that belonging to a foreign nation, the company could keep Knight Errant out of their business. That ought to slow things down enough that the only thing Cross security would find when they tracked down the missing Whitehorse was a dead end. It was one of the main reasons Talon had been willing to try such a risky plan. It had worked, at least so far.

He hopped into the passenger side of the van, and Valkyrie drove deeper into the Rox. The van was a bit cramped with Boom and Hammer in the backseat and their six unexpected guests laid out cold in back.

"Let's take them to the chapel," Talon said to Val. With a nod, she turned at the next corner.

Talon keyed open his commlink. "Trouble, how are we doing with security?"

Her voice came in clearly over the link. "Null sheen, from the look of it," she said. "I concealed your movements from metroplex air-traffic, so they haven't got any clear radar. Of course, they'll figure out the landing site based on your previous vector when they pick up the Whitehorse again. Looks like Cross is still trying to figure out exactly what happened, and you were right about them putting the brakes on Knight Errant. It was the first thing they did when you entered metroplex airspace. I'd say we're clear."

Talon smiled. "Good work, Trouble. Meet us at the chapel. We're going to keep our uninvited guests there until the heat dies down, then we'll dump them and call this thing a wrap."

"Will do," Trouble said. "Out."

The chapel was actually an old Catholic church in South Boston, damaged during the quake and the Bloody Thursday riots. Boom had "acquired" it shortly after Talon returned to Boston from DeeCee, and it had served as one of their safe houses since then. They were using it today because they were planning to retire it soon rather than make some expensive repairs. Compromising its security by bringing outsiders there was no longer a big concern. If Cross found out about it, the team would simply move on to another.

The building was constructed mostly of heavy stone. The windows were boarded up or covered with heavy sheets of construction plastic to replace the once-splendid stained glass. Anything else of value had long since been stripped by squatters and junk dealers. That left a stone shell with a few small rooms in the back and a good-sized basement. Stocked with the right supplies, it could keep a team of shadowrunners going for several weeks, though Talon didn't plan to spend that much time there. The heat would die down after a day or two, and they would let their prisoners go.

The van pulled up to the back doors, which were protected with rusting chains and padlocks, along with "KEEP OUT" signs posted on the walls. Talon got out, fishing in his pocket for the keys to the doors, then stopped at a flash of movement at the corner of the building. His trained reflexes went on alert, expecting an ambush. Was it possible that Cross security had found them, he wondered? Then he saw who the shadowy figure was.

Jase! The familiar features gazed back at him, exactly the same as nearly fifteen years before.

Talon turned and sprinted toward him. "Jase!" he shouted, but the figure ducked around the corner, disappearing into a flood of light as if he'd walked into a bright passageway. Still calling his name, Talon followed Jase around the corner, and nearly ran into a car driving down the alley. The driver slammed on the brakes, which gave an earsplitting squeal. Talon tried to do the same, but he hit the front of the car and rolled onto the hood before smashing into the windshield. The car stopped, and he rolled forward to keep from being thrown to the ground. He was a little banged up, but not seriously hurt.

"Talon, my God!" Trouble said as she jumped out of the car and rushed over to him. "Are you okay? I tried to stop, but—"

"Did you see him?" Talon interrupted. He levered himself into a sitting position on the hood as Val and Boom also came rushing around the corner.

"See who? All I saw was you nearly getting turned

into roadkill." Then Trouble's face paled slightly. "It was Jase again, wasn't it?"

Talon nodded. "I saw him, as plain as day."

"Maybe it was someone else," Trouble began, "a squatter, or—"

"It was him," Talon insisted. "I know it. Damn it, I'm not crazy. It was him."

"Nobody's saying you are, term," Boom said, helping Talon down off the hood of the ZX. "But whoever it was, he's gone now, and we've got some other things to deal with."

"Yeah," Talon said, glancing around one final time. "Yeah, you're right. Let's get our new friends inside."

But once the prisoners were secure, Talon knew what he had to do. This thing with Jase had him turned inside out, and he was going to find out what the frag was really going on.

17

Roy Kilaro slowly regained consciousness, vaguely remembering a strange dream about being a corporate agent investigating espionage, then confronting a group of shadowrunners aboard a Cross-owned plane before . . . shadowrunners! The plane!

As he bolted awake, a hand touched his shoulder. He spun to see who it was in the dank, musty room where he was lying on the floor. It was dark, and he didn't recognize the man's face.

"Easy," the man said. "Take it easy. Everything's okay. You're all right, for now. I'm Frank Connell."

As his vision and his head began to clear, Roy recognized the pilot of the Whitehorse, who'd been dragged out of the cabin by the shadowrunners. He dropped his hand, which had been raised to strike out, and looked around.

There wasn't much to see. It looked like they were in some sort of basement. On one side, a set of old wooden stairs led up to a closed door. On the other side, what looked like an old metal bulkhead was at the top of a set of concrete stairs. Some thin foam pads had been laid out on the bare concrete, which was covered with a thin layer of dust and dirt. He could see exposed metal pipes and insulation between the ceiling beams. The only light was the glow of a couple of small chemical lanterns.

"Where are we?" Roy asked, slowly getting to his feet. Everyone else from the plane was there. Sitting nearby were the pilot and the co-pilot. Dan Otabi sat huddled against one wall, hugging his knees to his chest and not moving. Cary Greenleaf sat near him, looking equally despondent. Gabriel, who had been examining the bulkhead, came down the stairs.

"We don't know where we are," he said in a low voice. "Probably somewhere in the Boston plex, since that's where we landed. According to my headclock, we've only been unconscious for a few hours. That door up there is locked and probably guarded, and the bulkhead door looks like it's been welded shut. There's no way out of here."

"What about magic?" Roy asked.

Greenleaf shook his head. "I'm a security mage," he said. "I don't know the kind of spells that could get us out of this. Besides, we're being watched."

"What?" Roy said.

The elf nodded. "Up there," he said, and pointed at the opposite wall, near the ceiling. "There's some kind of spirit up there in astral space. A pretty powerful one from the look of it, and it's keeping an eye on us. It can hear everything we say. If I try to use magic, it will know and probably react before I even finish casting a spell."

"Can't you banish it or something?" Roy asked.

Greenleaf paused, and seemed to be listening for a moment. "It told me that wouldn't be a good idea, Mr. Kilaro. Its master is close at hand and would know. If

I even attempted magic, it would, quote, kick my skinny hoop around the block, unquote."

"It can talk?"

"It's quite intelligent," the mage said. He stopped and looked up toward the empty space. "And he doesn't like being called 'it.' He's probably the street mage's familiar."

"So, what are we going to do?" Roy asked.

"Nothing, for now," Gabriel said.

"Nothing? But . . ."

Gabriel held up a hand for silence. "There's nothing we *can* do, Kilaro, except wait and be patient. If these shadowrunners had wanted to kill us, we would never have woken up. They could just as easily have used live ammo on us in the van or onboard the plane. They want us alive for some reason. For now, we've got to wait and find out what that reason is . . ."

There was a clicking of locks as the door at the top of the stairs opened, letting in a shaft of light. Silhouetted were the dark-skinned ork and the street mage Kilaro had taken to be the leader of the shadowrunners. They closed the door and descended the stairs, both of them holding weapons.

This time they weren't carrying dart-guns, and Roy felt a chill of fear. The mage held a slim pistol, while the ork cradled a stubby submachine gun in one arm. Roy wondered if he and the others were about to be executed. He heard Otabi whimper behind him, but Gabriel's face was as impassive as stone.

The ork stood near the foot of the stairs, protecting the mage, who stepped forward. His gun was still leveled, but he didn't get any closer.

"Before you try to do anything stupid, I should

warn you that my chummer here is faster than a cat on speed and three times as mean. He'll drill you full of holes before you can take even two steps. Don't do anything stupid and you'll get out of this alive. If not, we'll have to kill you."

He glanced over at Greenleaf. "My ally tells me you're already aware of the wards around this place and of him watching you. You were smart not to test either one of them. Give me your word that you won't try to, and we won't have to keep you drugged unconscious."

The elf cringed slightly. He looked up at the wall and then at the mage and then up at the wall again. "I won't cause any trouble," he said in a small voice.

"Good," the street mage said.

"What do you want with us?" the pilot of the Whitehorse asked.

"With you? Nothing," the mage said. "You were simply in the wrong place at the wrong time. We were planning to clear all of you out before taking the Whitehorse, but the Cross security response-time was a little better than we expected. We hadn't planned on there being so many people onboard, either. Especially him." He nodded his head toward Otabi, who cringed against the wall. "So we had to take you all with us."

"Isn't Otabi working with you?" Roy asked, feeling completely confused.

"Not exactly," Gabriel said before the street mage could answer. "Otabi has been conditioned with a special type of simsense chip to believe he's a corporate agent working undercover as a shadowrunner. He thought he was working with them, and in a way he was—though he's rather confused at the moment."

"That'll pass," the mage said. "The chip wasn't designed to do any permanent damage, although I can't speak to Otabi's habit."

"How nice of you," Roy sneered, then remembered he was treading on thin ice. Here he was mouthing off to a hardened criminal holding a gun pointed in his direction.

The mage's eyes narrowed dangerously. "I'm not here to discuss our methods with you," he said. "I'm simply telling you how it's going to be. If you cooperate and don't frag with us, you'll get out of here alive and in one piece. If you don't, then things will get messy. It's that simple. Whatever you may think, we're not in the business of wetwork, so don't give us a reason to kill you, *so ka*?"

Everyone except Gabriel nodded, but the mage seemed satisfied. He slid the bag he was carrying off his shoulder and tossed it onto the floor.

"That has food and water packs—survival rations. If you've got a problem with that, you can take it up with the management."

He took a step back, then turned and began ascending the stairs. The ork was still there, keeping an eye out as the mage went up. Then he sidestepped and backed up the stairs, watching them the whole time.

The mage rapped on the door, and it opened. He and the ork passed through, then the door closed and locked behind them.

Roy looked up at the empty space where Greenleaf said he'd seen the spirit, then moved toward the bag. Otabi began to sob softly in the corner.

"Who wants something to eat?" Roy asked.

Soon they were sitting on the pads and eating the foil-packed rations, which they washed down with mouthfuls of tepid water that tasted like plastic. Roy tried to get Dan Otabi to eat or drink something, but he refused. He stayed curled up against the wall, occasionally muttering or whimpering and brushing his fingers over his datajack like he wanted to be sure it was still there.

"C'mon," Roy said. "You're not doing yourself any good."

"It doesn't matter," Otabi moaned. "It's hopeless. They'll never let us go. Not after we've seen them and know who they are."

"Hey, he's got a point there," said Simms, the Whitehorse co-pilot. "How do we know they'll really let us go, now that we know what they look like and all?"

Gabriel snorted and shook his head like someone dealing with an ignorant child. "They're shadowrunners," he said, as if that explained everything. "It doesn't matter what we've seen. They can easily change their appearance even if we've seen what they really look like. The names are just street names, and these people don't even exist as far as the rest of society is concerned. Knowing their names or what they look like doesn't matter because they'll just disappear back into the shadows when this is all over."

"What about you?" asked Frank Connell, the pilot. "I thought it was your job to protect us from people like them. Isn't that what you Special Security people do?"

"Keep your voice down," Gabriel said. "And I am

protecting you by telling you to stay calm and keep your head. This isn't a game, and 'these people' you're talking about are professional criminals.''

"And you still think they're going to just let us go?"

"Yes, as long as we do what they say. Shadowrunners have their own code of conduct, and there's no reason for them to kill us. It's not what they're being paid for, and it has the potential to cause them a lot of trouble. They'll release us as soon as things quiet down. They've got no use for us as hostages. They've already got what they want, and they know that the company doesn't negotiate with criminals.''

Yeah, Roy thought, they hire them to work Special Security instead. How different were Seraphim black ops from what these shadowrunners did? Still, he thought Gabriel should have a secret ace up his sleeve, like a hero in one of Dan Otabi's sims. Apparently, the others did, too. They expected the company—and its representative—to take care of them. Gabriel and Greenleaf's helplessness—or unwillingness—to do anything about the situation came as something of a shock.

In the end, all they could do was wait and hope that the shadowrunners were as principled as Gabriel seemed to think they were.

"So?" Boom asked as Talon and Hammer came into the small kitchen at the back of the church. They'd outfitted it with some camp equipment to make it reasonably functional. Talon turned one of the chairs around and sat down, leaning over the back of it while Hammer raided the cooler for a can of beer. He set his Ingram smartgun on the countertop, then popped the can open and took a long swig.

"I don't think they're going to give us any problems," Talon said, "but we still have to keep an eye on them."

"A company man and a mage," Boom said. "I don't like it."

"The mage won't be any trouble. Aracos and I both checked him over. He's not that hot, but he knows enough not to frag around. He knows that Aracos is watching and that if he tries anything, Aracos will be all over him like flies on drek. Plus, he's a wagemage, not really trained for combat or infiltration stuff. I checked out his aura and he's justifiably scared. They all are."

"What about the company man?" Hammer asked. "He didn't look scared to me."

"You're right. He's the only one who's not afraid of us. He's a mystery, a real iceman. He's good at hiding his feelings. Even reading his aura didn't tell me much. He's got the most cyber of anyone in that room, but not more than you, or even Boom. He seems pretty confident, but for the moment, he's cooperating."

"That being the operative term," Trouble said from the opposite side of the table. She'd been going through their prisoners' few possessions—mostly wallets and credsticks, along with the company man's briefcase and sidearm.

"His ID says he's Mr. Gabriel, with Cross Special Security," she said, fingering the ID case. "Seraphim. That could mean they've been on to us for a while."

"If that was true, they'd have found us already,"

Boom said, "or hit us harder at the airport or even when we pulled the data-steal. I doubt the Seraphim sent him. It's more likely an agent routinely looking into a break-in like the one we staged. I mean, that was the response we wanted, right? To get the company to think their project was threatened so they'd move the biosamples to where we could get at them?"

"Boom's right," Talon said. "Things went pretty much according to plan, so I don't think the Seraphim is on to us." He gestured toward the items on the table. "Have you checked over everything?"

"Mostly what you'd expect," Trouble said. "Just ID and drek like that. This is the interesting part." She picked up the briefcase and set it on the table. "It's got a thumbprint scanner lock, and it's armor-plated under here." She rapped the side for emphasis. "Whatever's in it is pretty heavy, probably compact electronics, maybe a cyberdeck. There's also a deck in the bag Kilaro was carrying. It's a Cross Babel-series and looks like it has all the legit corporate coding, so it's not really good for serious decking without some work."

"Do you think the case is worth cracking into?" Talon asked.

"Be good to know what our company man was carrying," Trouble said, "especially if it relates to our run." She grinned. "Besides, I'm curious."

"Curiosity killed the cat," Hammer said and downed the last of his beer.

"Yeah, but satisfaction brought him back."

"Okay," Talon said. "See what you can do, but be careful."

Val joined them at that point, shrugging into her

leather jacket. They'd been taking turns sleeping in short shifts, and she was just coming off hers. "Anyone need anything while I'm out?" she asked.

"Actually, yeah," Talon said. "Hold on."

He reached inside his jacket and pulled out his pocket secretary, jotting some things down on the screen and talking to Val as he did so. "You know the Silver Moon, right? The lore-store over near the old overpass?"

Val nodded.

"I need you to pick up some things for me for later. I'd go, but I've got to babysit our guests and be around to give Aracos a hand if he needs it. It's just some stuff I need for a circle." He finished the list and slid the stylus back into the case as Val pulled out her own pocket comp.

Talon beamed the list over to her, and she glanced at it. "Should be no problem," she said.

Talon had no doubt she would handle it. Besides him, she was the team member who knew the most about magic, having spent some time working and living with a coven of witches in her native Germany. She went out to the van, which was parked in back.

Boom stood, stretched, and ambled over to the sleeping mats. "Wake me in a couple hours," he said, "and be gentle. I'll be glad when this is wrapped up and I can go back to sleeping in a real bed."

Talon and Trouble traded smiles, then Trouble gathered up the briefcase and other junk and settled down in the corner to begin tinkering with it.

Hammer tossed Talon a soda from the cooler, then sat down across the table. He produced a deck of cards from one of the many pockets on his vest and gave Talon a grin.

"Five card stud?" he asked.

Talon shrugged. "What the hell."

"Just remember, you still owe me fifty nuyen from last time. And don't forget, no magic."

"Want to make it double or nothing?" Talon asked.

Hammer started dealing the cards, and Talon found himself agreeing with Boom's sentiments. He'd be glad when this run was over because there was something else he needed to do.

18

Although the wait seemed to take forever, the prisoners remained well behaved. Thirty-six hours after Talon and the others had grabbed the Whitehorse, they let their guests go. They were tranquilized once more and loaded into a van Hammer and Val had "acquired" for that specific purpose. Then they drove the van to an isolated spot in South Boston and left the locked vehicle in a parking lot. A Knight Errant patrol car spotted it and matched the registration to a stolen vehicle. When the occupants of the van woke up, they were in a Knight Errant holding cell with a lot of explaining to do.

Knight Errant couldn't hold them for long, of course, but they made it difficult, and expensive, for Cross to spring its people; just the kind of red-tape war Talon had been hoping for. Although Cross security began an immediate search of the area, they had virtually no leads to work with, and the pointless search turned up nothing.

Boom proposed a night out to celebrate the successful conclusion of the run. Talon reluctantly agreed, and joined them around the table at the CyberClub. He spent most of the evening staring into space, mulling over his thoughts and plans. Finally, he set down his glass and stood up.

"I'm sorry, but I've got to go," he said. "I've got things to do that aren't going to wait."

"All right," Boom said. "If you need any help . . ."

"I know just the people to call," Talon replied.

"I think I'm going to call it a night, too," Trouble said, and turned to Talon. "Walk you to the door?"

They left together, leaving their three teammates talking over drinks and watching the action on the dance floor.

"When is that girl going to give it up?" Hammer said, as Talon and Trouble made their way through the crowd.

"What do you mean?" Val asked.

"She's still got it bad for Talon."

"What? But she knows Talon's gay!" Val said.

"Well, her brain knows it," Hammer returned, "but I'm not so sure about the rest of her. The heart wants what the heart wants."

Boom took a swig from a big mug, which looked like a shot glass in his massive hand. "I dunno. Seems to me that Ms. Trouble has been rather . . . preoccupied of late, and not with Talon, if you know what I mean?"

"You think she's got a thing going on?" Val asked.

Boom shrugged and leaned forward, dropping his voice to a low tone. "Let's just say I didn't get the job of faceman for this crew for my incredible looks. I know people, and I can tell you this, whatever else Trouble may be feeling about Talon, she's definitely got someone else."

"I sure as hell hope so," Hammer said. "I've

worked with Trouble longer than anyone else on this team, and she deserves a chance to be happy. I mean, Talon's a good guy, and I know he'd never do anything to hurt her intentionally, but he can be kinda . . ."

". . . dense? obtuse? oblivious?" Boom supplied helpfully.

Hammer nodded. "When it comes to women who are interested in him. She should give up on him and find herself some nice, available, straight guy."

Boom sighed. "Ah, to have Talon's problems with women."

Valkyrie grinned, stood up from the table, and laid a hand on each of the men's forearms. "I'm tired of talking about everyone else's lack of a love life," she said. "Talon and Trouble will work things out on their own. In the meantime, we're here, we survived another run, and, for the time being, we're flushed with cred. So, let's party!"

Boom and Hammer looked at each other and smiled as Val pulled them toward the dance floor, giving a wild whoop.

"Thanks for walking me out, but you didn't have to," Talon told Trouble as they emerged from the club into the cold December night.

"I wanted to," she said. "What Boom said, if you need any help . . ."

"Don't worry. I won't bite off more than I can handle. I've just got to find out what's going on."

"Okay, but if you need any other help—you know, just someone to talk to instead of somebody to crack a security system, kick some hoop, or shoot a missile, well, I'm here for that, too."

"Thanks." Talon took Trouble's hand and gave it a squeeze. "I appreciate it."

When they got as far as the alley, Talon called out to Aracos with his thoughts. The darkness of the alley seemed to shimmer, and then a red, black, and silver motorcycle appeared, the engine already running. Talon swung one leg over the seat and slipped his helmet over his head.

"Have fun," he told Trouble. "I'll be in touch." Then he revved the engine and pulled out onto the street. Trouble stood and watched until he was out of sight, then walked to her car. She had an appointment to keep as well.

She drove out to the Rox, the traffic thinning out quickly when she reached the outskirts. Most Bostonians knew enough to avoid places like the Rox, especially at night when the streets were largely controlled by go-gangers who charged "tolls" for the use of "their" roads or whose idea of fun was smashing the heads of any norms who wandered into the area from downtown.

Trouble wasn't worried. She knew which routes to take and which ones to avoid. And where she was going, the local gang knew her and had been told to expect her.

She pulled up to the old mill building and drove around to the lot in back. It was surrounded with rusting chain-link and razor-wire, erected to deal with gangs who could have been the grandparents of the ones watching her come in. Except that most of these kids' grandparents probably hadn't lived here until thirty or so years ago, she thought. She set the car's alarm system and walked boldly up to the back door of the building, which looked abandoned from the outside. There were no signs of habitation, except perhaps by squatters or less pleasant inhabitants of the Rox, like ghouls.

She rapped on the door, and a freckle-faced kid in his late teens or early twenties let her in. She'd barely stepped through the door, when Ian was there, taking her in his arms.

"I'm glad you could come," he said after kissing her hello. He led her away from the door with a smile from the sentry, who seemed pleased that his commander was so happy.

"Did you have any trouble getting here?" he asked.

"No, your directions were perfect," she said, "and I know my way around the Rox pretty well. I never dreamed you were using this place." She looked around, taking in the crumbling brickwork and rusting pipes and fittings. The ceilings were high and the corridors wide. The building had probably been a textile mill or something similar when first built a couple of centuries earlier. It had clearly gone through several other incarnations before becoming the safe house for a group of terrorists.

"That's the idea," Ian said. "We couldn't base ourselves out of South Boston anymore. It was getting too hard to keep out of sight. That's why we came here."

"Which explains the warring between the Bean Sidhe and the other gangs in the Rox." She knew the Bean Sidhe gang worked with the Knights. They were the organization's foot soldiers, and they idolized Ian

O'Donnel and what he stood for, a free homeland they had never known.

"Yes," he said simply. "They've been clearing space for us, and the fights with the other gangs keep everyone thinking it's just business as usual."

"Commander," said an unfamiliar female voice, and Trouble started. She hadn't seen the woman approach until she was standing just arm's length away. She was young, probably in her early twenties, with pale skin and fiery red hair. Her eyes were a deep blue, but something about them was hard. The look she directed at Trouble was almost withering.

"Yes, Bridget, what is it?" Ian asked.

"Sorry to interrupt," she said, with just the slightest hint of sarcasm, "but we've gone over the data and wanted to get your approval . . ."

"I'll have a look at it later," he said. "Call a meeting in the morning."

"Very good . . . sir." Bridget turned away with one final glance in Trouble's direction, then stalked off down the hall.

"Sorry about that," Ian said. "She's a new recruit and very . . . intense."

"I can see that," Trouble said. "Where'd you find her?"

"She found us, actually. That's one of the reasons we took her on. She knows what she's doing."

Trouble wondered about that. If Bridget had located the Knights on her own, could she be some kind of spy? She almost said something to Ian, but reminded herself that she was the newcomer.

"Let's not talk about business right now," he said as they walked to a door at the end of the hall. With a half-bow, he reached out and opened the door, and Trouble gasped.

The room beyond was the same brickwork and mortar as the rest of the building. It had probably been an office once, but the dozens of candles placed around the room transformed it into an enchanted glen of soft golden light. It illuminated a small table set for two. Just beyond the table was a bed covered with a scattering of roses, blood red against the soft white blanket.

"Ian, it's . . . it's beautiful," she breathed as he led her in by the hand and closed the door behind them.

"Not nearly as beautiful as you," he said, leaning in to kiss her. She pressed her body against his, hungry for his kiss, his touch. Their passion carried them toward the bed, the food and drink and all other concerns forgotten in the heat of the desire. Their lovemaking was more passionate than ever before. It was as if they wanted to seize and hold this moment where there was nothing but each other.

Afterward, as they lay twined together in bed, Ian sat up slightly and looked at Trouble, his eyes sparkling in the candlelight.

"I couldn't believe my good fortune when I walked into that bar and saw you there. It made me realize just how much I missed you, how much of a fool I was to ever let you go. We're so good together, Ariel," he said. "We belong together."

"Ian, I . . ."

"Shhhh," he said, pressing his fingers against her lips. "Please, let me finish. I know I was a fool, and I know that the life I've chosen is not an easy one. But I want you back in my life, Ariel. Come back to me and the Knights. We need you. I need you. Please say you will."

He reached over to the small table beside the bed and picked up a tiny box, which he held out to her.

Trouble took it with trembling hands and opened it. It held a ring of white gold, cut with a Celtic knot-work design and set with diamonds.

"It was my grandmother's," Ian said softly. "I want you to have it. I want you to marry me, Ariel."

19

The next day, Talon set up a circle of eight candles in the part of his apartment he called his "work room." He sat in the center of the ring on a rug embroidered with mystical symbols, focusing on the flame of a ninth candle that he'd set in front of him. He tried to clear his mind of all other thoughts and concerns except the task ahead, though it wasn't so easy to center himself for some reason. Slowly, he prepared himself by letting his breath become deeper and deeper until he felt that he was ready.

"Aracos," he called out in his thoughts, and the call traveled out across the manifold planes of existence. The air on the other side of the candle shimmered as if from the heat of the flame, and the ghostly image of a silver-furred wolf appeared to Talon's mystic senses. The regal head dipped in acknowledgment, and Talon returned the gesture of respect.

"Watch over and guard me while I journey," he told Aracos, and the spirit nodded again. Talon lay back on the meditation rug, relaxing deeply as he began to sink into a trance. Waves of peace and calm washed over him as he let his grip on the physical world slip away, opening himself to the larger world beyond, the world of the astral and the infinite mystery of the metaplanes.

His awareness of the physical world faded and narrowed to become a dark tunnel through a realm of infinite shadow—the borders of the metaplanes. He flew through the tunnel toward a glowing light visible ahead. As the light grew, he could see a figure silhouetted against it, the Dweller on the Threshold.

No one knew who, or what, the Dweller was, exactly. Many traditions believed the Dweller was the guardian of the gateway between the physical world and the deeper realms of the astral plane. More modern magicians said the Dweller was a construct, a creation of the traveler's unconscious, the essence of the id or the shadow, the deep, repressed side of the personality. Powerful spirit or figment of the imagination, the one thing that could not be denied was that every traveler to the metaplanes encountered the Dweller, and was tested before he or she could move on.

In Talon's experience, the Dweller often took the form of people from his past, masks it used to unnerve him or confront him with some mistake. The Dweller knew everything about the travelers who came here, every secret, every hidden shame, every deepest fear, and wielded its knowledge like a weapon to carry out its tests.

As Talon approached, the Dweller was nothing more than a living shadow, a dark shape against the white light beyond it. Talon steeled his nerve and moved closer as the Dweller seemed to drift into his path, blocking his way into the metaplanes.

Talon felt a flare of anger. "I don't have time for

this drek," he growled at the Dweller, reaching out to push it away.

As he did, the shadows seemed to fall away from the Dweller's figure, and Talon found himself staring at his own face staring back at him, the features twisted into a look of smug satisfaction.

"Don't ask the question unless you are certain you want the answer," the Dweller said in his own voice.

Then suddenly the figure burst into flames, becoming a living torch. Talon screamed and pulled his hand away from the burning figure. Pain seared through him. His flesh burned, and his nostrils filled with the stench of charred skin as he squinted against the blazing light of the burning man. He clutched his burned hand to his chest as he fell back into the darkness, the light of the fiery figure drifting further and further away. As the darkness began to claim him, he thought he heard a familiar voice.

"Tal, help me!" it said. "Please, help me!"

"Jase?" he called out. "Jase!"

Talon was jolted from his trance and sat bolt upright with a gasp. He looked down at his right hand. It was unharmed, although he still felt a twinge, recalling the touch of the fire that had engulfed the Dweller. Aracos stood nearby in wolf-form, startled by Talon's sudden return to consciousness and looking at him with concern.

"Are you all right, boss?" he asked.

Talon nodded slowly. "Yeah, but I didn't get very far. The Dweller kicked me out of the place before I even got started. But it did give me a clue as to what might be going on. If I'm right, I'm definitely going to need some help."

He stood up and waved his hand. The candles immediately went out, plunging the room into darkness. Talon flicked on the electric lights and started pulling on his boots.

"C'mon," he said to Aracos, "we're going to Trouble's place. I'll meet you outside." The spirit instantly vanished. Talon reflexively checked to make sure he had his gun and his mageblade before locking the apartment door behind him.

He let himself into Trouble's apartment, but it was quite some time before she showed up. She was surprised to see him sitting there when she came in through the front door.

"Talon! What are you doing here? How'd you get in?"

"It's not hard when you're a mage," he said by way of explanation. "Sorry to barge in this way, but you weren't around. I tried to get you on your phone, but . . ."

"I turned it off," she said abruptly. "Sorry, but I needed some personal time."

"I understand, but something's come up, something important."

"Actually, I've got some news, too," she said, but Talon held up a hand.

"I think Gallow's back," he said.

Trouble took in a breath slowly. "Are . . . are you sure?"

"Not a hundred percent, but yeah, pretty sure. I had a vision while I was on an astral journey earlier tonight. I saw someone who looked like me, but burst into flames when I tried to get past him. That says Gallow to me."

"Oh, God," Trouble said, coming over to sit next to Talon on the couch. The two of them had met because of Gallow, the rogue fire elemental the seventeen-year-old Talon had conjured to avenge Jase's death at the hands of a Rox gang. Talon had completely forgotten about the elemental after he'd commanded it to kill the members of the Asphalt Rats. The spirit, created out of Talon's anger and grief, had somehow continued to exist after fulfilling its only purpose for being. It had possessed one of the dying gang members and, hungry for more lives, had a short-lived career as "The T-Slasher," a mysterious serial killer the Boston authorities never caught.

That was because the spirit's host had managed to gather the strength to end his own life, trying to take the elemental with him. He hung himself in the abandoned area of the Catacombs where the spirit was hiding out. That didn't destroy the elemental; it merely trapped it in a dead and slowly decaying body. The mad spirit, calling itself Gallow, eventually contacted a human mage named Garnoff, and the two formed a pact. Their plan was to draw Talon back to Boston so that Gallow could take possession of his summoner's body. Gallow ultimately betrayed Garnoff and took over his body, but Talon and his friends managed to overcome him. The last time Talon had seen Gallow was when Garnoff's body hit the third rail in a subway station near the Rox. The body burned to a crisp. Gallow, however, was a spirit, and the death of its host body was only a temporary hindrance.

"It might not be him," Trouble said. "Maybe it was just a vision or a warning of something else."

"Maybe," Talon said, "but I don't think so. Anyway when . . . when I was falling away from the burning figure, I heard a voice." He bit his lip and blinked back the tears forming in his eyes. "I heard his voice, T. I heard Jase calling out to me, begging me to help him . . . to help save him."

Tears began to run down his cheeks. "And the Dweller, it said to me 'don't ask the question unless you're certain you want the answer.' And I understood why I couldn't get past. It's because I'm not sure I want to know what's going on and whether it's Jase who's trying to contact me, or just Gallow or someone else trying to frag with me." He turned his tear-streaked face toward her. "Gods, I thought this was all over and done with, that I'd finally laid Jase to rest, and now . . ."

Trouble took Talon in her arms as he began to cry, and she held him close.

"I don't know if I could face seeing him again," he whispered as sobs wracked his body.

"No," Trouble said gently. "It wasn't your fault, Tal. There was nothing you could have done to save him." She stroked his hair, and gradually his tears subsided. He pulled away slightly, his mouth set in a grim line.

"Gallow *is* my fault, though. If it weren't for me, that thing wouldn't exist. I'm going to make sure it's destroyed this time, once and for all."

Trouble laid a hand on his arm. "You didn't know what you were doing when you summoned Gallow," she said. "You were crazy with grief, you were . . ."

"I should have known better than to let something like that loose with nothing to control it. I taught it

to kill and then expected it to stop without bothering
to make sure it did. How many people have died because of me? How many more are going to die now?"

He stood up and said, "I've got to stop it
somehow."

"Where the hell do you think you're going?" Trouble said, jumping up to grab Talon's arm and spin him
around to face her.

"I'm going to find a way to track down Gallow and
finish this once and for all. I'll make it tell me what's
happened to Jase, and then I'll make sure it never
threatens anyone again."

"Alone?"

"It's my responsibility," he said.

"Are you crazy? You can't go up against Gallow
alone!"

"I'll have Aracos . . ." he began.

"What about the team?" Trouble said. "What about
your friends? Don't you think we might have something to say about all this?"

"It's not your problem. I can't ask you or the others
to risk—"

"Jesus Christ, Talon!" Trouble burst out, her face
flushed with anger. "What do you think we do every
time we work together? What about the risks we take
every fraggin' day for some corporate suit with a fat
credstick who we don't even know? Don't you think
we'd be willing to take the same risks for a chummer,
somebody we care about?"

The set of Talon's jaw became even grimmer. "I
can't ask that of you . . ."

Trouble stood up too. "You don't have to ask.
We're your friends. We care about you. I care about

you." She drew him to her. "I love you," she said, pulling his face to hers and kissing him firmly.

Talon's eyes widened, and he grabbed Trouble by the arms and pushed her away.

"Trouble, hey, what are you doing?" he said.

She shook off his hands and turned away from him. "I'm sorry, I . . . I don't know. I don't know why I did that."

"I didn't know you felt that way," Talon said. "I mean, I thought you understood . . ."

"You're not an easy man to get over," she said. "Look, can we just forget about this? There are more important things to worry about." She wouldn't meet his eyes. "I don't really want to talk about it. I think I've made enough of a fool of myself for one night."

"Don't say that," Talon said. "I'm really flattered, but . . ."

"Yeah, but," Trouble interjected. She took a deep breath, fighting back tears. "How about I start doing some checking. You know, Knight Errant reports, drek like that, see if I notice any of Gallow's old patterns. You can get everyone else together and fill them in, okay? And don't even think about arguing with me that it's too dangerous, all right?"

Talon wanted to object again, but he knew it was useless. "All right. I'll give you a call after I've talked with the rest of the team, and you can tell us what you found, okay?"

Trouble nodded and tried to give him a smile.

"Thanks," he said. "For everything."

"Shush," she said and waved him to the door.

"I'll call soon," he said, closing the door behind him.

Talon was disturbed by what had just happened with Trouble. It was awkward, embarrassing. It was sad, too, to think that he was causing pain to a good friend without meaning to.

Right now, though, he thought work would be the best medicine for both of them.

20

Roy Kilaro was not a happy man. He'd come to Boston looking for intrigue and a chance to prove himself to the big bosses, and he'd done it in spades. First, he tagged Dan Otabi as a potential security leak. Then he managed to survive getting kidnapped by shadowrunners after even Cross Special Security failed to protect whatever it was the runners were after. Now that it was all over, however, CATco was giving him less than a hero's welcome.

Both he and Otabi were being housed at a company condoplex in Methuen, an anonymous sector inhabited mostly by lower-paid CATco employees and not far from the decay of the Lowell-Lawrence Zone. Though Roy and Otabi were supposed to be free to move about, it was abundantly clear that they weren't to go anywhere without informing a company representative. Security personnel were on-site "for their protection." The guards kept a closer eye on Otabi, though it hardly seemed necessary. The guy was so despondent he could barely get out of bed in the morning, and when he did, he spent all his time watching the trid. Roy knew they were watching him, too, like they suspected him of something.

Then there were the "debriefings," though Roy thought interrogation was more accurate. Endless rounds of questions, starting from the moment he had discovered signs of unusual activity in the Boston logs right up until he walked through the doors of the Merrick Valley facility under the watchful eye of Gabriel. The Seraphim agent personally conducted many of the interrogations. He even questioned Roy about events where he'd been present. Roy got the distinct impression that Gabriel was trying to catch him in a lie or to trip him up about some of the facts. He stuck to what he knew and told his interrogators everything he could remember, but they were never satisfied. They wanted to go over the same things again and again and again. And this had been going on for two full days now.

All of Roy's requests to speak with someone else from the company were met with the same response. They could not allow it "for security reasons" until they'd learned as much as possible about the crime perpetrated against Cross.

By the time they finish interrogating us, Roy thought glumly, those shadowrunners will be retired. He probably would be, too, though much sooner than expected. No one had said so, but Roy was starting to realize that his involvement in this affair had somehow tainted him in the eyes of others. Though there was no evidence of wrongdoing on his part—except, perhaps, that he hadn't reported his suspicions immediately because he wanted a shot at investigating them himself—Roy felt like he was being treated like a criminal.

He could only guess at how they were treating Dan

Otabi. It was hard to tell. Deprived of his simchips, Otabi spent all his time either watching the trideo like a zombie or staring off into space, responding only when the guards arrived to take him for another "debriefing."

Otabi's career with the company was finished, of course. He could easily end up out on the street when this was all over, still hooked on chips—assuming the enforced isolation didn't cure him of it (which Roy doubted). So, if Otabi was finished with the company, what did that mean for him?

The strangest thing of all was the focus of the questions. Roy had thought that Gabriel would be most interested in tracking down the shadowrunners and recovering whatever it was they stole. But his questions focused more on Roy's own actions. The questions also seemed to be directed at finding out how much he knew about what the shadowrunners took and why, even though Roy hadn't a clue. It was as if Gabriel wanted to pretend that the shadowrunners didn't exist and focus the investigation on him and Otabi.

He's setting us up, Roy thought. Gabriel needed a scapegoat to pin this on because he'd hosed up and let those runners get away. That had to be it. After all, the Seraphim took their duty to the company very seriously. The fact that Gabriel had let a band of street-runners not only steal company property, but steal it right out from under him, couldn't look very good. Gabriel was probably trying to divert attention from himself by making it look like Roy had misled him, in cooperation with Otabi.

Well, Gabriel had another thing coming to him if he thought he was going to set Roy up for a fall.

He got up and went over to where his few belongings were stacked up in the corner of the room. Company personnel had recovered his things from the hotel where he'd been staying and brought them here. He took his deck out of its case and sat on the bed with it in his lap. The sounds of the trideo coming from the other room told him that Otabi was occupied, and probably would be for a while.

He jacked into the deck and plugged the connector into the wall-jack. It was time to find out what was really going on. He booted up the deck's systems and hit the Go button. Instantly, his senses were filled with a wall of hard static before he emerged into the virtual reality of the Matrix. He was standing next to the small, glowing, white pyramid that represented his cyberdeck, and around him saw the various polygons of the local computer systems. He started with them. They were strictly low-level systems, but they told him that the security at the housing facility was fairly light. It looked like no security cams were spying on him and Otabi, at least not any connected to the main computer systems of the building. That, thought Roy, was a ray of hope.

He sped through the Matrix at light-speed to the Cross Bio-Medical offices in Boston. The building's icon loomed up out of the virtual cityscape, topped with the golden cross of the corporate logo. Roy's pass codes got him through the public section of the host into the employees-only areas. Naturally, the inter-departmental bulletins and such had no mention of the incident in the Merrick Valley bio-med facility or any sort of theft. He'd have to dig deeper than that.

Think, he told himself, think. There had to be something to go on. He turned up some routine information by inputting a search relating to the research facility, but it was nothing he hadn't seen before leaving Montreal. He thought about the Whitehorse and the airport, but those searches also came up blank. He even did a search on Gabriel, but it was no surprise that he could learn nothing. The Seraphim were top-secret, as were most of their activities.

Then he thought about the cylinders that got loaded into the Whitehorse. He recalled the biohazard symbol, indicating that their contents was potentially dangerous or infectious, and the lettering on the sides. He focused and tried to remember what the writing said.

Pandora, he recalled. That's what was stenciled on the sides of the cylinders. He inputted a new search with expanded parameters, feeling his heart beat faster back in the real world while he waited for the search to run. A screen appeared in front of him with the results:

Pandora, Cross Bio-Medical Project No. X140-762, Security Clearance, Level Three or above.

Bingo. Roy didn't have the necessary security clearance to access the file, but he knew a few tricks. He'd been working on company security files and systems long enough for that. He quickly started piecing together a program to do the job. It wasn't as elegant as he would have liked, but he didn't have a lot of time. The shape of a silvery key took form in front of him in virtual space as he completed work on the program. He touched the key to the screen to activate it, then held his breath.

There was a moment where he thought he'd hosed it, that the system was going to lock him out. But then the screen cleared and turned into a small white cube spinning in space—a data-packet. Roy reached out and touched the cube, commanding it to open and display the data it contained. He glanced over the index of the file, and his eyes widened. Then he touched parts of the index to scan highlights of the file.

Cross Technologies wasn't going to find the shadowrunners, he realized. They weren't even looking for them. It all made sense to him now: Gabriel's presence at the MV facility, the theft of the Whitehorse, Gabriel's apparent lack of concern about the shadowrunners or the loss of company property. He understood why his interrogators were focusing on his and Otabi's actions during the incident. They were building a scaffold from which to hang them.

He collapsed the file back into a cube and put it into his pocket. That triggered the file to download onto his deck. Then he quickly backed out of the system and returned to his starting point, hoping he'd done enough to cover his tracks.

Back at his jackpoint, he investigated the relatively simple computer system of the building he was in. It handled routine functions like telecom traffic and simple security like electronic locks and such. Roy didn't find it difficult to gain access to the system as an authorized user. The program he'd used in the Cross system worked just as well here, and this one's security was childish by comparison. He made a few adjustments, then made sure they were set correctly. Once things were set in motion, there would be no going back. He pressed the virtual button that would start his program, then logged off the system and jacked out.

Nothing had changed back in his room. No Seraphim agents or security personnel were trying to break down the door, and the trideo was still blaring in the other room. He briefly regretted not having done more to help Dan Otabi, but there wasn't much he could do. Otabi had probably been doomed from the start, before Roy ever spotted anything unusual in the logs of the MV facility. He quickly gathered up a few necessities and put his deck into its carrying case.

He was just finishing up when he heard the scream of the fire alarm. He knew the windows in the room would unlock automatically, so he dashed over and threw one open to climb out onto the fire escape. As he ran down it to the alley three floors below, he could see other people starting to emerge from the building. He didn't look back, but focused on getting to the ground. The metal fire stairs rattled, impossibly loud, and other occupants of the building poked their heads out to see, but he ignored them.

He hit the ground running. There were a fair number of people on the sidewalk, but a large enough crowd to disappear into. He headed for the subway station they'd passed on the way here. Only when he reached it did he dare take a moment to look over his shoulder. He saw no sign of pursuit, but that wouldn't last long. He rushed down into the station and fumbled for his credstick, which he slotted into the turnstile like all the other people on their way to the trains.

Please, God, he prayed, let there be a train. He was in luck. One was filling up as he reached the platform. It sounded the all-aboard signal, and Roy dashed for the doors, slipping in just before they closed. As the train began to pull away from the station, he dropped into a seat and looked out the scratched and dirty window. He thought he saw a familiar figure in a long, dark coat come racing onto the platform in time to see the train pull away. Roy hunched down in his seat, but tried not to be too obvious about it.

He got off the train a few stations later, just long enough to use the bank machine in the station. He slotted his credstick and downloaded all but a few francs from his personal account onto a certified stick, converting the funds into nuyen. The certified stick was almost as good as cash and virtually untraceable, since it contained no ID codes. He pocketed both sticks and boarded the next train, which would take him to downtown Boston.

As long as he didn't use his personal credstick, it would be harder for the company to track him. Now he was on his own in a strange city, with only limited funds. He'd probably given Gabriel more than he could have hoped for by running off. It would be proof of his guilt and complicity with whatever the Seraphim were trying to pin on him, and would probably damn Otabi by association, too. The hopelessness of his situation nearly overwhelmed him, and he gripped the support bar of the subway car as if his life depended on it.

No, he thought, he couldn't give up. He had to get to the bottom of it, find some evidence that he could bring to the company brass so they would know the truth. Assuming they weren't the ones who'd authorized this scheme in the first place. That was a sobering thought. If it were true, then Roy really didn't have a single place to turn. Who would be willing to help him against a megacorporation like Cross Applied Technologies?

The answer came easily: the same ones people always called on when they needed to take on a corp.

Shadowrunners.

When the train reached downtown, Roy got off the train and found a public telecom. He slotted his certified stick and touched the screen for directory assistance.

"The number of the Avalon nightclub," he said when the prompt appeared. A few moments later, he had the number and a printout map with directions for getting there folded up in his pocket. He was glad to see that the address wasn't far from one of the stops on the red line.

All he had to do was keep from getting caught before he got there.

21

Talon walked into the Avalon the way he always did, and the various bouncers acknowledged him with a nod. It was almost eleven o'clock, and things were just starting to pick up as a line of people began forming at the front door. Talon immediately headed up the stairs to Boom's office on the top floor.

"All clear, boss," Aracos said in his mind. "Everyone's there."

Talon thanked the spirit as he cleared the last few steps. He was thinking of what had happened when he'd gone to tell Trouble that he thought Gallow was back. As if he didn't have enough problems without Trouble revealing that she'd been harboring feelings that were more than friendship for him.

Trouble had made no secret of the fact that she was attracted to him when they'd first met. At first he didn't tell her he was gay because that wasn't the kind of information he went around telling people he barely knew. They did talk about it eventually, and he'd assumed that was the end of it.

Jase was his first love and, in many ways, the only one. As he'd told Trouble, it was the only serious relationship he'd ever had. Besides, keeping a relationship going wasn't easy even for a straight shad-owrunner. Deep down, though, he knew that he never again wanted to hurt like he did when Jase died. Losing Jase had nearly killed him, though it was other people who died as a result of it. He took his revenge against the gangers who'd killed Jase and, in doing it, had unleashed an evil force that kept coming back to haunt him.

Seems like, where love is concerned, all I do is make a mess of things, Talon thought as he turned the knob of the door to Boom's office.

Boom, Hammer, and Valkyrie were already waiting for him when he came in. He sat down near Boom's desk, not bothering to take off his jacket.

"So, term, what's up?" Boom asked. "Don't tell me you managed to find more work for us already?"

"No," Talon said. "I've been doing some checking, and I think Gallow's back." There was a pregnant pause as the words sank in.

"So, what's the plan?" Hammer asked calmly. Nobody asked Talon if he was certain or whether they had to get involved. They simply asked what he wanted to do next, offering their help unconditionally, without question. He wondered what he'd done to deserve such good and loyal friends.

"Trouble's doing some checking now," he said. His face got hot with embarrassment at the mention of her name. "She's looking for Gallow's usual pattern of kills. That might give us some clue about where it is and what it's doing. Then we track it down and take care of it once and for all."

Hammer and Boom nodded their assent. Then Talon's headware phone rang, and the incoming call icon flashed in the corner of his vision.

"I've got a call," he said. "That might be her now."

He sat back and mentally signaled his headware to answer the call. Instead of Trouble, however, he saw something else. It was a woman's image projected directly onto his optic nerves by his headware display link. She was perfectly formed, beautiful and sensual like a woman straight out of a high-class erotic sim. She was dressed head to toe in leather as red as blood, and her lips were colored to match. She looked at Talon with soulful eyes, and he smiled at her. Talon knew that the real woman behind the erotic image used it as a little joke on those fooled by appearances.

"Jane," he said. "Long time no see. What's going on?"

"Hoi, Talon," she replied, her voice transmitted directly to his audio centers. "Hope I'm not calling at a bad time."

Jane-in-the-Box was a decker, one of the slickest Talon had ever known. She worked with Assets, Inc., the team of shadowrunners employed by the Draco Foundation and funded by money from the late dragon Dunkelzahn's estate. Talon had worked for Assets before coming to Boston, traveling the world as well as taking part in some harrowing shadowruns. Then the business with Trouble and Gallow brought him back to his home town. He hadn't heard from any of the Assets crew in a while, and Jane's sudden appearance made him think this wasn't a social call.

"Could be better," he said. "What's up?"

"A consultation," Jane replied. "There's something unusual going on down in DeeCee, and Ryan wants you to come down and have a look at it. Usual rates, of course."

Talon sighed. "This is a bad time, Jane," he said. "We're pretty deep in some weird things around here, too. What's up?"

Jane's image shrugged slightly, a subtle nuance to the programming. "Well, I don't know from magic, but Ryan says it's got something to do with the astral rift near the Watergate. I guess people are picking up some strange vibes from it or something."

"Don't you have a mage who can check it out? What about the Foundation? They must have more mages on the payroll than you can shake a wand at."

"They do," Jane said, "and plenty of them have checked out the rift, but they don't know what to make of it. Ryan says he wants someone with experience 'dealing with things from the other side.' That means you, chummer."

Talon grimaced as he recalled some of those experiences with "the other side," the bizarre reaches of the metaplanes and the things he'd seen there in his first run with Assets. It still gave him the occasional nightmare, and he wasn't anxious to revisit any more unpleasant memories.

"I can't come just now," he said. "Tell Ryan I might be able to come down in astral form in a few days. That's the best I can do."

"All right," Jane said. "I'll tell him." She didn't ask for more details on what he was doing. It wouldn't have been proper street etiquette to inquire. "Good luck, chummer."

Then the image blinked out, and Talon returned his attention to the room.

"Was that Jane?" Boom asked.

"Uh-huh. Assets has something they want me to look into."

"Never rains but it pours," the troll muttered.

"I'll say," Talon said.

"I hate to interrupt, term," Boom said, looking down at his desk, "but it looks like there's another country being heard from. Come take a look at this."

They all clustered around the desk to look at the windows open on its glassy surface. They showed surveillance-cam images of a man making his way through the nightclub below, carrying a flat-sided bag slung over one shoulder. They recognized his face and reddish hair.

"It's Kilaro, the guy who was following Otabi," Hammer said.

"What's he doing here?" Boom asked.

"Looking for us, probably," Talon said. "He followed Otabi here before. Maybe he recognized one of us from here."

"Or maybe he told Cross security about it, and they're using him as bait," Boom said, his expression turning sour. He didn't care for anything that threatened his nightclub. The Avalon was considered neutral territory, like many such places in the various plexes across the country, but it wasn't unknown for corporations to use stalking horses to invade them when need be.

"I'm gonna have him thrown out," Boom said, reaching for the hot button on his desktop.

"Wait," Talon said. "Let me have a look first."

He sat down, sinking quickly and easily into a trance

and loosing his astral body. He floated away from
his physical form, then dived down through the floor
of the room, with Aracos close behind him. He
passed through the physical structure of the nightclub as if it wasn't even there, reaching the main
room in moments. He oriented himself among the
flurry of unleashed emotions and desires coming off
the crowd like waves of heat, and quickly zeroed in
on Kilaro.

Talon scanned the colorful aura around his body,
which reflected the man's emotions as well as his general state of health and well being. Talon saw the telltale signs of cybernetic implants that he'd noticed
when assensing Kilaro's aura previously. He looked
carefully before zipping back up through the building
and returning to his physical body.

"Well?" Boom asked when Talon opened his eyes.

"He's scared," Talon said. "Confused and scared
out of his wits, but also determined underneath it all."

"Do you think he's trying to draw us out?" Val
asked.

"Yes, but I don't know if he's doing it for the corp
or not. I'd like to talk to him before we just try to
ditch him."

Boom frowned, then nodded slowly. "All right,"
he said.

"Hammer, you and me," Talon said. The ork nodded, following Talon out the door. "We'll be right
back," Talon said.

They descended the stairs and pushed through the
crowd of people to where Kilaro was standing. Talon
was always impressed with the speed and stealth at

which someone the size of Harlan Hammarand could move. The ork faded back into the crowd, allowing Talon to approach their target from the other side. Kilaro started slightly when he noticed Talon, but he didn't see Hammer until the big ork laid one massive hand on his shoulder. Talon thought he was going to jump out of his skin.

"Mr. Kilaro," he said. "Fancy seeing you again. Is this business or pleasure?"

Kilaro gulped visibly as he tried to regain his composure, glancing from Talon to Hammer and back again.

"Business," he said finally. "I've found out some things I think you might like to know."

Talon allowed himself a raised eyebrow. "Really? Well, then, why don't you come with us and you can tell us all about it."

Kilaro knew he didn't have much choice in the matter, so he allowed Talon and Hammer to escort him away from the dance floor and up the stairs. They went into Boom's office, and Talon gestured to an empty chair.

"Have a seat," he said. "So, was it our charming company or something else that wouldn't let you stay away?"

Kilaro gave Talon a hard look. "I've probably destroyed my career over this," he said bitterly. "The least you could do is listen."

"We're listening," Boom said.

"How much do you know about that stuff you were hired to steal?" Kilaro asked.

Talon glanced over at Boom, letting him answer. "Crowd control agent," Boom said. "Engineered bug intended to make everyone feel like drek for a few days; fast-acting with an aerosol vector."

"Is that all?" Kilaro asked.

Boom leaned forward, elbows on his desk. "Why? Is there something else we should know about it?"

Kilaro nodded. "The virus is called Pandora, and you're right, it's an anti-riot agent. But that's not all. It's a binary product based on some experiments with a riot-agent called Vigid back in the early fifties. Normally, it's a fast-acting, incapacitating agent with symptoms similar to a bad stomach flu. Victims feel nauseous, dizzy, and so on. Spray a crowd with it, and they'll all be puking up their guts in about a minute. But include a special catalyst and the Pandora bug mutates rapidly into something much, much nastier."

"How nasty?" Talon asked.

Kilaro turned to look at him. "Deadly," he said. "Kills in a matter of minutes, but it isn't contagious. It dies quickly when it's exposed to air, so it's safe to enter the area just a few minutes later. I guess the idea was to create a tool for broad-range military use, so you could either incapacitate an enemy or make sure he never got up."

Kilaro reached down toward the bag sitting at his feet, then stopped for a moment when he saw everyone's hands drift toward their weapons. Moving his hand very, very slowly, he took an optical chip from the bag's inner pocket and slid it across the desk toward Boom.

"There's the data," he said. "Direct from the company's files. Interesting thing is, around the same time you stole the samples of the virus, the only samples of the catalyst went missing, too. Did you have something to do with that?"

"No," Talon said. "We didn't know about any catalyst. Whoever hired us must have hired someone else to get the catalyst for them."

"Which means whoever's got it has a massive lethal weapon," Boom said.

"Why are you telling us this?" Talon asked.

Kilaro looked down, seeming to gather his thoughts. "Two reasons, I suppose," he said, looking up again. "First, I think somebody at Cross wanted you to get away with this stuff. The investigation is focused on finding scapegoats to blame for the theft of the virus rather than tracking it down again."

"Well, wouldn't you say that's standard corporate procedure?" Talon asked.

Kilaro shook his head. "No, it's more than that. The data in the files I found shows that the company has started inoculating its own personnel in Boston against the effects of the Pandora virus, but nowhere else. They've got a vaccine for it, but they haven't said word one about it, or about how dangerous the virus is, to the authorities. It's like they expect Pandora to get used here and want to be ready for it."

"And second?" Talon prompted.

"And second, because I didn't have anyone else to turn to who'd believe me without the company being able to cover it up," Kilaro said.

"Frag," Boom muttered. "We've been set up."

"But why?" Val said. "Why would Cross get involved in letting someone steal a weapon from them? If they use it, they'll only end up looking bad."

"Not necessarily," Boom said. "Think about it.

Cross gets two potential benefits from letting the Pandora virus get used. One, it's a field test of the technology under 'actual conditions.' If it works as advertised, Cross will have no lack of military buyers wanting some of their very own. That will drive the price up and create demand even if there's a public outcry against it. What's more, think about who holds the security contract for Boston."

"Knight Errant," Talon said.

"Right. If somebody manages to set off a major viral weapon in the metroplex, Cross can come forward and say they contacted Knight Errant about the theft, but that Knight dragged its feet. They'll make them look incompetent. And Knight Errant is controlled by Ares Macrotech, Cross's biggest rival. Getting their contract with Boston pulled would cripple Ares's presence in the New England area."

"Leaving it ripe for somebody else to move in," Hammer concluded. "Frag."

"And you can bet Cross will be pointing fingers our way when the drek hits the fan," Boom said. "They'll blame everything on the big, bad shadowrunners, or should I say 'terrorists'?"

"Never rains but it pours, huh? Looks like we're going to have to find that virus," Talon said, looking around at the others.

A beeping from Boom's desktop interrupted any further discussion.

"Oh, frag me," Boom said. "We've got another problem. Looks like Mr. Kilaro here has friends."

"What?" Talon said, coming around to Boom's side of the desk. The security monitors showed the crowd down below, and Talon quickly picked out another familiar face in the crowd.

"Drek," he said.

"What is it?" Kilaro asked.

Talon looked up at him. "It's your buddy Gabriel. He must have followed you here, and I don't think he came alone."

22

"Okay, chummers," Talon said. "It's time for us to be going."

"Out the back way," Boom said, rising from his desk and hitting a switch to shut everything down. Val and Hammer went out quickly, though Hammer stopped to check the camera pickups outside.

"What about me?" Kilaro asked.

Talon grabbed him by the armpit and pulled him out of the chair. "You're coming with us," he said. "Stick close and do exactly what you're told, understand?" Kilaro nodded numbly, clutching the bag with his cyberdeck to his chest.

"All clear," Hammer said.

"Go," Talon said.

Hammer opened the door and began moving down the hall, gun at the ready. Val went next, then Kilaro and Talon, with Boom bringing up the rear. The troll drew a heavy pistol that looked almost childishly small in his massive grip, but it had enough power to punch through an engine block, much less a human target.

"The van?" Talon asked Val.

"Ready out back," she said.

They heard a loud report from a gun and the thudding sound of running feet.

"They're coming up the stairs!" Aracos said in Talon's mind.

"They're coming," Talon said. "Go! Go!"

They raced for the door leading to the emergency exit. When they reached the intersection of the corridors, three men, all human, were coming up the stairs from the main floor. Gabriel was in the lead, and each of the three held a semiautomatic pistol in his hand. They wore heavy long coats over nondescript corporate wear and dark sunglasses that seemed not to hinder them at all in the dim hallway.

Hammer flattened against the wall, and Talon did the same as the men opened fire. Boom did his best to get out of the way, but there wasn't anywhere in the hall for a three-meter-tall troll to hide. He leveled his pistol at the men and returned fire as Hammer leaned out around the corner to do the same. Gabriel and his companions dived for cover as bullets chewed up the walls around them.

"Get going. We'll hold them," Talon said to Valkyrie, who then sprinted down the hall toward the exit. Talon pushed Kilaro after her. "Go with Val," he said, and Kilaro didn't argue.

"Trouble, boss," Aracos said. "They've got spirits with them!"

Oh, great, Talon thought. "How many?"

"Two, and they look like elementals."

"Can you handle them?"

"Maybe one, but I'm not sure about both," Aracos said. "They look pretty powerful."

Talon reached down and drew the gold-hilted dagger at his hip. The cool metal came alive at his touch, and the fire-opal set into the pommel began to glow faintly with an inner light.

"Watch out," he told the others. "Enemy spirits incoming."

No sooner had he spoken than a roaring wind blew down the corridor. It resolved itself into a humanoid shape of dark mist, whirling like a miniature tornado the size of a man. A pair of glowing eyes looked out from within the dark funnel. At the same time, a spark further down the corridor appeared in the air and blossomed into a raging cloud of flames. At its center was a floating, lizard-like creature nearly two meters long from head to tail, surrounded by an aura of flames. It lashed its tail from side to side and glared at Talon with black reptilian eyes before charging toward him.

"Aracos, take the fire spirit!" Talon thought as he brought his blade up to defend himself. He shifted his attention to the astral plane to better assess the threat the spirits posed and to use his magical abilities against them. The invisible astral form of Aracos as a silvery wolf came between him and the oncoming fire elemental, grappling with it in combat. In astral form, Aracos was immune to the withering flames that surrounded the elemental, but Talon wasn't. He turned his attention to the air elemental as it leapt toward Hammer, who was firing off shots in the direction of Gabriel's group.

"Aw, frag, not again," Hammer said as the spirit lunged toward him, seeking to smother him with its gaseous body. This time, however, Hammer was ready for it. He rolled back and away from the spirit, and Talon stepped between them. He struck with Talonclaw, driving the magical dagger into the elemental spirit. Although it was nothing but mist, the blade's enchantment let it bite into its spirit body. Talon felt his thrust strike home and saw the elemental writhe in pain, recoiling from him and gathering for another strike.

Boom's gun roared as he fired off multiple shots down the hall, forcing their attackers to keep their heads down for the time being. The air elemental had recovered from Talon's strike and turned its attention back toward him. A being of spirit and wind, the elemental moved with inhuman swiftness, lunging at Talon and wrapping him in a thick blanket of mist. A hideous, nauseating stench filled Talon's nostrils, making him want to wretch as the air was squeezed from his lungs, driven out and replaced by the noxious mist. His eyes began to burn like they'd been exposed to tear gas. He held his breath as best he could and laid about with Talonclaw, striking at the spirit as it surrounded him.

Then something cut through the fog in front of him. The air elemental peeled away, coalescing in the air nearby for another strike. Talon didn't stop to question his good fortune or wait for the elemental to attack again. He lunged forward and stabbed into the cloud. There was a crack like thunder that echoed through the astral, and the dark cloud began to break up, the spirit slain.

Talon turned his attention back toward Gabriel's team. He whipped around the corner and fired off several shots with his Predator, calling out to Boom across the intersection.

"Go!" he shouted as their opponents tried to return

fire. One took a round in the shoulder for his trouble, spinning him back around behind cover.

Talon leveled his gun around the corner to cover Boom, but stopped suddenly when he saw a translucent form standing there, heedless of the danger of gunfire.

"Jase!" he called out.

"Tal," said the ghostly form of Jason Vale. "They're coming back, Tal."

"Who, Jase? Who's coming back?"

"The dead. The dead are coming back."

As the image began to fade, Talon cried out, "Jase! Jase, wait!" But it was too late. He was gone.

Boom made a dash across the hall just as Gabriel took careful aim and fired. The round hit Boom just before he reached cover. He went down on one knee near Talon, who moved to help him.

"It's okay," Boom said, getting back to his feet. "I can handle it." Talon saw blood staining Boom's brightly colored shirt. They had to get out quickly, but the only way out was blocked by the fire elemental.

Aracos grappled with the reptilian spirit in astral form. The two seemed evenly matched, but Aracos had the advantage of greater intelligence and more experience. Though servitor elementals were often quite intelligent, they tended to be rather limited, and fire spirits were particularly dominated by their passions.

Aracos managed to dodge another of the spirit's attacks, then lunged in, grappling with the elemental and driving it toward the ceiling. Although Aracos was immune to the flames surrounding the elemental, the ceiling tiles were not, particularly the sprinkler cap where the spirit's shoulder struck.

The heat of the flames instantly triggered the building's sprinkler systems. A fire alarm clanged as water sprayed into the corridor from all sides. The fire elemental hissed and shrieked at the touch of the water, and steam rose from its body. Its reptilian form dissolved almost instantly as it fled back into the astral plane, away from its elemental nemesis.

"Two can play at that game," Talon muttered. He cupped one hand and held it under the spray of water, murmuring words under his breath, focusing his magical powers and sending out the call across the astral plane. He had some spirits at his command as well. The call was answered when the water spraying from the ceiling took the form of a snake made up entirely of liquid. Talon pointed in the direction of the company men.

"Attack," he said, and the watery serpent lunged forward. Talon heard a cry of alarm coming from down the hall as Hammer stopped firing. The empty clip popped out of the ork's gun as he slammed a fresh one home from the cartridges on his belt.

"Let's go," Talon said, and they ran for the door.

"The fire elemental is going back to help the suits," Aracos said to Talon.

"Good. That's just what I figured it would do."

They burst out of the door and raced down the fire escape to the alley, where Val had the van running, its side door open. Kilaro was huddled in the back as they climbed in, soaking wet. Hammer ran around to get into the passenger seat while Boom hauled himself in back along with Talon.

"Go!" Talon said, pulling the door closed. Val floored it, and the van burst out of the alley like a shot. The tires squealed as they pulled out into the street, and Talon's headphone started ringing.

"Oh, frag it," he growled and mentally signaled the phone to switch off. Whoever it was, he couldn't afford the distraction at the moment. He turned his attention to Boom, who had a hand pressed against the side of his sopping wet shirt, the blood partly washed away but more of it covering his fingers.

"Let me see," Talon said, and Boom pulled his hand away. Talon ripped the shirt open. It was a clean entry and exit wound, and that meant the bullet wasn't lodged anywhere. He pressed his hand against the wound and heard Boom gritting his teeth in pain.

Talon closed his eyes and concentrated, blocking out the roar of the van's engine and the sound of angry horns from other cars as Val wove her way through the late-night traffic. He felt his hand heat up as magical energy poured from it into Boom, strengthening the natural systems of the troll's body, giving them the energy they needed to heal. When he pulled his hand away, all that was left of the wound was a bloody tear in Boom's shirt. No break in the skin, no indication that he'd been injured at all.

"Nice work," Boom said admiringly, poking at the injured spot.

"We're not out of this yet," Val said from up front. "Looks like we've got company, two MCT roto-drones coming in."

"Frag," Talon said. "Got any antiair in this thing?"

"Yeah, you," Val replied.

"That's what I was afraid of." Talon settled back

against the bench seat, closed his eyes, and concentrated. He sent out the call again, feeling a response, a growing presence. "Come," he called, "come to me."

"Yes, master," came the reply. Then Talon slipped the bonds of his material form, entering the astral plane. He flew up and away from the racing van, finding two spirits hovering obediently before him, similar to the elementals controlled by the company men, one fire elemental and one air elemental. He reached out with his senses but could not feel the presence of his water elemental. Most likely, the spirit had been destroyed, but it took the enemy fire elemental with it. That was one down, leaving Talon with only three other elementals at his command. He hoped he'd have time to conjure another water elemental, but his primary concern was to deal with the problem at hand.

The spirits hovering in front of Talon were in their astral forms, one a cloud of mist vaguely shaped like a woman with small wings, the other a pillar of flame. Talon could see the two drones Val had mentioned closing in on the van. They were cylindrical, about a meter high, with thick, metal-plated hulls and dark lenses that reminded Talon of an insect's eyes. A rotating collar near the top of each drone held the whirling blades that gave it lift, and a machine gun was slung under its "chin," swiveling to track the escaping shadowrunners.

"I don't think so," Talon said. He turned to the spirits.

"Those drones," he said, pointing toward them. "Materialize and destroy them."

"As you command," the spirits said in unison. They rocketed toward the drones, and Talon followed.

When they neared the flying machines, the spirits took material form, appearing out of thin air from the point of view of the drones, and attacked. The fire spirit engulfed one of the Roto-Drones in a cloud of flames. Although the drone's metal and composite body was resistant to fire, this was an intelligent fire, running across its surface, seeking areas of weakness.

The drone pivoted and gained altitude, turning and banking, trying to shake off the spirit, but it was futile. Talon heard a squeal of superheated metal, then the fire elemental found the drone's ammo bin, which exploded like a bomb. The Roto-Drone rained fragments down onto the street below, while the bulk of its burning hull crashed down onto a parked car, crushing the roof and blowing out the windshield.

The air elemental appeared as a whirlwind around the second Roto-Drone. The drone fought against the spirit's raging winds, its rotors whining in protest as they were pushed to their limits. The wind roared, and the drone veered off course, slamming into the corner of a building hard enough to crack brick and concrete and damage its rotor. Talon watched as the drone bounced off the side of the building, then listed and crashed to the sidewalk, its armored casing cracked and leaking smoke.

"Good job," Talon said to his spirits. "Follow me."

He flew off after the van. He slid through the back doors, through the seat and into his body again, feeling the weight of solidity upon him again as he opened his eyes.

"Nice show," Hammer said from the front seat, and Kilaro was looking at Talon with an equal measure of respect and fear in his eyes. It was obvious he'd never really seen a mage cut loose like Talon had tonight. Although most mundanes tended to overestimate the kind of power a mage had at his fingertips, the fearsome reputation of the Awakened was still well deserved.

"Well, chummer," Talon said to Kilaro, "I think you can safely assume that your bosses have decided you're as expendable as the rest of us. Welcome to the shadows."

Boom shifted a bit in his seat. "I heard you call out Jase's name in the club," he said. "You saw him again, didn't you?"

"Yes," Talon said with a grimace. "I'm sorry about . . ."

"Null sheen," the troll replied, running the fingers of his other hand across where the gunshot wound had been as if testing whether it was still healed. If Gabriel's shot had been a bit more to the right, things might have turned out differently.

"None of you saw him, did you?" he asked, and the others shook their heads. A golden falcon appeared out of thin air and alighted on the back of the seat between Boom and Talon.

"I saw him," Aracos's thought-voice said. "Someone, or something, was there all right."

Thank gods, Talon thought. Maybe I'm not going crazy.

"Any idea what it was?" he asked.

Aracos gave a very unbirdlike shrug. "Not really. I've never seen anything quite like it. Of course, I also didn't know the real Jason."

"What did he say?" Val asked, expertly weaving them through the traffic.

"He said, 'the dead are coming back.' "

Val shuddered slightly, and Hammer asked, "What the frag does that mean?"

Talon shook his head. "I don't know, chummer, but I've got a feeling we're going to find out."

23

God, I'm such an idiot, Trouble thought after Talon left. How could she have done something so stupid? She dropped down onto the couch and reached into her pocket for the ring Ian had given her when he'd asked her to marry him. Marry him! And here she was actually thinking about it!

So, of course I kiss another man who I know isn't interested and tell him I love him, she thought, turning the ring over in her fingers, letting it catch the light. Am I really that hung up on Talon, or am I just looking for excuses not to give Ian an answer? Like she really needed any other reasons. Whether or not she was interested in Talon or he in her, there were plenty of other reasons not to get involved with Ian O'Donnel. Not the least of which was that he was a wanted terrorist.

And you're a wanted criminal, Trouble reminded herself, a shadowrunner. In a lot of ways, the authorities probably considered her as bad as Ian, if not worse. Ian didn't go after the corps, after all. His goals were political, something he believed in.

Trouble sighed. What did she believe in? She didn't even know anymore. She used to be proud of being

one of the best deckers in the shadows. She'd loved
the challenge of taking on the best systems the megacorps had to offer, and showing those arrogant corp
programmers that a slip of a girl from the Boston
streets could foil their very best. And she'd enjoyed
the camaraderie of her team, especially since teaming
up with Talon.

Talon, she thought. God, why did she always fall
for the unavailable ones? First it was Ian, dedicated
to his cause above anything else, including her. Then
it was Talon, unavailable for a completely different
reason. But now Ian said he wanted her back, said he
was a fool for letting her go, and part of Trouble
wanted to agree with that. She didn't want to think
that she was only seeking solace in his arms because
it brought back the thrill of the days when she was
making her first real forays into the shadows. Back
then, she was full of fire, ready to take on the world.
Then a dashing and heroic man from back home, the
outcast rebel fighting to free Eire, had swept her off
her feet and given her something to believe in. Now
she'd let his passion and his charm almost carry her
away again, but seeing Talon so vulnerable made her
realize that what she felt for Ian paled next to her
feelings for Talon. It made her so glad that he'd come
to her, and she'd let some tiny part of her begin to
hope again.

Now Gallow might be back, too. The spirit hated
Talon and everything connected with him. He would
do anything to destroy Talon, and Trouble wasn't
going to let that happen. She set Ian's ring on the
table, then took out her cyberdeck, which she set on
her lap. She plugged its optical cable into the jack

behind her ear and snapped the other end into the wall jack.

Time to go hunting for information, she thought, and tapped the Go button. She let the virtual world of the Matrix unfold around her, leaving all her doubts and fears behind. In the Matrix, she was one of the best: confident, capable, unbeatable. In the Matrix, she wasn't afraid. If Gallow was around, she'd track down the information.

A short while later, Trouble logged off and pulled the cable from her datajack with a deep sigh. It wasn't a lot to go on, but she did discover one lead that made it look like Talon was right. Knight Errant had logged a burned body found in an alley, tagging it as one of the many Jane Does that turned up in the metroplex every day. The difference was that the routine autopsy didn't find any signs of what caused the burns, and the forensic mage on duty had tagged it a possible magical crime, perhaps by a wizzer gang or even a rogue spirit.

The charred body fit the pattern of other victims killed by Gallow. Equally disturbing was that the killing had taken place only a couple of klicks from her doss. Was it possible that Gallow was stalking her? The spirit had tried to use her against Talon before. It had held her hostage, and Talon had given up the chance to banish Gallow in order to save her life. Trouble shuddered at the memory of the spirit's burning touch.

She reached over and tapped Talon's number into the telecom. The number rang a couple of times, then stopped as a musical tone came over the line. "We're sorry," a pleasant synthesized voice said, "but the number you're trying to reach is temporarily unavailable. If you'd like to leave a message, you may do so after the tone."

Trouble left a brief message, asking Talon to get back to her. She wondered why he'd turned off his phone. He'd gone off saying he was going to get the rest of the team together, so she decided to go over to the Avalon and see what was up. She put the cyberdeck back into its case and zipped it shut.

Just as she was putting on her jacket to leave, a knock at the door almost startled her out of her wits. God, I really am jumpy, she thought.

When she checked the spy-port, she was surprised to see who was at the door. She opened it cautiously, ready to draw the pistol packed in her shoulder harness if need be.

The red-haired woman breezed past her into the apartment before Trouble could stop her.

"Ian sent me to find you," Bridget said.

"What is it?" Trouble asked. "Did something happen? Is he all right?"

"Yes, he's fine," Bridget said, and her eyes dropped to the ring lying on the table. The way she stared at it made Trouble wonder if the other woman was jealous of her relationship with the leader of the Knights.

"He gave you that?" Bridget asked. It wasn't really a question.

Trouble was annoyed by her presumption and more than a little concerned by her motive for asking. "I don't see that it's any of your . . . urk!"

She gasped as Bridget moved with incredible speed, grabbing her by the throat and pinning her against the wall with inhuman strength. Trouble fumbled for her gun, but Bridget batted it away like a toy. It clattered to the floor.

"Excellent," she said in a hoarse whisper. "Things do have a way of falling into place. He was here, wasn't he?"

Trouble gasped and struggled. She could barely breathe in Bridget's iron grip. How could she be so strong? Was she cybered up?

Trouble shook her head. "No," she choked out. "Ian hasn't been here . . ."

"Not him," Bridget hissed. "Talon."

Then Trouble saw the hate glittering in Bridget's eyes, felt the heat of her skin, like a fever, the inhuman strength.

"Oh my God," she whispered. "Gallow."

"That's right," Bridget said, an evil smile spreading over her face. "He was here, wasn't he? My dear creator—I can sense his presence, his stink, on you." Bridget leaned closer, her breath hot on Trouble's face. "And you hate him, don't you?" she whispered, smirking.

"Frag you," Trouble said, struggling.

Gallow tightened the grip on her throat, and her vision started to swim. "Yes," the spirit said, drawing the word out. "You hate him. You think you love him, but you know he can never return your love, not in the way you want, not in the way you long for, deep down inside. And that poisons that little, hidden part of you, doesn't it? Such a thin line between love and hate . . . Admit it. A part of you hates him, a part you feel so guilty about."

Trouble glared as defiantly as she could at the spirit

in a woman's body. "Not as much as I hate you," she gasped out.

"That's just what I needed to hear," Gallow said. Then it leaned in close and kissed Trouble, Bridget's lips so hot they seared like the touch of a branding iron. Trouble screamed, but something hot, dry, and burning invaded her mouth, choking off her cry. She struggled feebly against it. Then her struggles subsided as Gallow held her pinned against the wall, slowly slumping against her. Bridget's clothes and hair began to smoke, then burst into flames. Trouble pushed the limp, burning body away from her, letting it fall to the floor, where it was consumed in flames.

As the fire spread across the carpet, she calmly picked up her cybercase and her gun, which had fallen to the floor. She slipped the gun back into its holster and went over to get Ian's ring. Slipping it onto her finger, she admired its gleam in the light of the fire beginning to spread across the room. She opened the door, glancing back into the burning room as the smoke detector in the hall began to blare an alarm.

"I hope you'll be happy to see your bride-to-be, Ian," Gallow said in Trouble's voice. "There's still much work to be done, and I wouldn't want to miss the finale."

The spirit walked out of the building, then stood nearby and watched it burn. Only when the firefighters arrived did Gallow take its leave.

Talon had Valkyrie drive him home to pick up some things he would need. After Aracos verified that the coast was clear, he ran in and gathered up the items. Back in the van, he directed Val to pick up Trouble at her place. As they drove, he checked his headphone and found a message from her.

"Tal," it said, "I've been doing some digging and I found a Knight Errant report of a Jane Doe burned to death in an alley not too far from here the other night. They've labeled it an unsolved crime, possibly magic-related. Call me back."

He mentally keyed Trouble's cell number and waited. It rang several times, then the message function came on. He hung up without leaving a message. They'd be at her place soon enough.

"Holy drek!" Hammer said as they turned onto Trouble's street. Her building was in flames, with several firetrucks clustered around the building working to put out the fire. It looked like they had it contained and that only the top two floors had been damaged. People were crowded along the sidewalk, and uniformed Knight Errant officers were keeping them back to give the firefighters room to work. It looked like most of the crowd had been rousted out of bed and been forced to evacuate the building.

The mass of people, the barricades, and the rubbernecking drivers slowed traffic to a crawl, even at this late hour. "Keep it casual," Talon said to Val, as they merged into the traffic moving slowly down the street. "Just keep driving past like everyone else and find a place to park a few blocks from here." He leaned back. "I'm going to go and check it out."

Talon let his head fall back against the seat and sank quickly into a trance. His astral form glided from his body and the van, with Aracos close behind.

They flew over to the building, passing heedlessly

through the streams of water from the fire hoses. When they reached Trouble's apartment, Talon felt a jolt of shock. The interior was blackened and charred, a total loss. The furniture and appliances were burned amid the water-soaked morass. More important was the lingering aura in the place, the distinctive astral residue of magic.

He floated through the ruined door and looked around. Aracos moved on ahead, alert for any signs of danger.

"Boss, over here," Aracos said. Talon felt a chill ripple through his being as he saw it too. There, curled up on the floor in an almost fetal position, was a badly burned corpse, charred beyond all recognition.

"Oh my gods," Talon said, and a terrible fear welled up inside him. He reached out with one insubstantial hand to brush his astral fingers a few centimeters from the surface of the body. The aura of the recent and sudden death was heavy in the ether, hanging over the whole room like a shroud.

"Is it . . . her?" Aracos asked, his voice dropping to a whisper.

"I don't know." Talon forced himself to look closer at the body, praying like he hadn't prayed for a long time. He felt sick, but he forced himself to move closer, hovering over the burned corpse.

"Thank gods," he said finally. "I don't think it's her." He pointed to the head and neck. "Look. There's no datajack."

The fire had burned away most of the flesh, but there was no telltale gleam of a datajack's metal or wires. The body couldn't be Trouble's.

"Then who is it?" Aracos asked.

"I don't know, but we'd better find out."

Talon gave a quick look around the rest of the apartment, but sensed nothing unusual. The damage was too extensive to determine anything more, particularly from the astral plane.

Nothing more to be done here, so they returned to the van, which Trouble had parked a few blocks away. Talon slipped back into his body and opened his eyes. The others were looking at him anxiously.

"It looks like the fire started in Trouble's apartment," he said. "There's a body in there, but I don't think it's hers. I didn't see any sign of a jack or other wire."

"Then who is it?" Boom asked. "And where's Trouble?"

Talon shook his head. "I don't know. Maybe whoever started the fire got careless. Before we got there, I picked up a message from her. She must have called when we were leaving the club. The fire probably started right after that, because the message didn't sound like she was in any danger."

"Maybe Cross went after her, too," Kilaro said, speaking up suddenly. "It could have been a bomb or something."

"It didn't look like there had been an explosion, just a fire," Talon said. " I think we've more than a problem with your corp, chummer." A glance at Boom and Hammer told him they understood what he was saying. A fire certainly fit Gallow's style.

"What now?" Val asked. "We probably shouldn't stay here too long."

"You're right," he said. "Head north."

"Where to?"

"The L-Zone. I know some people who'll give us a safe place to lie low for a while. I've got some magic to do."

24

Gallow walked through the dark tunnels of the Catacombs in Trouble's body. As it approached the entrance to Mama Iaga's lair, a pale-skinned troll covered with warty bumps and nodules of bone stepped from the shadows to block the way. It wore leathers crudely stitched together to fit its bulk and a harness across its massive chest. The troll carried no visible weapons, but its size and strength were enough to tear most opponents limb from limb with his bare hands.

"Stand aside," Gallow said. "Mama is expecting me."

The troll reached out a massive hand, but Gallow smiled poisonously, and Trouble's body was instantly shrouded in an aura of fire. The troll cried out, his scream echoing through the tunnels as it pulled back its burned hand and whimpered. Gallow glared. The troll scuttled to one side, letting it stride through the door and into the inner sanctum of its mistress.

As the velvet curtain fell into place behind Gallow, a voice spoke from the shadows near the dim hearth.

"You shouldn't have injured Albin, my dear," Mama said like a mother scolding a wayward child.

"Now I'll have to heal him after he's had a chance to think about what happens when you play with fire."

"He shouldn't have blocked my way," Gallow said.

"He was only protecting his dear old mother," Mama said, leaning forward and allowing the dim light to reveal her gaunt and wrinkled face.

As if the old hag required protection, Gallow thought. It knew better than most just how powerful Mama was. She might command its loyalty for the moment, but Gallow knew that a time would come when they would have to test who would be the master and who the slave. The spirit looked forward to the day. It had no intention of losing that struggle.

"Besides," Mama continued, "Albin obviously didn't recognize your new . . . outfit." She smiled, showing her sharp little yellow teeth. "Quite nice. I think it suits you."

"It does, doesn't it?" Gallow smiled back. He turned this way and that to show off Trouble's form. "Still, not as well as Talon's body will suit me."

"Soon, my dear, very soon. Is everything else ready?"

"With O'Donnel and the Knights? Oh, yes, even more than I'd expected." Gallow held out its hand, fingers splayed out, letting the gold ring on Trouble's finger catch the light of the candles. "It seems dear Ian is quite enamored of his fair lady."

"Wonderful," Mama said, clasping her bony hands together in a ghoulish parody of girlish glee. "And I have just the present for the happy couple."

She picked up a small, metallic cylinder from the table beside her chair and held it out to Gallow. He stepped forward to take it from her.

"That contains the catalyst for our little Pandora's box," she said. "See that it's used properly, and the plans of O'Donnel and his little band will be successful beyond their wildest dreams. Too bad they won't have the opportunity to see the fruits of their labors."

"And then I get to take Talon?" Gallow asked.

"Oh yes, my dear. I'm sure you'll have no difficulty finding him. In fact, I'm sure he'll come looking for you."

"Good," Gallow said.

"Never let it be said that I don't try to keep my boys happy," Mama returned with a wicked smile. "Now hurry back to 'your' man. I'm sure he can't wait to hear the happy news from his blushing bride-to-be."

A slow smile spread across Trouble's lips, then she bowed and withdrew from the room.

Mama gave a high-pitched cackle. "Soon, very soon," she whispered, alone in the dimness of the room. "Soon, my time will come."

The Lowell-Lawrence area, or the "L-Zone," as it was known to its inhabitants, had seen far better days, but not recently. The area had been in decline for nearly a hundred years. With the formation of the Boston metroplex, areas like the Rox and the L-Zone were written off as worthless. They were too difficult to police and too expensive to clean up. Left to their own devices, the residents of places like the L-Zone either got out or dug in and did the best they could. Homeless refugees, squatters, illegal immigrants, metahumans, and other outcasts had swelled their numbers over the years. The area was home to a particularly large number of orks, most of whom had been forced out of many of the "nicer" areas in the sprawl. With their faster maturation and birthrates, orks quickly came to dominate the L-Zone, which generated resentment and led to gangs, late-night shootings, and other violence.

Talon wasn't as familiar with the L-Zone as he was the Rox, but he knew it well enough. Places outside the metroplex—and outside the rule of law—were havens to shadowrunners. Talon and his team kept an apartment building for occasions just like this one. They didn't object to its use by squatters and street people because a local gang was paid to keep their own area clean and locked up when not needed. The team had reinforced security with arcane graffiti and by spreading rumors that powerful spells were in place to keep intruders out. Of course, those were tall tales, but most people in the Sixth World knew better than to mess with a mage, so they left the place alone.

Talon had taken over the living room as his working space, banishing the rest of the team to the kitchen and the two smaller bedrooms. He felt a little guilty claiming the biggest room in the place, but the demands of his work didn't leave him with much choice. Boom and Hammer had helped him clear out the space and tack up sheets of plastic garbage bags to close off the open doorways from the kitchen and front hall. It was crude, but enough to block out distractions and remind the others not to intrude while Talon was working. The symbolic boundaries were as important as the actual privacy.

He would have liked to ward off the whole place, but there just wasn't time. Getting immediately to work, he took some small paint cans and a box of colored chalk from his kit bag. The room, which was about four meters square, was only barely large enough for his purposes, but he didn't have the time to look for a bigger one. First he painted a large circle in black, then another inside it in red. Between the two circles, he painted four red triangles pointing outward to the four cardinal directions, then four white triangles at the cross-quarters. Inside each triangle went the appropriate mystic symbol of power and warding. At the tip of each triangle, he placed a small white candle.

He drew a white circle within the red one, then a circle of mystic runes in white and red all the way around. In the center, he painted a white, six-pointed star big enough to contain his body lying down. The top and bottom points were aligned east-west, and he drew magical symbols at each of the star's points. Finally, he painted other small symbols of mystic power along the ring of the inner circle. As he worked, he focused his intent on the subtle energies of the circle, building it up as a place of power and safety for his magic.

When he was done, Talon stood back and examined his work. He checked everything twice for flaws or errors in his workmanship. Finding none, he was ready to begin. He stepped into the center of the circle, closed his eyes, and gave a wave of his hand, making the candles spring to life. Then he withdrew a small lock of black hair from a sealed plastic pouch. It was a great token of trust that the other members of the team had allowed him to take magical links to them in case something like this happened. The tiny lock of

Trouble's hair would be his connection to her, the means for using his magic to find her.

Talon gathered the energies of his spell and began chanting in a low, sonorous voice. He focused his attention on the lock of hair between his fingers, fixing Trouble's image in his mind. As best he could, he put aside his concerns over what might have happened to her. If Gallow had harmed her . . .

Talon brought his attention back to the ritual. The working had to be exact.

After several hours' work, he lifted aside the dark plastic curtain over the doorway and stepped into the kitchen. Boom was leaning back in a chair, staring off into space and mumbling to himself. Talon smiled faintly, realizing that must be how he looked when conversing with someone over his headphone or when trancing to do magic. Boom acknowledged Talon with a nod and a slight wave of his hand. Then he blinked a couple of times, apparently ending his call.

"Any luck?" the troll asked.

Talon shook his head, dropping down into a chair. "No. Wherever Trouble is, she's behind a ward too powerful for me to penetrate. I couldn't reach her."

"You did the best you could," Boom said. "We'll just have to find another way. I've been checking around, too, and it sounds like our friend Kilaro is telling the truth about at least one thing. I heard from a friend of a friend that some runners pulled off another job against Cross recently. Seems they got hold of a canister of some kind of bio-agent. Sounds like that catalyst he was talking about."

"Did you learn anything about the runners who did it?"

"Just one thing: they're all dead. Nobody knows who did it, but the street buzz is that they got careless and were double-crossed, probably by their Johnson."

"And nothing on who that was?" Talon asked.

"Not so far, but I'm still checking," Boom replied. "It could have been the Seraphim, too," he said, "tying up loose ends."

"Yeah, like us," Talon said. "It could have been someone within Cross who did the hiring in the first place. They wouldn't be the first corp to hire runners to pull off a job against their own assets as a cover for something else."

"Paranoia as a way of life," Boom said, then got serious again. "Do you think it might have been the Seraphim that set fire to Trouble's apartment? I mean, maybe they went after her, she took one of them out, and they decided to torch the place to cover their tracks."

"Could be," Talon said slowly. "I don't know, but something tells me it was Gallow. It's back. I just know it."

"Any way we can find out for sure?" the troll asked.

Talon nodded. "Yeah, but I'm going to have to get some rest before I try it."

Boom laid a hand gently on his shoulder. "Go ahead and catch some z's," he said. "You're no good to anyone if you exhaust yourself. I'll keep an eye on things."

Talon went back to where they'd laid out some sleeping mats. He dropped onto it gratefully, but it was a long while before sleep came.

Talon tried to sleep, but his rest was fitful. He finally woke up in a cold sweat after another nightmare about

Gallow and the death of the Asphalt Rats. He got up, and went into the kitchen, where Boom and Val were laying out some takeout food. They all sat down at the rickety table to talk over deli sandwiches, except for Talon, who thought his work would go better on an empty stomach.

Roy Kilaro was in the same subdued mood as the previous night. The full reality of his situation was apparently just starting to sink in. He had probably never seen a neighborhood like the L-Zone, except maybe on the trid. Talon decided that if they had to keep Kilaro with them for a while, they might as well put him to work doing something useful. It would also take his mind off his problems.

"What kind of deck have you got?" he asked, gesturing toward Kilaro's gear bag. Kilaro didn't answer right away, maybe wondering if Talon was planning to take it and sell it.

"Cross Babel-series," he said finally.

"Not bad," Val put in. "You any good with it?"

"What do you think? I found out about what was going on with Otabi, didn't I?"

"The more I think about it," Boom said, "the more I think you were intended to find out about that, chummer. At the very least, your bosses decided it was in their interest to have someone to hang this on."

"Don't forget I found out about the Pandora virus, too," Kilaro said defensively.

"Yeah, and led the Seraphim right to us," Hammer grumbled.

"I didn't have any choice . . ."

"Doesn't matter how we got here," Talon cut in. "We've got to deal with it. It's a good thing you know how to use a deck, Roy. Without Trouble, we're going to need you to dig up some data for us."

"I know a coupla other deckers, Tal," Boom said, but Talon shook his head.

"No, I don't want anyone else to know about this. Not until we learn more about what's going on and who we can trust."

"Does that mean you trust me?" Kilaro asked.

Talon gave a short laugh. "Not on your life, chummer, but if you frag us over, you're going down with us. That's reason enough to think you won't. Anything more than that, you've got to earn it."

"What about the signature of his deck?" Val said.

"We've got Trouble's emergency bag in the van," Talon said, then turned back to Kilaro. "Think you can swap out some of the chips in your deck for some of Trouble's extras and load up some of her backup programs?"

Kilaro nodded. "No problem if they're compatible. Give me a microtronics tool kit and an hour or two, and I should be able to do the mods so my deck won't leave fingerprints in the Matrix."

"You sure?" Talon asked.

"Don't worry. I know all about the standard security measures in legit decks versus shadow cyberdecks. I've seen the mods lots of times. It's all part of working in computer services. I know what I'm doing."

"Let's hope so," Talon said.

"So what information am I after?" Kilaro asked.

"First, you've got to dig up the scan on what happened at Trouble's place last night. We need to know more about it, especially whose body I found there. It might tell us where she is now."

"What about the Pandora virus?" Kilaro asked.

"That's next," Talon said. "Find out what you can, but only after you track down the intel on Trouble's place. Boom, can you talk discreetly to a few people about . . ."

"Wait a minute," Kilaro said. "That virus could kill thousands—tens of thousands—of people! And all you're going to do about it is make some calls and have me dig around in the Matrix?"

"Listen, chummer," Talon said. "We didn't ask for this run. We'll do what we can to make sure no one gets killed, but you should understand one thing up front. My first loyalty is to the people on my team, and that includes Trouble. If she needs our help, then the rest of the plex is on its own. Besides, the thing she's dealing with could be a hundred times worse than your virus if we don't stop it now while we still can. Understand?"

"What could be worse than this stuff?" Kilaro asked.

"A rogue spirit named Gallow," Talon said. "It's potentially more dangerous than any weapon. It's done something with Trouble, and I want to know what." He turned to Hammer, who was washing down the last of his sandwich with a long swig from a can of soda.

"Hammer, talk to whoever you can trust on the military circuit. See if anyone has gotten their hands on something like this virus and who would have an immediate use for it."

"That's a pretty tall order," Hammer said. "I can think of about a dozen right off who'd love to get their hands on something like that, but I'll see what I can do."

Talon pushed his untouched food away and slid back from the table. "I'm going to do some astral work and see what else I can find out," he said. "I'll probably be out of it for a while, so Boom, you're in charge. Kilaro, get to work on your deck. Val can help you with it."

Val nodded and wiped her mouth with a paper napkin, then crumpled and tossed it on the table. She got up and went to get the tool kit they'd need to make the modifications to Kilaro's deck.

Talon also grabbed his kit bag and got up to return to the other room. Boom reached out to stop him with one massive hand on Talon's shoulder.

"You're going to try and find out more about these visions of Jase, aren't you?" he asked, though it wasn't really a question.

"Boom, I'm no use to anybody until I figure out what the frag is going on," Talon said, "and I'm more convinced than ever that this whole thing ties in with Gallow somehow. It might be using something that looks like Jase to frag with my head or it might really be Jase trying to tell me something. Whatever it is, I can't ignore it. Don't worry. I'm not forgetting about Trouble, but we need to know what we're up against if we're ever going to find her."

Boom gave Talon a lopsided grin. "Hey, chummer, I wasn't arguing with the magic expert. I just wanted to know the plan. For what it's worth, I think you're right. We're all of us worried about Trouble, but I know we'll get her back."

"I sure as hell hope so," Talon said.

That wasn't entirely true. In his heart, Talon *vowed* to find Trouble and stop Gallow, no matter what it took. And if that meant he had to face down the Dweller on the Threshold again, he was ready for it.

25

Talon spent an hour or so rearranging the hermetic circle to his liking. Then he went back to the kitchen to check in with Boom before he got started.

"How are Kilaro and Val doing?" he asked.

"We're all set," Val said, coming into the room and wiping her hands on a dirty rag. "We made the mods to Kilaro's deck, and he jacked in. Looks good so far, but I'm going to keep an eye on him in case something goes wrong."

"Or in case he decides to rat us out to his Seraphim buddies," Boom muttered.

"I don't think so," Val said. "If he wanted to do that, he's had opportunities before this. Just call it a feeling, but I think he's for real. He's been hung out to dry just as much as we have, even more. He didn't really ask for this. At least we knew what we were getting into, sorta."

"Okay, keep an eye on him," Talon said. "I'm ready to get down to work. You guys know the drill."

"Right," Boom said. "Any idea how long this will take?"

"A while," Talon said.

"That's helpful," the troll said dryly.

"It'll take as long as it takes," Talon said. "At least a few hours or maybe as much as all day and all night. I don't know for sure."

"Well, good luck, chummer."

"Thanks, old friend. I'm gonna need it."

Talon closed the plastic curtains behind him and stood in the center of the circle he'd drawn. He concentrated, and the candles around the outer edge of the circle sprang to life, casting a golden glow over the room. With the windows and door blocked off, they provided the only light.

"Aracos," he said, and his ally spirit appeared before him in astral form, the silvery-gray wolf seeming to step from the shadows to enter the circle. Talon told his familiar to watch over him while he was traveling on the astral plane and to alert the others if anything went wrong. Then he lay down in the center of the circle, breathing deeply as he let his body relax completely. Soon he was in a deep and comfortable trance. He focused his intention on reaching the metaplanes to discover the truth of his visions. This time, nothing was going to keep him from his goal.

He felt a familiar sense of weightlessness, like he was floating in an endless void of nothingness. Then he saw a pinpoint of light in the distance and moved toward it. The light grew larger and larger, illuminating a dark tunnel down which he traveled, continuing toward the light. As the light grew brighter and closer, Talon could see a figure silhouetted by the brilliant glow, a shadowy shape that blocked the way between him and the light.

The Dweller on the Threshold.

As he approached, the Dweller moved toward him, its features becoming clearer. It appeared as a mirror image of Talon, wearing the same clothes and the same expression on its face.

"Don't ask the question unless you want the answer," the Dweller said in Talon's voice, then with a whoosh! the figure was surrounded in flames.

Talon didn't flinch or fall back this time. He just looked directly at the Dweller's fiery face.

"I want to know," he said and moved boldly forward. He could feel the heat of the flames, but ignored it. He passed through the burning figure as if it was nothing more than a hologram, an illusion. He could feel the heat, but it did not burn him. He moved toward the light that filled his field of vision, leaving the Dweller behind him. Whiteness was everywhere for a moment, like the blackness when he'd first entered the metaplanes, then the light dimmed.

Talon found himself standing in a corridor of rough-hewn stone. It was about three by three meters and stretched off into the darkness ahead of him. Behind him was a solid stone wall that did not yield to his touch. Flickering torches lined the walls of the corridor at intervals, shedding a faint light and making the shadows on the walls dance and leap.

Talon looked down and saw that he was wearing the same clothes as when he'd begun his journey, including his armored jacket. The front of his shirt was damp and sticky, with a livid red stain across it. He touched it, then brought his fingers to his lips.

It was blood, but not his. He didn't seem to be injured in any way. He quickly checked for Talonclaw, and reassured himself that it was securely strapped to his hip. His gun, though, was missing from its holster. Talon didn't miss it much. The mageblade was by far the superior weapon on the astral plane anyway.

He moved down the corridor and came to a T-intersection. The corridor looked the same in both directions, so Talon chose the right. He soon realized that he was inside some kind of maze. The corridors branched off regularly as the path twisted and turned, sometimes doubling back on itself, other times coming to a dead end, forcing him to retrace his steps to the last junction and take another route. The walls all looked the same as he went, and Talon wasn't certain he could ever find his way back. The maze seemed to go on forever, with no sign of anyone or anything else. He wondered if it was a trap.

Talon had never heard of anyone being able to set up something like this, but who knew what abilities Gallow might possess? The Sixth World held more than its share of mysteries, and that included the limitations of magic and magical beings. These days, with the SURGE producing all kinds of new metagenetic changes because of an apparent spike in the levels of magic, that was truer than ever. He'd never seen a metaplane like this one. In fact, he wasn't entirely sure which metaplane he was on.

How would he ever find his way back without some way of knowing where he'd already been? He remembered the story of Theseus, who marked his path with a thread given to him by Ariadne when he entered the labyrinth to fight the Minotaur. But Talon had no Ariadne and no thread . . .

His hand went to the front of his shirt. He touched the blood-soaked cloth and wiped his fingers against the wall, leaving a livid smear of blood, bright red against the dark stone. He grimaced and continued on, leaving a blood mark every few meters along the way. It helped him get a better feel for where he'd been, and he realized that he'd retraced his steps more than once. That allowed him to choose different paths with at least some clue about finding his way. The blood soaking the front of his shirt never seemed to run dry, although Talon felt like he'd been walking for hours.

Finally, he came to a room, the first he'd seen since entering the maze. It was square, roughly ten meters across, with three other doors leading out of it. Was this the center of the maze, or just a part of it? Gods, did this thing go on forever?

He despaired of ever finding what he was seeking, but quickly pushed away the thought that he might never get out of here. More than a few magicians had gotten lost in the metaplanes, their spirits trapped and their bodies withering away without food and water. Some were kept on life support for years, complete vegetables. Had some of them stumbled into a place like this? Was it possible that there were places on the metaplanes from which there was no return?

I can't just keep wandering forever, Talon thought, but that gave him an idea. He drew a small circle in blood on the stone floor. Stepping into the center, he raised his arms and began to intone in a strong voice, his words echoing strangely through the maze of corridors.

"I seek a guide to help bring me through this maze of confusion," he said. "Hear me, spirits of this place. Send me a guide to show me the way!"

Talon stood silently, straining to hear a reply as his words echoed—way, way, way, way, way—and slowly died away. The echoes blended into the sound of footsteps coming ever closer, and a figure stepped through one of the doorways. She was human, hardly more than a girl, and dressed like a street kid. Her short hair was a vivid, almost neon purple. She wore a close-fitting Concrete Dreams T-shirt under a short synthdenim jacket, black shorts over torn fishnets, and black combat boots. Metal gleamed from the piercings through her ears, nose, and eyebrows. She looked strangely familiar, though Talon couldn't quite place where he'd seen her before.

"Hello, Talon," she said. "You look kind of lost."

"I am," he admitted. "I could use a guide."

"That's what I'm here for," she replied. "We owe you one."

"What do I call you?" Talon asked, politely refraining from asking the girl her name. "And who's we?"

"You can call me Vi," she said, gesturing for Talon to approach. He took a few steps forward, and she turned toward the same doorway by which she'd entered. Talon caught his breath when he saw the logo emblazoned on the back of her jacket. She turned to look at him over her shoulder.

"You're . . ." was all he could say.

The patch on the back of Vi's jacket showed an evil-looking rat wearing a helmet and goggles and riding a motorcycle. It was the insignia of the Asphalt Rats gang.

"Yeah," she said. "One of the ones you killed. You don't have to ask forgiveness. You already did that.

You asked us back in the alley, and we gave it. We don't hold a grudge. Being here changes the way you look at things. Like I said, we owe you one."

"I . . . thank you," Talon finished lamely, not knowing what else to say.

"Null sheen," Vi said. "You may not thank me when this is all over."

Then she continued down the tunnel, and Talon picked up his pace to keep from losing her. Although she was shorter than Talon by at least a head, Vi moved rapidly. But then she could probably move as fast as she wanted to, Talon thought. The denizens of this place were not limited by the laws of the physical world.

He wondered briefly if he should continue to mark his path, just in case Vi wasn't what she seemed. When he touched the front of his shirt, the blood was starting to dry. He almost said something to Vi, then changed his mind.

Vi led him through a maze of passages, so many that Talon was certain he'd be hopelessly lost if he tried to get back on his own. The light became dimmer as they went, the shadows heavier. In fact, the shadows were possessed of movement that had no relation to the light, as if they were alive. Then he saw another faint light ahead.

Vi slowed her pace and held up a hand for him to stop. "Here we are," she whispered.

"Where's here?" Talon asked, and Vi pointed toward the end of the tunnel.

It opened out onto a sheer drop that plunged down as far as the eye could see, though a dull red glow came from somewhere below. It was a giant shaft cut from solid rock, at least thirty or forty meters wide, by Talon's guess. Other tunnels led into it, some of them spouting a dirty-colored liquid, which fell away into the mist below. Hanging in the shaft were dozens of small metal cages, each suspended by a heavy chain that stretched upward into darkness, each at a slightly different level than the others and containing a huddled figure. Around the cages flew creatures resembling gargoyles, demonic figures carved from the same stone as the walls, with curling horns, batlike wings, and hands and feet tipped with sharp claws. Some alighted on the tops of the cages or clung to the chains, while others lofted about, completely silent except for the beating of their wings against the hot, misty air.

"Welcome to hell," said Vi.

26

Talon looked out onto the strange vista to which Vi had led him.

"That's what you came for," she said, pointing to one of the cages near the middle of the shaft, about five or six meters above them.

Talon looked up at it.

"My gods, Jase!" he whispered. He turned to Vi. "How . . . ?"

"You're asking me? You're the mage. You came to find him, and there he is. Now all you have to do is get to him. Wish I could help, but there's nothing more I can do."

"You've done more than enough," Talon said. "It's up to me from here." Too bad I can't fly, he thought, looking down into the pit. He even tried putting all his will into getting himself aloft. Nothing happened. He tried a levitation spell, but that too failed. It looked like he was going to have to do this the hard way.

He drew Talonclaw and held the blade in his teeth. Then he touched the crystal claw pendant around his neck, whispering a silent prayer to whatever gods there were as he leapt out into space. He grabbed the chain of the closest hanging cage and started to climb up, which immediately drew the attention of the gargoyles circling overhead. One of them banked toward Talon as he climbed onto the top of the next-nearest cage. Some of the occupants of the cages cried out and rushed to the bars when they saw him, while others paid no heed, remaining huddled on the floor or against the bars.

As the gargoyle came shrieking in, Talon leapt for the flat top of another cage, landing with a thud and grabbing at the chain so he wouldn't roll off. The thwarted gargoyle shrieked in anger and banked around for another pass as Talon started climbing, hand over hand, up the chain. As the creature swooped in, Talon extended one hand and focused on a manabolt spell, but once more, nothing happened. Damn! His magical abilities were obviously limited on this particular metaplane.

The gargoyle slashed at Talon as it flew past, leaving three lines of blood along his arm and shoulder. Hanging on to the chain with one hand, Talon grabbed his dagger with the other, waiting as the gargoyle swooped in again. He glanced toward the other gargoyles circling above and below him. Why weren't they attacking, too? Then the creature swooped at him with a shriek. At the last moment, Talon thrust upward, his mageblade sinking deep into the stony flesh. When he pulled the blade out with a jerk, the gargoyle spun out of control and plunged into the pit below. With a grimace, Talon put the blade between his teeth again and resumed climbing.

When he was high enough, he jumped to the next cage. He grabbed at the chain, but missed, losing his balance and tumbling over the edge. He scrambled to grab the upper part of the cage, then held on for dear life as the pit yawned below him. The motion set the cage to swaying slightly as Talon struggled to climb back up.

Suddenly, he felt hands reaching for him from one side of the cage. He looked up and saw a withered old visage with filthy white hair, but it was impossible to make out whether the figure was male or female. It wore rags and reached for Talon with long, bony fingers.

"Please," it croaked, "help me!"

Fighting down a wave of revulsion, Talon kicked away from the cage and pulled himself up onto the top of it, ignoring the cries and pleas for help. He dropped flat as another gargoyle swooped in, missing him by mere centimeters. Taking hold of the chain with one hand, he pulled himself to standing. He held Talonclaw in his other hand, waiting for the gargoyle to move in again. When it did, he ducked down and slashed up, slicing into its leathery wing. It spiraled out of control and plunged into the pit. Talon again began climbing up the chain.

Jase's cage was the next one over. Talon could see him slumped inside. Jase didn't seem aware of Talon or anything else going on around him. When Talon had climbed high enough, he began to swing the chain, building up enough momentum to carry him the remaining distance. Then he leapt out into the air.

Something slammed into him forcefully in mid-leap. One of the other gargoyles, observing the fate of its fellows, had bided its time, waiting to strike when Talon was the most vulnerable. Spinning out of control, Talon threw one arm around the neck of the gargoyle and held on with all his strength. The creature tried to shake him off, but Talon's weight was unbalancing it.

The two of them crashed down onto the top of one of the cages, the gargoyle shrieking and thrashing its wings. Talon felt one wing-beat slash open his cheek and another cut across his thigh. He brought his weight to bear and flipped the gargoyle onto its back, then struck downward with Talonclaw. The enchanted dagger drove straight through the gargoyle's body, piercing the metal of the cage. The creature howled and shuddered, then lay still.

"Tal?" came a voice from within the cage.

"Jase!" Talon called, leaning over the side.

"Oh, Tal, thank gods." It was Jason Vale, looking up at him. His face was dirty and his dark hair disheveled, but his green-gold eyes and his expression were just as Talon remembered. Tears of joy glistened in his eyes as he looked up at Talon.

"You heard me," he said. "You finally heard me."

"Hang on, Jase," Talon said. "I'm going to get you out of here." He meant what he said even though he really had no idea how to do it. The cages didn't appear to have locks, or even doors. They were of a single piece as if they had been woven or forged that way. He had to act, though. It was only a matter of time before he was attacked again. Then he heard a strange noise and turned to see something sizzling and smoking on the surface of the cage. He heaved the body of the gargoyle off and saw that some drops of blood were smoking and eating into the metal of the cage like acid.

He looked down at his chest and saw that the blood-stain was dry and shrinking. He brought a hand up to the wound the first gargoyle had inflicted on his arm and smeared some more blood on the cage. It hissed and smoked like the first, and Talon smiled.

"Stand near the side of the cage, Jase!" he cried out. Then he began to draw a thin line in blood along the top, creating a circle about a meter in diameter. The line of blood smoked and began eating through the metal. Within moments, the inscribed area tumbled into the cage with a clang. Talon reached down with one hand, and Jase reached out to clasp it. He felt a surge go through his body as he pulled Jase out of the cage and onto the roof. Tears were pouring down his cheeks, stinging him where the gargoyle had cut him.

"We've got to get out of here," Talon said. "Are you strong enough to jump across to the next cage?"

"There's another way out," Jase said. "Do you trust me?"

Talon looked into those deep green eyes, recalling the time Jase had saved his life, glowing like an angel.

"With my life," he said.

"Then jump."

"What?"

"Take my hand and jump. It's the only way." Jase extended his hand to Talon, who took it and held on tightly.

"I love you," Talon said, then leapt out into space. Together, they plunged down, down into the bottomless pit. As they fell, Talon looked up and saw the iron cages, opening up like strange, mechanical flowers and the people in them also leaping out into the air, with the shrieking gargoyles in hot pursuit.

They seemed to fall forever. The sides of the pit gave way to an endless darkness all around them, with only a faint reddish glow far, far below to light the way. Talon could hear the strange cries of the prisoners, the gargoyles, and other things echoing in the distance. Jase gave his hand a little squeeze of reassurance, but the wind howled too loudly around them to speak.

Suddenly Talon felt something move in the darkness, a massive presence, like feeling a whale moving past in the water. There was a rush of chill wind and a howl of triumph that sent chills through his astral body.

A voice echoed all around them. "Free! Free at last! The Ghostwalker has returned!"

Talon caught a brief glimpse of bone-white scales, felt the rush of powerful wings, then his senses were consumed by a blinding light, red as blood.

Talon's awareness of the physical world returned slowly.

"Talon?"

He heard someone call his name as if from a very great distance.

"Tal, can you hear me?"

"Hmmm?" He opened his eyes and, when he saw the familiar face leaning over him, was instantly awake.

"Jase! You . . . you're here. I found you!" Talon reached out, but his hand passed through Jason's body. That was when he noticed that Jase was somewhat transparent and floating a few centimeters off the ground.

"You're a spirit," Talon said slowly.

"So it would appear," Jase said, looking down at his hands and turning them over. "Or maybe 'ghost' would be more appropriate. I did die, after all."

"Jase, I . . ." Talon began.

Jase's ghostly form held up a hand. "No, me first. Tal," he said. "I'm so sorry I let you down."

"You let me down?" Talon said. "Jase, I let you die!"

"There was nothing you could have done. I should have been more careful. I hated to leave you all alone like that, but it looks like you've found some friends."

Talon followed Jase's gaze and saw Aracos in wolf form, sitting on his haunches and watching the spirit cautiously.

"Is this . . . him?" Aracos asked suspiciously.

"Aracos, this is Jason Vale," Talon said. "Jase, this is my familiar, Aracos."

"Celtic for 'falcon,' " Jase said, then smiled. "It's a pleasure to meet you, Aracos, even if the circumstances are kind of strange." Aracos inclined his head toward Jase, but otherwise didn't move.

Talon turned back to the ghost of Jason. "You said you'd been trying to contact me for a while. For how long, and why did you only get through to me now?"

"A long time," Jase said, "but it's a long story."

Talon held up a hand. "I should check with the others first," he said. He moved to the doorway, hardly daring to take his eyes off Jase, lest he vanish like a mirage. He reached up and tore down the plastic curtain.

"Boom, Hammer, Val, anyone out there?"

In a moment, Hammer appeared at the doorway, Ingram in hand and ready for anything. "Welcome back, boss," he began. "Kilaro's got some . . ." As he caught sight of the ghostly form of Jason Vale, Boom's voice trailed off in mid-sentence. "Who . . . what is that?"

"Get everybody together," Talon said, "and I'll try to explain."

A short while later, the whole team had gathered around the rickety old table in the kitchen of their hideout. Roy Kilaro looked tired, with dark circles under his eyes, but he also radiated an air of satisfaction. Val looked like she hadn't been sleeping much either; she seemed distracted and more than a little taken aback by the new turn of events. It was hard for any of them to get used to the idea that the ghost of Talon's long-dead boyfriend was there with them, "sitting" tailor-fashion in the air near the table. The whole team had seen a lot of strange things in the Awakened world, but this was a new one on all of them.

With the magic level rising and all the craziness over the return of Halley's comet and the SURGE, these were strange times for everybody in the UCAS, Talon thought. Apparently, even shadowrunners weren't exempt.

Jase glanced around the group, looking as self-conscious as a ghost could. "I guess Talon has told you all how I . . . died. What you don't know is what happened afterward. I wanted more than anything to help Tal and to stay with him. I think that gave me a kind of anchor, a hold on the physical plane. Still, I found my astral body drawn through the metaplanes to that place where Talon found me, imprisoned inside a cage I couldn't break."

"Who imprisoned you?" Talon asked. "Those creatures I saw?"

Jase shook his head. "No, they were just jailers of a sort, I think. I saw a woman, if you can call her that, who lived in the catacombs under Boston. I'd dealt with her a few times . . ."

"Mama Iaga," Talon said immediately, and Jase's eyes widened.

"You know her."

"Oh, yes. We've had some dealings with her before. The first time I met her, she said she knew you. I just didn't know how well. Why did she capture your spirit? And why hold you like that?"

"I don't know. She never told me. She only said that I was very valuable to her. I tried calling out to you, but I didn't know if you even heard me. I couldn't tell how long I was there. Time passes differently on the metaplanes."

"Almost fifteen years," Talon said softly.

"Fifteen years . . ." Jase murmured. "You're ten years older than I was the day we met."

"That was almost half my life ago," Talon said.

Jase gave Talon a longing look before returning to his narrative. "For some reason, I've been feeling stronger lately and that gave me courage. I gathered up all my strength to reach out to Talon, to call out to him, but my contact with the physical world was fleeting and confused. It was hard to get anything across."

"You kept trying to tell me something," Talon said.

"Yes. There's something happening on the metaplanes, something is changing. I don't know what, but I think Mama Iaga does. She's been expecting it for some time, and she's got some kind of plan. I think I'm part of it, but I don't know for sure. I heard her say something about 'the dead coming back.' "

"That may be true," Kilaro said. "Around the time Talon got back from . . . wherever, there was a live netcast from DeeCee about some kind of mass hallucination. People said they were seeing things coming out of that astral hole near the Watergate Hotel where Dunkelzahn died. Some said they saw a dragon emerge from the rift and fly off, and some said they saw other things, like a horde of spirits. The news cams didn't pick up anything, though."

Talon looked stunned. "A dragon," he said, turning toward Jase. "Just before we came out, I thought I sensed something move past us on the metaplanes, something big."

Jase nodded. "I felt it, too."

"Then it's happening—what Mama Iaga predicted."

"Great," Hammer said, "as if we didn't already have enough trouble with Gallow and this virus drek."

"Gallow?" Jase looked sharply at Hammer, then back at Talon. "Do you know Gallow?"

"Yes," Talon said. "Do you?"

"It's a spirit bound to Mama Iaga. She kept it in one of the cages for a while, a powerful spirit."

"Oh my gods," Talon said. Mama was controlling Gallow. That meant the spirit wasn't just out for revenge. There was some other reason, something else behind it. He thought he knew what it was, and it gave him a chill.

"What about the virus?" Talon asked Kilaro.

"I've done some checking," Kilaro said, "and Cacti definitely isn't looking for it, no matter what they might be telling everyone else. From the looks of it, they've been immunizing their own people against the virus and setting up for a siege. They've informed Knight Errant about the theft, but KE is swamped these days, trying to keep up with security for everything else going on in the streets these days."

"Gods," Talon said, "is today the day? The anniversary of the Awakening?"

Kilaro nodded. "You've been out for over fourteen hours, Talon. It's December twenty-fourth. There's all sorts of drek happening all across the metroplex tonight. Just about any one of those events would make a great target for some anti-Awakened terrorists like Alamos 20K or Human Nation."

"And there's no way for us to know who has the virus or what they're planning to do with it," Talon said. "We have to try and find Trouble."

"But what about the virus?" Kilaro said. "Pandora could kill thousands of—"

"What a minute," Jase broke in. "Did you say Pandora?"

"Yeah. That's what the virus is code-named," Talon said. "Why?"

"Something else Mama said. She talked about 'opening Pandora's box on the night of the comet.' I didn't know what she was talking about, but could there be a connection?"

"Maybe Gallow and Mama have the virus," Hammer said. "She sure as hell has the connections to hire runners to do the job."

"That makes it all the more urgent that we find Trouble," Talon said, "and I think I have a way."

27

"I really shouldn't be doing this," Lt. John Brady of Knight Errant said to Boom.

Brady flicked on the flourescents in the sterile white and chrome room. "It's against regs, and with all the other drek that's been going down . . ."

"Don't worry, chummer," Boom said smoothly. "We'll be in and out before anyone even notices. I really appreciate it." It was only five p.m., but on Christmas Eve a mere skeleton crew was on duty at the KE facility.

"Well, I owe you one after what went down in the Rox last summer," Brady said. "Just don't be too long, okay?" Boom, Talon, and Val followed him down a row of steel drawers built into one wall, with Brady stopping occasionally to check an ID tag.

"This is the one." He pulled out the long steel drawer and looked down at the form shrouded in black plastic.

"Merry Christmas," he said, though no one laughed at his graveyard humor.

"I hate morgues," Val said with a shudder as the lieutenant walked off, leaving them alone here. She wrapped her arms around her chest, and her eyes darted around like she thought a gang of spooks might attack at any moment.

Talon understood how she felt. Morgues were creepy enough to ordinary people, but even more unpleasant to Awakened beings. The fact that so many of these bodies had met violent ends made the emotional impressions and lingering spirit influences even stronger.

Talon momentarily wondered if Val's unease had anything to do with her own latent magical abilities, which she'd lost as a teenager when she chose to get cybered up as a rigger. Like Talon, she had grown up in a conservative religious environment, but she only began fearing her magical gifts after she'd already crippled them by getting cyberware and abusing sims. Talon knew there were times when she regretted it. Perhaps moments like this were painful reminders.

Boom checked the door while Talon unzipped the body bag. Inside was the charred corpse he'd seen in the ruins of Trouble's apartment. He checked the datapad magnetically clipped to the drawer, but it revealed very little. The body was tagged only as "Jane Doe #12-61-754," and the cause of death was given as burns and smoke inhalation. The autopsy report indicated no signs of foul play, so the case was tagged as low-priority.

Talon took a deep breath to steel himself before closing his eyes and opening his awareness of the astral plane. The atmosphere of the morgue washed over him like a pall, as oppressive as the stench of disinfectant and chemicals and the hint of decay underlying them. Aracos and Jase hovered nearby, invisible and inaudible to the mundane world.

Talon looked down at the body, his mystic senses probing deeply, searching for some clue in the lingering traces of the woman's aura. He moved his hands above the body, as if he could use them to part the layers of time to find what he was looking for. Then he spotted it.

"There it is," he murmured. "There's a faint trace, a lingering astral signature. Gallow was here."

He reached into his jacket and withdrew a small plastic bag containing tweezers and a small glass vial. He used the tweezers to pluck small bits of charred skin from the corpse, then dropped them into the vial. Val turned slightly green and turned away.

"Gallow didn't materialize the first time we encountered it," he said slowly as he worked. "It possessed host bodies—first that ganger, then Anton Garnoff. It looks like this was another one of its host bodies, which he then discarded like an old set of clothes."

"Does that mean Gallow is possessing Trouble?" Boom said softly.

Talon capped the vial. "It might."

Boom looked shocked by the implications, and Val was shivering in spite of the leather jacket she wore. The room was cold, but no colder than the late December weather outside.

"It's okay, Val," he said. "I'm done. We can leave now."

"Oh, God," she whispered, "something's wrong. Talon, we've got to get out of here!"

Talon and Boom both gasped at what happened next.

"Val!" Talon said. "Your eyes!" Small drops of

blood were coming from the corners of her eyes and streaming down her cheeks like gory tears.

"They're here," Val whispered, and Talon sensed a swirl of motion and energy seeming to fill the astral plane.

"Who's he . . ." he started to say. That was as far as he got before a bony hand grabbed his arm. Talon spun to see the charred body, which clung to him as it pulled itself up and out of the body bag. An unnatural light, like the pale violet of a UV lamp, glowed in its eye sockets.

"Holy drek!" Talon said. He tried to yank his arm free, but the corpse held on with inhuman strength. Even before he could draw the mageblade at his hip, Aracos swooped in, raking at the face of the corpse, loosening its grip. Talon drew his enchanted dagger, feeling the rush of power down his arm as he joined his magic with it and stabbed at the creature. The blade bit into the charred flesh, plunging in to the hilt. The corpse opened its jaws in a silent scream even as it slashed out at Talon with bony hands, clawing at him like a wild beast.

Talon jerked the blade free as Boom launched across the room to backhand the corpse with enough force to send it flying against the opposite wall. Talon heard a crunching noise, but the corpse began to get up again. Then, Jase and Aracos fell upon it, each striking at its astral body. Along with the damage inflicted by Talonclaw, it was too much, and the astral form faded. The burned corpse collapsed to the ground, just a dead body again. No sooner had it done so than Talon heard the sounds of movement and of fists banging against the insides of the closed steel drawers.

"Let's get out of here!" he said to the others. Boom grabbed Valkyrie by the arm, and they ran out of the room, heading for the emergency exit. They passed Lt. Brady in the hall.

"Hey! What are you—" he called after them, interrupted by the cry of a nearby lab technician spotting several animated corpses coming out of the morgue.

"Holy drek!" Brady said, reaching for his sidearm. The building alarm sounded as Boom pushed open the emergency exit, and the three of them made a beeline for the van. Boom got in back with Val, and Talon hopped into the driver's seat, wishing they'd brought Hammer along. He was a better driver.

Talon gunned the engine, and they sped out of the parking lot. "How's she doing?" he asked, glancing into the rearview mirror.

Boom shook his head. "I don't know. She's still bleeding. Val, can you hear me?"

"My head hurts," she mumbled, feebly wiping at the blood on her cheeks, which Boom also tried to wipe away.

"Don't worry," Talon said. "We're going to Doc's."

In short order, they were bursting through the front doors of Doc's clinic on the edge of the Rox. Hilda glanced up from trying to restrain a young ork who looked like he was fragged up on something.

"We need help!" Talon said.

"Get her down to room three!" Hilda said. "I'll be right there!" She pressed a tranq-patch against the ork's neck, and his struggles began to subside.

They brought Valkyrie into one of the examining rooms, where Boom laid her gently on the examination table. A few moments later, Doc and Hilda came in, both looking haggard. Doc immediately began to examine Val. He shone a light in her eyes while Hilda took her vital signs.

"What happened?" he asked.

"We don't know," Talon said, "but I think there's magic involved. Something's going on with her aura, but I've never seen anything like it before."

Doc frowned. "Magic, just great. Whatever it is, it seems to be going around, because I've already had over two dozen patients this month with a variety of weird symptoms I can't explain."

"Can you do anything for her?" Talon asked.

"I'll do what I can," Doc said, "but I don't know magic from a hole in the ground. Could you stay and see if you can give me some help?"

Talon hesitated, caught between his duty to Val and the knowledge that time was probably running out for Trouble and a large portion of the rest of the city.

Val must have read the look on his face. "Go on," she said, levering upright a bit. "I'll be fine. Sorry I can't hel . . . oh!" She gasped, falling back again with one hand pressed across her eyes.

Talon touched her arm gently. "We'll be back as soon as we can," he said, then turned to Doc MacArthur. "Take good care of her."

Soon Talon and Boom were back in the van, heading north and west toward their safe house.

"What the hell is going on, Talon?" Boom asked.

"Remember Dr. Gordon, that doctor Mama Iaga

sent us to see the first time Gallow showed up? When she said she was helping us for reasons of her own?"

"Yeah," the troll said, "what a nutter he was."

"Maybe so, but I keep remembering what he told us. It was something like 'the Awakening is far from over—in fact, it's only begun.' I think what's happening is part of that, something Mama's been waiting for. She's been playing us for more than a year, ever since I came to Boston. This has been a long time coming."

"Do you think the stuff you took from that body will help you find Gallow and Trouble?" Boom asked.

"It had better, chummer, because I think time's running out. For all of us."

When they returned to the safe house, Talon and Boom told Hammer and Kilaro about what happened at the morgue and about Val's mysterious ailment.

Kilaro listened intently, then said, "It sounds like the same thing that's been happening in other cities. The newsnets are full of it. At first, they thought it was an outbreak of some strange new disease, but now they're comparing it to what happened on Goblinization Day. This time, it started in DeeCee, with people coming down with mysterious symptoms. The 'nets say some of those people are transforming now."

"Transforming?" Talon asked. "Into what?"

Kilaro shrugged. "Nobody knows. It's like Goblinization all over again, but this time it's not only humans being affected. They're reporting metahumans coming down with . . . whatever it is, too."

"Frag," Hammer said. "It's going to be chaos out there. Pure chaos."

"Keep monitoring the newsnets," Talon told Kilaro. "And see if the shadow servers have got more than what you picked up on the regular media."

He turned to Hammer. "You ready?"

"I'd rather have some of Val's drones backing us up," Hammer said, "or at least time to get me a minigun or something, but I guess we're as ready as we're gonna be. That is, as soon as you tell me where we're going."

"That's what I'm going to find out right now," Talon replied. "Wish me luck."

28

Talon returned to the room where he'd drawn his hermetic circle, drawing the dark sheets of plastic to close himself off from the outside world. He double-checked the circle to make sure every glyph, every angle, was in place before he began the ritual to link the scraps of burned flesh to the spirit that had once inhabited them and then destroyed them. He couldn't afford any mistakes with this one.

Also present was Jase, hovering near Talon in his astral form.

"You know," Talon said, "before you found me, I used to think I was loco because of some of the things I saw and felt from my magic. Now I'm getting that feeling again. Things coming out of the metaplanes, the dead walking and . . . you . . . showing up again. It's like the world is going mad. What's happening, Jase? Where's it going to end?"

"I don't know," Jase said. "I wish I did. In fact, you probably know more about magic than I do. I'd only been practicing the Art for a few years before we met. You've been doing it for half your life by now. Looks to me like you're a damn good mage, Tal. I always knew you would be."

"Thanks," Talon said, looking up at Jase's ghostly form. He couldn't help letting out a sigh. "Gods, Jase, this is so crazy. I . . . I feel like everything's falling apart and if I let go, even for a minute, I'll go down with it. And having you here . . ."

"I know," Jase said. "Think how it is for me. I still remember dying in your arms, and now I'm here and I don't even really know what I am. Am I the real Jason Vale or a ghost or just a memory of him wrapped up in spirit-stuff? I mean, I feel real, but how long will that last? How long can I exist like this?"

"I don't know," Talon said, shaking his head. "But I promise, I'm not going to lose you like I did the last time."

"You may not have any choice in the matter, Tal. None of us really do when the time comes."

Talon gave him a faint smile. "Jase, my love, if being a shadowrunner has taught me anything, it's that we can beat the odds—if we try."

"I wish I could help with this," Jase said.

Talon stood up, dusting off his hands. "Better you should conserve your strength. We don't know how much ritual magic might drain your energies. Besides, I've already got all the help I need."

He called out to Aracos, and his ally spirit appeared alongside him in the form of a silvery-gray wolf, nodding his noble head.

"Ready?" Talon asked, and Aracos dipped his head again. "And, Jase, keep an eye out for anything going on in the astral, okay?"

Talon raised one hand, and the candles placed around the circle burst into flame. He held a piece of the charred skin between his fingers and focused on the spirit connected with it, chanting the words of his spell.

"Ready?" Ian O'Donnel asked Trouble an hour later as she checked over the equipment for the last time.

She favored him with a dazzling smile as she closed the pack and stood up. "All set," she said. "I've checked it over, and your people did a wiz job with the release device."

"Well, we've had plenty of practice with things like that," Ian said with more than a hint of irony in his tone.

"Soon that will come to an end," Trouble said, slipping her arms around him. "When that delegation of elves arrives at the Dunkelzahn Institute to bask in the glory of their so-called 'good deeds,' they'll find a very different reception waiting for them."

"Yes," Ian said. "It will make an impression on them, that much is certain. I just hope . . ."

"What?"

"I just hope it will be enough. I wouldn't say this to the others, but I sometimes wonder if releasing some riot gas and making the elves and their friends puke up their guts for a while is going to make a difference. Maybe you were right, Ariel, in walking away from all this."

She pressed a finger to his lips to silence him. "No, my love, it was you who was right all along. Of course our actions can make a difference. We have to believe that. You have to believe that."

"God," he said, a smile spreading across his face.

"What would I do without you? You're a pillar of strength for me." He pulled her into a fierce embrace.

Rory MacInnis poked his head in the door. "We're ready to go, sir," he said to Ian.

"Be right there," Ian said, then turned back to Ariel. He looked deeply, almost regretfully, into her eyes. "We should go."

"I'm ready," she said. "Very ready, my love."

It was a small team, consisting of only O'Donnel, MacInnis, a woman named Colleen, and Trouble. They drove across the river to Cambridge, where Ian led them down some of the old subway tunnels running beneath the part of the metroplex not connected to the Catacombs across the river. Ian carried the backpack holding the viral bomb as they made their way through the tunnels toward the site of the Dunkelzahn Institute for Magical Research.

The Institute had been founded with money from the dragon's will as a private, nonprofit organization devoted to pure research into the arts of magic and supporting Awakened causes. One of the members of the Board of Directors, Cormac McKilleen, was from Tír na nÓg. Although it was rumored that McKilleen was out of favor with the Tír government and that his position with the Institute made him something of an exile in the eyes of the ruling Danaan Families, he was still a propaganda tool of the elven regime. In honor of the anniversary of the Awakening, the rulers of Tír na nÓg had gifted the Institute with a number of Celtic artifacts for study, artifacts that were part of the heritage of Ireland, now an elf-ruled nation less than fifty years old. They weren't the Tír's to give, which was why the Knights were going to demonstrate their disapproval by making everyone as sick as the Tír made them.

The old access to the tunnels had been closed off years before the Institute was built, but a small shaped charge, properly placed, would take care of the layer of metal and concrete separating the tunnel from the outside world. The opening would allow the virus they'd acquired to spread through the Institute and the surrounding area for blocks before dying out. It was more than enough to make their point and give the Sidhe lasting memories of their visit to Boston.

Some rats squealed and scattered as the group's lights penetrated the dark chamber Ian had chosen. Ian lowered the pack gently to the ground, and they got to work, keeping a careful eye out as they labored by the harsh halon glow of their flashlights. He did most of the work himself, with some help from Mac-Innis and Trouble, mostly in the form of handing him the right tools, while Colleen kept watch.

As Ian worked, Gallow watched eagerly through Trouble's eyes. The spirit felt a faint brush against its aura, which wrapped around that of the woman. Its astral senses could make out faint indications of a power reaching out across the ether toward it, like a featherlight touch, a tenuous thread of magic connecting it to someone far away. That thread tasted of a familiar power, and Gallow was unable to keep a broad smile from Trouble's face. Let the others think it was satisfaction with their work. Gallow knew it was because Mama Iaga had been proven right. Talon had found it, and would come, as she said.

All Gallow had to do was prepare and wait.

*   *   *

From an apartment in the L-Zone, Talon reached out, forging the link between the piece of Gallow's abandoned host body and Gallow's spirit, hidden somewhere within the city. He spun out the thread of their connection, strengthening it with the power of his will and with energy drawn from Aracos. Then, he saw it stretching before him like a ghostly tether, stretching out, out toward Gallow. He kept the thread firmly in the grip of his will and began to work the spell. Its energies coursed down the thread like a vibration down a violin string, but Talon remained prepared for the danger of a backlash or a sudden attack from the astral plane.

The spell reached out and, in a flash of insight, Talon knew where Gallow was. It was in the depths of the Catacombs, where they'd confronted the spirit the first time, but in a different area of the tunnels. Staying focused on the spell, Talon strode to the doorway and pulled open the plastic curtain. The others were waiting for him in the kitchen.

"I've found them," he said. "Let's go."

Gallow felt the touch of Talon's spell and did not resist as the mage who had created it sought to find it again. It was so easy, the spirit thought, feeling the spell play across its aura like a faint shimmer of heat and light. Now Talon knew. He would be on his way. Gallow glanced up into the open shaft above where Ian O'Donnel was working.

"How much longer?" Trouble asked, and Ian glanced down.

"Nearly finished," he said, using his sleeve to wipe away the sweat and grime from his face. Gallow forced down feelings of urgency and the desire to command Ian to work faster. Patience, patience, it thought. Savor the moment. But the moments ticked by too slowly before O'Donnel finished his work, climbed down the shaft, and dropped the last two meters to the floor.

"Done," he announced proudly. "It's only too bad we can't wait around for the show to begin."

Trouble slid smoothly into his arms. "Well, it depends on the sort of show you want to see," she said wickedly, drawing him to her lips for a kiss.

Watching them, Rory chuckled. "Get a room, you two. We've got to get going." When the two lovebirds ignored him, he laughed again before tapping Ian on the shoulder. "Hey, boss, we got plenty of time for—"

Rory and Colleen gasped as Trouble released her hold on Ian, and he slumped to the floor, eyes wide and staring, his mouth open in a silent scream, but unmoving.

"What the . . . ?" Rory said, reaching for his gun.

"I'm sorry," Trouble purred, "but your usefulness to me is at an end."

No sooner had Trouble spoken, than an aura of flames surrounded her, throwing a hellish light across the room. She gestured toward Colleen, the fingers of her left hand opening like a blossom. A jet of flame shot from her aura, spraying the young woman like a fire hose, igniting her hair and clothing. Colleen shrieked and dropped to the ground, rolling to try and put out the flames.

Rory fired a shot at Trouble, but his surprise and fear sent it wide of the mark, and the shot ricocheted off one of the walls. Before he could begin to take aim for another, the fiery woman was upon him, her hands seizing him. He screamed as Trouble's touch seared his wrist and his throat like hot irons. In a moment, the room was full of the stench of burning skin, hair, and clothing.

Trouble threw back her head and laughed as Rory struggled frantically to break her grip. She loosened it enough to let him slip free, and he stumbled back, falling to the ground, his charred wounds beginning to weep red. He fumbled for the gun he had dropped.

Gallow never gave him the chance to use it. Trouble took a deep breath and huffed out a blast of fire that engulfed Rory, who screamed in anguish. The flames charred his exposed skin and set his clothing on fire, the heat so intense that, to Gallow's regret, he didn't live long enough to feel much more pain. The spirit turned to where Colleen was just getting up from the ground, having managed to put out her burning clothing. She was covered in raw, bleeding burns and dirt from the ground, with most of her hair burned away by the blast.

"No, please . . . ," she said, trying to scramble away on hands and knees as Gallow moved closer. ". . . Please don't." She spied her gun on the ground nearby and made a grab for it. Gallow could have stopped her, but didn't bother. As she picked up the gun and turned to point it at Trouble, Gallow gestured contemptuously with the flip of one hand. Suddenly, the gun in Colleen's hands was red hot, and she dropped it as it scorched her hand.

Then Trouble was upon her. The flame aura died away as she grabbed the girl's throat with one hand, forcing her to her knees with incredible strength. Colleen clutched at the hand locked around her throat, but her struggles were feeble, no match for the inhuman creature inhabiting Trouble's body. Tears of terror rolled down Colleen's face as she looked up into Trouble's eyes.

"Please," she whispered one more time, helplessly, as Gallow gave a sigh of pleasure and tightened Trouble's hand around Colleen's throat. There was the hiss of burning flesh, then the flames flared around Trouble's body once more. Colleen gave a gurgling scream that was cut off when Gallow snapped her neck like a dry twig, then dropped the smoldering body to the ground. Trouble turned to where Ian O'Donnel lay helpless, but still alive, paralyzed by the spirit's power.

"Poor, darling Ian," Gallow crooned in Trouble's voice, bending down to look into his eyes. "So caught up in your little cause that you never dreamed you were just a pawn in an even bigger game, did you? You never thought your precious little Ariel would betray you."

There was a gurgling sound as Ian tried to find his voice, but couldn't. All he could do was look at Trouble with pleading, confused eyes. Gallow drank in the waves of fear and pain coming from O'Donnel as his heart ached at Trouble's betrayal.

"You're never going to see a free Ireland, I'm afraid," Gallow continued, "but then, neither is anyone else. You and your kind need to learn an important lesson, Ian. This is the Sixth World. The time of you and yours has passed. This is our time, our world now. It is a world of magic, and it won't be long before nobody remembers when it was otherwise. I'd gladly tell you all about it, but I have a few other things to do, so I'll just leave you with that."

Gallow reached down and gently caressed Ian's cheek. He whimpered at the heat of Trouble's touch.

"Good-bye, my dear," Gallow said as the leader of the Knights of the Red Branch burst into flames. He recovered enough of his voice to scream, then he thrashed weakly before collapsing back onto the floor. A cloud of greasy black smoke billowed up toward the ceiling, filling the room with haze and the stink of burned flesh. Gallow watched the spectacle for a few moments before turning back to other business.

It climbed up to where Ian had affixed the viral bomb and made a few adjustments. Then it reached into the bag Trouble always carried and drew out a small cylinder with the catalyst from Mama Iaga. In a matter of minutes, the catalyst was attached to the viral bomb, turning the otherwise harmless Pandora virus deadly. The visitors to the Dunkelzahn Institute would soon be dead, along with everyone in the immediate area.

Gallow looked again at the faintly glowing thread in astral space, stretching from its aura out to wherever Talon was. Now, all it had to do was wait.

29

Hammer took the wheel of the van as they raced toward the Cambridge area, Talon's spell guiding the way. Talon silently wished they had Val along. Hammer was right that some of her drones would have gone a long way toward evening the odds. He also wished they'd had a chance to engage some additional backup, but there wasn't time. He could count on Hammer and Boom, but Kilaro had never fired a gun in his life. As always, Aracos would provide magical help, but Jase was an unknown quantity. Even Jase didn't know what abilities he retained in his ghostly form.

Talon hadn't wanted him to come along, but Jase insisted. "What am I going to do?" he asked. "Hang around here and haunt the place?"

Talon didn't want Jase endangered, but when Jase pointed out that the feeling was mutual, Talon relented. Besides, it wasn't like he could really keep Jase from following them. As a ghost, he could move faster than their van and keep up with them no matter where they went.

Talon thanked the gods that traffic was relatively light as they made their way along Massachusetts Avenue in Cambridge. Then he spotted the distinctive flashing lights of Knight Errant patrol cars parked along the road in various spots.

"They've got road blocks up," Hammer said, spotting it at the same time. "What the frag's going on?"

"Take a left up here," Talon said. "We're going to have to ditch the van and go through the Catacombs. Gallow is definitely underground."

Roy Kilaro was sitting in the back of the van, scanning a portable datapad. "The police are out in force," he said. "They're even calling in help from local corp security. It looks like what's been going down in DeeCee and all the commotion around the anniversary of the Awakening has got everyone edgy."

"Maybe it's got something to do with the Pandora virus," Boom said.

Kilaro shook his head. "There's no way Pandora could cause the symptoms they're talking about. In its regular form, it's like a nasty, fast-acting flu virus. Add the catalyst, and it becomes deadly. People would be dropping in the streets. They wouldn't even make it to the hospitals."

Hammer took the van along a side street and found a parking spot. They all got out, and Talon led the way through alleys and side streets to avoid attracting police attention. The last thing they needed was to be stopped and questioned.

Talon led them down a dark cul-de-sac and stopped near the end of it. "There it is," he said, pointing at a small, blocky structure. The entrance was covered over with heavy sheets of construction plastic bonded into place, but the faded "T" logo of the Massachusetts Bay Transit Authority was still visible on either side and over the door.

Boom and Hammer quickly set to work peeling back one of the plastic panels, which broke with a snap loud enough to be heard around the block, but no one came to investigate. The runners slipped through the narrow opening, though Boom barely managed to squeeze through.

Beyond the entrance, the old subway station was dark and covered in a thick layer of dust. Talon produced a flashlight to light the way as they descended the cracked concrete steps. Hammer and Boom didn't really need the light; their metahuman eyes adjusted easily to the dimness. Neither did Aracos or Jase, with their astral senses, but Talon and Kilaro still did. They hopped over the rusting turnstiles to the platform, then continued on down through the well of the tunnel itself.

"I thought these tunnels were sealed off after the earthquake," Kilaro said, noticing the many large cracks in the concrete walls.

"They were," Talon said. "In fact, this one collapsed a few hundred meters that way." He gestured down the tunnel with the flashlight. "The metroplex government abandoned most of the old T system and built newer tunnels further down using more modern materials. But after the Awakening and Goblinization Day, a lot of squatters and metahumans took refuge down here and in other parts of the old subway system. They cleared out the debris in some areas and in others took over abandoned tunnels and stations. The collapse that blocked this tunnel has been mostly cleared."

In fact, when they reached the area where the tunnel had fallen down, it was just as Talon said. Debris still choked most of it, but a path had been cleared through the pile of concrete, rock, and steel. The hole was just large enough for Boom to fit through, and he grunted a bit as he squeezed out the other side.

Kilaro ran his hand along the side of the tunnel as he crawled through.. "It's smooth," he said. "Like they used some kind of cutting torch. What did they use to cut through here?"

"Magic," Talon said.

Hammer and Boom took the lead now. Talon and Kilaro were next, and the spirits stayed close by in astral space. They were invisible to mundane sight, but Talon knew they were there through his link with Aracos. He still felt the old connection to Jase, too, the same ties that had bound them together from the moment they'd met.

"Not far now," Talon said to his companions. "Watch out. There could be just about anything down here."

Following Talon's directions, they took a branch off the main tunnel. It sloped downward at a slight angle, then took a turn ahead that made it difficult to see what lay beyond. Talon kept the light aimed low, trying to minimize the chance that anyone, or anything, would see it. There was just enough light to show him what was just ahead as they went. It was more than likely that Gallow would know they were coming. If it had sensed Talon's spell, it was probably lying in wait for them.

Hammer gestured for them to stop as he took a

single cautious step forward. He tilted his head, listening to something none of the others couldn't hear.

"Get ready," he said, taking a step back. "We've got company."

Then Talon heard the sound Hammer's enhanced hearing must have picked up. It was a faint squealing, skittering noise that steadily grew louder and louder.

"Devil rats!" Boom cried as a living carpet of mottled flesh and glowing red eyes rounded the corner, squealing as they charged at the invaders of their underground domain. Devil rats were an Awakened variety of the common Norway rats that plagued cities all over the world. Unlike their mundane cousins, devil rats were virtually hairless, covered in wrinkled folds of loose, pinkish-gray skin. At a meter in length, they were much larger than normal rats, with a vicious and evil disposition.

Hammer and Boom sprayed gunfire into the front ranks of the onrushing creatures, eliciting squeals and shrieks of pain as the 9mm rounds chewed up many of them. The rest simply climbed over the fallen bodies of their comrades in their frenzy. Talon spoke the words of a spell and pointed at the head of the surging mass of rats. A jet of flame shot from his outstretched palm, sweeping across the front ranks of the horde and burning several of the rats to a crisp. But still the devil rats kept coming.

A pair of them broke through the line being held by Hammer and Boom, their charge aimed at Kilaro. He shot one of them as the other leapt onto his chest and barreled him over.

"Help!" he screamed as the vicious rat tried to bite him with its razor teeth.

"There's too fraggin' many of them!" Hammer yelled as he continued mowing the things down.

"Aracos, help me!" Talon said to his familiar. Fighting the devil rats one-on-one was a losing proposition—there were dozens of them. He focused on the crystal claw pendant around his neck, feeling the cool pulse of its power, and then he felt the addition of Aracos's strength as he worked another spell. Several devil rats rushed toward him as if drawn by the power of the focused magical energies.

"Close your eyes!" he said to the others.

He extended his arms, and a sphere of light appeared between his outstretched hands. The light was blinding, as bright as the sun, and it illuminated the whole tunnel. Squeaking and squealing in pain and fear, the rats immediately began to retreat from the source of the light, scattering down the tunnel and escaping through narrow holes and wider cracks in the walls. Talon lowered his hands, and the light dimmed.

Boom helped Kilaro back to his feet. "Nice work," he said to Talon.

"It won't keep them away forever," Talon said. "We've got to keep moving."

They hurried down the tunnel and around the bend. A faint, flickering light became visible on ahead. Talon glanced at Hammer and Boom, who nodded, and they all charged toward the light, weapons at the ready.

The tunnel opened onto an old subway platform. When they reached it, a sheet of flame shot with a giant whooshing sound across the space above their heads.

"Get down!" Talon cried out as the flames roared overhead. They were standing down on the rusted tracks, deep enough that Talon could stand upright without touching the fire above them. Boom and Hammer had to crouch down, and Kilaro ducked, covering his head with his hands. The heat from the flames was blistering, but not harmful. When the fire cleared a moment later, they looked up to see Trouble standing on the edge of the platform, smiling down at them. Talon shifted to astral sight and saw that the aura surrounding her body was not hers. It flickered with ghostly flames of triumphant hate and pulsed with mystic power.

"Hello, Father," Gallow sneered. "It took you long enough to get here. Dear Trouble has been missing you."

The spirit leapt off the edge of the platform and landed smoothly in the gravel some four meters from where they stood. Trouble wore a gun at her side, but Gallow had no need of weapons. It glanced past Talon, its astral senses aware of the spirits hovering nearby in astral space.

"Interesting company you keep, Talon. That thing must be my replacement. It seems your conjuring skills have declined since you summoned me. And what have we here? A spirit in the form of the dear, departed Jason Vale or . . ."

A slow smile spread across Trouble's features. "Ah, the genuine article! How rich! Hello, Jason. A pleasure to meet you. I'm Gallow, the spirit Talon summoned to avenge your death. How fitting that I shall now have the opportunity to end your existence again."

Jase's eyes went wide as he looked from Gallow to

Talon and back again in disbelief. Talon felt his face get hot with anger and shame.

"You're not threatening anyone," Talon said, stepping forward. "Let Trouble go."

Gallow only laughed, a chill sound that echoed down the tunnel. "Why should I? I know you want to destroy me, Father. But if you try, you'll only harm dear Ariel's body. Don't you already have enough blood on your hands?"

It glanced back at Aracos and Jase. "Besides, if you try to attack me, what will become of your friend's spirit, eh? Or them, for that matter?" it said, pointing toward the rest of the team. "Can you keep me from destroying them?"

"What do you want?" Talon asked, gritting his teeth, already knowing the answer.

"That's simple: you. I want you to give yourself to me willingly, without resistance. Let me take your body, and I will free Trouble and the rest of these misfits you call friends."

"Tal, don't do it!" Jase said, becoming visible and audible to everyone. "It's lying!"

"Don't trust it, Talon!" Aracos added, but Talon paid no attention.

"Swear by your true name," Talon said.

Gallow smiled in triumph. "I swear by my true name that I shall not attack your friends."

"Or harm them in any way," Talon said.

"Or harm them in any way." Gallow nodded inside Trouble's form. "Are we agreed then?"

Talon glanced at Jase, who returned the look with pleading eyes. Then he turned again to Trouble, his friend.

"Yes," he said.

"Yes!" Gallow roared.

Instantly, Trouble was surrounded by an aura of fire that licked out at Talon. Something like a face appeared in the flames, and laughter echoed through the tunnels as Gallow reached out to claim what was his.

"No!" Jase said. Moving with the speed possible only to a spirit, he leapt at the surge of flames reaching for Talon, grappling with it in midair and pulling Gallow back from its prize.

"Jase, don't!" Talon screamed, but it was too late.

Gallow roared in anger, rearing up as it struggled with the ghost of Jase. "The oath is broken!" it shrieked. "Kill them all, but leave him to me."

The sounds of squealing and scrabbling feet came from all directions as devil rats poured down the tunnel and over the edges of the platform, diving down onto the tracks to attack the shadowrunners. Boom and Hammer opened fire, hosing down the oncoming rats with 9mm rounds, but as before, the next wave trampled over the bloody corpses of the dead ones and kept coming. Kilaro drew his gun and shot one of the rats in the throat as it leapt from the platform.

Talon drew his enchanted dagger, while Aracos leapt into the fray to help Jase, who was clearly overwhelmed by Gallow's power now that the spirit had recovered from its surprise.

"How fitting," Gallow gloated. "I'll be able to destroy these weaklings before claiming you for my own. Prepared to watch Jase die again, Talon?"

Gallow's flames encircled Jase like tendrils, catching his astral form in their grip. Jase struggled as Gallow squeezed, and he screamed in pain.

"Leave him alone!" Talon shouted, stabbing at Gallow with his blade. The spirit danced aside, and Talonclaw sliced through empty air.

Gallow had all the advantages on its home turf. In its true spirit form, it was a creature of quicksilver and shadow, incredibly fast, too fast for Talon to keep up with. But if Talon tried to confront it on the astral plane, he would leave his physical body at the mercy of the devil rats and anything else Gallow had up its sleeve.

He slashed at Gallow again, but the spirit easily danced out of his reach, still holding the struggling Jase. Talon knew he had no choice but to go astral.

He called to Aracos through the mental link they shared. "Manifest and protect my body, Aracos. I'm going after Gallow."

Talon thought that Aracos was about to object, then a silver-furred wolf appeared next to Talon and sank its teeth into one of the squealing devil rats. It shook the rat hard enough to snap its neck before tossing it aside and going after another. Talon sank to his knees in the gravel, discarding his body like a robe, his spirit rising up into the astral. Talonclaw glowed in his hand, and the crystal Dragonfang shone at his throat.

"Nice of you to vacate my property before I take up residence," Gallow said as Talon emerged onto the astral plane. "Come to watch your dear love's final death throes?" Fiery tendrils squeezed tighter around Jase. He thrashed against them, but could not break free.

Talon circled around the fiery spirit, mageblade in hand. "C'mon, Gallow. It's me you want. Let's finish this if you've got the guts to take me on."

The hate radiated from Gallow like a blast furnace. "I've been waiting for this moment," it said. "No more pawns, no more distractions." It hurled Jase's astral form away, but Talon didn't dare take his eyes off Gallow to see if Jase was all right.

"Today I become the master!" it bellowed, surging toward Talon with all its power.

Talon met the charge as Gallow's fury smashed into him. The flames could not harm his astral form, but the pain still seared through him like a burning spear. He struck back, plunging Talonclaw deep into the spirit's form. Gallow howled in rage and pain.

They grappled, Gallow spitting flames and clawing at Talon in elemental fury, while Talon jabbed and slashed with his mageblade, tearing at Gallow's very essence. Talon was skilled in astral combat, and his blade was a formidable weapon, but Gallow's fury lent it incredible strength of will. To Talon, it seemed that his strikes were little more than insect pricks to the spirit.

With a supreme effort of will, he managed to break free of the spirit's burning grip, tumbling away a short distance as Gallow gathered itself like a cobra preparing to strike.

"Now, mage," it roared with a voice like a furnace aflame, "you will belong to me, body and soul!"

Just as Gallow began to lash forward, it was seized from behind by strong, wiry arms that held it tightly.

"Haven't you forgotten something?" Jase said.

"Jase!" Talon cried, wanting to warn him off. But Jase's ghost held on to the raging elemental, despite the pain.

"Tal, get away," Jase said. "Hurry! I can't hold him for long!"

"I will kill you!" Gallow raged, struggling in Jase's grip.

"Sorry. You're a little late for that." Jase tightened his grip. "Tal, please, trust me—GO!"

Talon looked at his love for a long moment, prepared to rush forward to save him, then he looked down the tunnel, where his friends were battling the horde of devil rats. Some of the rats were going for Trouble, who lay on the ground helpless and unconscious. With one last look at Jase, he dropped back into his physical body and opened his eyes just as Aracos broke the back of another devil rat.

Talon rushed toward Trouble. He kicked one of the rats hard enough to send it sprawling a couple meters away and drove Talonclaw down into the head of the other one. He felt the bone crunch under his blade as the devil rat squealed out its life.

"Trouble! Wake up! We need you!" He cupped her face in one hand. "C'mon, Trouble. Wake up!"

"No!" Gallow cried, still fighting to break free of Jase's grip.

Trouble's eyes fluttered, and she looked up at Talon. "Hi," she said, somewhat dazed.

"Hi, yourself," he said, then got to his feet. Trouble also scrambled to get up and reached for her gun when she heard the squealing of the devil rats.

"You're finished, Gallow," Jase was saying. "You've lost your host, and you've got nowhere else to go. How long can you last without one?"

"Long enough to finish you!" With one final surge, Gallow broke free and materialized above the platform as a seething ball of fire. In the center of it was visible a vaguely humanoid shape whose red, scaly flesh glistened in the flames.

"DIE!" the spirit cried, lashing toward Talon.

Talon felt the heat from Gallow's flames, then heard the sound of wings as a golden falcon struck at the spirit. Talon staggered back as Jase pulled Gallow away, helping Aracos against the maddened elemental.

"Now, Tal!" Jase cried, and Talon lunged forward.

"Talon's Hate," he said, speaking the spirit's true name, "you are no more!" Then he drove his dagger directly into Gallow's fiery heart. There was a scream that tore at Talon's mind and spirit, and Gallow exploded. The force of the blast picked Talon up and sent him flying back into the platform, knocking the wind out of him. Talonclaw dropped from his hand, and he landed on his side. He was starting to feel cold, and he knew that Gallow had burned him badly. As his vision began to go black, he felt a hand gently caress his cheek.

"Now I know what I was here for," Jase said. "It was for this and to tell you to save your strength for the living, Tal. Gallow is dead. It's over, and we can both go on. I have only one more thing to do. Good-bye."

Talon reached out with a shaky hand and felt a gentle kiss. Then he passed out.

30

Consciousness returned slowly. The first thing Talon knew was a hand gently stroking his face. He stirred and opened his eyes.

"Jase?" he murmured.

"I think he's coming around," someone said, and Talon looked up into a blurry, unfamiliar face. As his vision cleared, he could see that it was a young man, probably in his mid-twenties. Golden highlights gleamed in his long hair, which was pulled back from his face in a ponytail or braid. His eyes were deep blue, with flecks of silver glimmering in their depths, and he flashed Talon a smile. He wore street clothes, including a T-shirt with an elaborate Celtic knot design on it, under a battered brown leather jacket.

"Who?" Talon said vaguely as he started to sit up.

"Don't you recognize me, boss?" the young man asked, his smile broadening. Talon looked deep into those eyes and saw the familiar spirit looking out through them.

"Aracos," he breathed, "but how . . ." Then he felt the empty space inside of him, and the subtle tension that had been there since he'd first summoned his ally was gone. "You're free, aren't you?"

Aracos nodded. "It happened when you passed out. I thought you were dead. I went to you, wishing I had human hands, and suddenly I did. I cast a healing spell so you would recover. If I'd known having a human body could be so useful, I'd have asked you to give me one a long time ago."

"Jase . . . Jase is gone," Talon said.

"Yes."

"It's okay," he said, and really believed it. "He was with me at the end there. He wants me to be happy. He wants me to live."

Aracos nodded as he helped Talon to sit up. Dead devil rats littered the ground around the rusted tracks, and there were pockmarks in the concrete from bullets, stitched in bloody lines. Trouble lay on the ground nearby.

"Trouble!" he said, but Aracos laid a hand on his shoulder.

"It's all right. She's alive," he said. "I've already healed her injuries. She's going to be fine."

"Thank gods for that," Talon said, then smiled weakly. "But if you went free, why are you still here? Why didn't you leave?"

"You have to ask? You called me here, Talon. You gave me a life in this world, and you've been a friend, not a master. I don't want to leave you."

Talon's smile quickly faded when he recalled all that had just happened.

He heard Trouble stir and bent over her. "Hey, how are you doing?" he said as she opened her eyes.

"What hit me?" she asked, sitting up. Suddenly her eyes widened in recollection, "Gallow! It . . ."

"Gallow's gone," Talon said. "It's all over."

"Well, not quite, chummer," Boom said from the edge of the platform above. "We've got one other little problem. It looks like there's some kind of bomb set in a maintenance shaft up above this station, complete with the Pandora virus, and it's counting down."

"Help us up," Talon said, reaching a hand toward the troll, who hauled him and Trouble up to the platform using one hand for each. Aracos simply walked on air up to the platform like someone climbing a staircase.

Hammer was standing under a circular opening in the ceiling, and three charred bodies lay nearby. Trouble took one look at them and gasped. "Oh my God! Ian!"

She ran over and dropped to her knees on the concrete. She reached one trembling hand toward the charred body, then jerked it back as she began to sob. Hammer came over and encircled her shoulders with one massive arm.

"Hey, kid," he said gently. "There was nothing you could have done. It's not your fault."

Roy Kilaro climbed up into the shaft above with a boost from Boom. For several long minutes, the only sound in the tunnel was Trouble's sobs, then Kilaro called down from the shaft. "I can't shut it down! It's got some kind of encryption lock! I don't dare tamper with it or I might set it off."

Talon knelt down beside Trouble and Hammer on the platform.

"Trouble, do you remember anything about what happened while Gallow was controlling you?" he asked softly.

She shook her head, wiping away tears with the

back of her hand. "No, it's a blank. The last thing I remember was being in my apartment. Then I woke up here, and Talon and Gallow were fighting, and then . . ." She looked at Ian O'Donnel's burned body and stifled another sob.

"We've got less than five minutes on the counter!" Kilaro said.

"Trouble, we need your help. Kilaro can't disarm the viral bomb," Talon said. "If we don't disarm it, a lot of people are going to die, including us. We need you."

Trouble glanced at the bodies once more. Then she closed her eyes and took a deep, shuddering breath.

"I understand," she said, opening her eyes again. "Just get me up there."

"Okay, kid," Hammer called up to Kilaro. "You can come down now."

Kilaro dropped out of the shaft, and Boom gave Trouble a boost. Talon and Aracos watched as she climbed up into the shaft.

"Anything we can do to help?" Talon called.

She looked down at him. "Did you kill Gallow?" she asked.

"Yes."

"Good enough for me." Trouble then disappeared from view. A tense silence descended again as they waited and she worked.

Finally, Talon turned to Aracos. "Is there something we can do to contain the virus if it gets out?"

"Maybe with the help of an air spirit," Aracos said.

Talon's eyes flicked away for a moment as he looked within himself, feeling for the links to the spirits he commanded, but finding only emptiness.

"Damn," he muttered. "They're gone." It would take far too much time to conjure another air elemental to do the job. "Don't suppose you've picked up any new spells in the last few minutes or so," he said to Aracos.

"Afraid not. We may just have to wing it. Maybe you and the others should clear out, just in case."

"No need," Trouble said from above them. Then she crawled out of the shaft, the terrorist bomb dangling from a strap slung over her shoulder. One of the side panels was off, and multicolored wires dangled from it. The tiny LCD on the side showed that the timer had stopped with just under a minute to spare. Trouble handed the whole thing over to Talon, who took it gingerly.

"The broken dreams of a good man," she said, looking at it with regret.

"I'm so sorry," Talon said, and Trouble turned to him with tears in her eyes.

"It's not your fault," she said. "I think he always knew he would die in the name of the cause. I just wish he hadn't died thinking I betrayed him. What . . . what Gallow must have made me do . . ."

Talon handed off the bomb to Hammer and took Trouble in his arms. "I think he knows it wasn't really you. In fact, I'm certain of it. If I learned anything from all this, it's that the people who cared about us are out there, somewhere, watching over us."

31

Mama Iaga waited impatiently in her lair deep below the city streets. Sitting by the fire, she felt the waves of magic spreading across the land, felt the fear and confusion they sparked. Soon those feelings would turn to anger as people lashed out at what they didn't understand.

She glanced at the antique clock resting on the mantel, its soft ticking and the crackle of the fire the only sounds in the room. The seconds passed, and the appointed time came and went. Mama reached out with mystic senses far beyond those of even most of the magicians in the city. She felt the growing power of the magic as it touched certain people here and there, awakening long-slumbering commands buried deep within their genetic code, instructions dating back to a time of ancient legend. Although the confusion was spreading, the fear growing, she could feel the moment slipping away.

Where is my sacrifice? she wondered. Where is the moment that will imprint my stamp on these events, turning the tide of power and emotion to me?

There was nothing.

The viral bomb should have gone off by now. She

should have felt the shift in power. Could Gallow have betrayed her? No, that was impossible. She held the spirit in unbreakable bonds, her mastery of it complete. There was no way Gallow could have knowingly betrayed her, though it could have failed her somehow. If so, it would pay dearly for the opportunity it had cost her.

She rose stiffly from her chair and went closer to the fire. She traced her fingers through the warm, still air as she chanted words in a tongue that was ancient when the history of the world was still unwritten. She gazed into the fire.

"I bid thee, Talon's Hate," she called to her servant, using Gallow's true name to draw it to her. "Appear before me!"

She spread her arms wide as she completed the call, but again there was nothing save the crackle of the fire and the ticking of the clock. Gallow did not appear or answer her call.

Destroyed, Mama thought. The only way Gallow would not appear was because someone had destroyed it. Someone who knew its true name, for that was the only way to demolish such a spirit.

"Destroyed!" she shrieked, knocking the clock off the mantel. It flew to the stone floor, where it shattered, scattering tiny gears and springs with a pitiful pinging noise.

She had planned so carefully, foreseen everything about this moment for so long! Gallow must have fallen into the hands of its summoner, the mage named Talon. Mama had underestimated him, but she would not make that mistake again.

"Oh, no," she murmured. "I'll deal with you, little mage, and I'll make you wish you'd never been born."

A stick cracked in the fire, and the flames flared up, glowing brightly at their center.

Gallow? she thought as she sensed a presence in the flames. But it wasn't the fire spirit. It was something, someone, else. The flames leapt up, and a form emerged from them, glowing brightly with a light that was painful to look at. Mama shielded her dark eyes with one bony hand as she squinted at the familiar face of the spirit that appeared before her.

"No, this can't be!" she said.

"It is," said the spirit of Jason Vale. "You've made your bid, and you've failed. Those souls you imprisoned are free, and many other spirits have come to this plane with the passage of the comet. Most will remain, and the living will have to deal with them in the fullness of time. Others of us are ready to move on once we have completed one final task."

"Arrogant pup!" Mama said, shaking her walking stick at him. "You think to dictate to me? Do you know who I am?"

"Yes, I do now," Jase returned. "The time for your vengeance is long past. You no longer have a place in this world. You are of the last world, Mama Iaga, and I have come to take you home."

"Pfah! You do not command me! Back to your cage, boy!" She pointed the head of her stick at Jase and uttered harsh, gutteral words. Then her eyes widened in surprise and fear when nothing happened.

"My . . . my power!"

"Is no more," Jase said. "You made your bid for power, and you failed. Now the time has come to put an end to this."

The flames in the hearth flickered, and Mama could see shapes moving among the shadows all around her. They slipped toward her, dark and silent.

"No!" she cried. "I will not be denied!"

The shadows rose up all around her, and Mama could see their eyes, glowing faintly in the light cast by Jason.

"Nooooo!" she cried out as the shadows reached for her. They dragged her, kicking and screaming, toward the fire. Her cane fell forgotten to the floor as the shadows contracted.

"Be grateful that you have a chance for the peace you denied others," Jason said. "If it were up to me, I would not be so merciful."

Her only reply was an inarticulate shriek as the shadows drew her into the fire. Then Jase, too, faded away, the light around him slowly dying out.

The flames in the hearth exploded outward with a sound like a scream torn from the depths of the soul. The flames roared through the underground lair like a purifying torch, reducing everything within it to blackened ash, scouring the walls and floor clean of the taint that had built up there and even partially melting the great metal door that led into Mama Iaga's domain.

By the time her loyal servants managed to pry open the door and dared to go inside, all they found was blackened and empty rooms filled with scattered ashes and the silence of a tomb.

*   *   *

The next night, Talon stood with Boom in the alley outside the Avalon nightclub and watched a dark limousine pull up, the glare from its headlights blinding in the darkness. A man got out, silhouetted in the harsh halon glare. He walked toward Talon and Boom, then stopped a short distance away. The two shadowrunners moved forward to meet him.

It was Gabriel, the Seraphim agent they had first encountered on the Cross Technologies tilt-rotor. He wore a dark trench coat, no doubt lined with armor and concealing more than one weapon. His blond hair was immaculately groomed, and he wore dark sunglasses despite the lateness of the hour. Talon had no doubt that Gabriel's eyes were able to adapt to any darkness.

"You have the item?" Gabriel asked.

Boom produced a bulging backpack and held it up, causing Gabriel to raise one pale eyebrow above the edge of his shades. The pack was vibrant purple and was covered with pictures of cartoon characters. Tied all around with colorful ribbon, it was clearly intended for a young girl. When Boom had first shown it to Talon, he explained that nobody would suspect that such a silly container could hold a vital corporate secret. Talon had to agree, and the look on Gabriel's face was priceless.

"You have the payment we agreed upon?" Boom asked.

Gabriel reached slowly into the breast pocket of his coat and produced a slim plastic wand. He held it out in one hand and reached out to take the bag with the other. After the items changed hands, Boom scanned the contents of the credstick while Gabriel unzipped the pack to look inside. He seemed satisfied with the contents and zipped it back up. When Boom also indicated satisfaction with the payment, Gabriel picked up the pack and hung it over one shoulder. Talon did his best to keep from chuckling at the sight.

"I hope we don't meet again," Gabriel said coolly as he turned back toward the car.

"Pleasure doing business with you," Boom replied cheerily. "Merry Christmas!"

They watched as Gabriel placed the pack in the trunk of the car and then got back into the limo. The driver backed the car out of the alley, then drove off into the moonlit night.

Talon and Boom returned to Boom's office, where Roy Kilaro was waiting.

"We could have cut a deal to get you back in with the corp, you know," Talon said. "Recovering the virus and all the data probably would have earned you some serious brownie points, maybe even gotten you a promotion or a chance to work for the Seraphim."

Kilaro shook his head. "I don't think so. I've had a taste of how the corp really works, and I don't think I want to go back to that. Besides, they'd never trust me again. They'd be much better off making sure I never get the chance to do anything with what I know. Right now, that information will keep me safe, since Cross would rather just forget all about me. I think it's best for Roy Kilaro to remain among the missing." He smiled a bit. "Kilroy, on the other hand . . ."

Trouble was leaning casually against the wall, arms crossed over her chest. "I like how he thinks. He's got potential," she said. "He handled most of it himself when we went into the Cross system to delete his records and other information. And I thought it was a nice touch to have the company set aside that offshore trust fund to take care of rehab for Dan Otabi and anyone else in the company with a simsense problem. The press release that went out to the newsnets means Cross isn't likely to renege. You know, with some practice and a real cyberdeck, this boy could kick some butt in the Matrix."

"If Trouble thinks you've got what it takes, that's good enough for me," Talon said. "We could use another decker from time to time—if you'd be interested, that is."

Kilroy smiled. "I'd be honored."

"An' I know lotsa folks looking for good Matrix talent," Boom said, "so I can keep you busy for as long as you want. You're gonna need the cred to start building your new toys. Trouble's got expensive tastes. Better start making out next year's Christmas list right now!"

They celebrated quietly that night, though things were still plenty interesting that Christmas of the year 2061—the spectral dragon appearing through the rift in DeeCee and the wave of changes spreading across the world like ripples from a pond. The science-types were calling it SURGE, "Sudden Recessive Genetic Expression." To most people it was another wave of "goblinization," though different from the day nearly forty years before when people began transforming into orks and trolls. Some of the newly changed people developed strange physical traits, and some were affected in other ways.

Val was one of those. Though physically unchanged, Doc still declared her affected by the SURGE.

"I had to remove her cybernetic optical implants," he explained. "It was the most amazing thing. Her biological eyes were actually regenerating somehow. The only explanation I can come up with is magic. Physically, she's in perfect heath, so I'm releasing her."

Val's eyes were moist with tears as she greeted her friends. The cool blue of her old cybernetic eyes had reverted to the warm brown of the ones she was born with.

"I've got part of it back," she said to Talon in an awed tone.

"Back?" he asked.

"My magic. I've got part of it back, at least a little."

Talon's eyes widened in wonder. She'd lost her magical gifts years before through the abuse of sims and the implantation of cyberware. She laughed and nodded at his look of surprise. "It's true," she said. "I can see again, I mean really see."

Talon hugged her and congratulated her. He promised to start immediately to teach her how to control her newfound sight and to understand what she saw. Val wasn't afraid of it any longer, just as the guidance of a wonderful and kind man had taught Talon not to fear his abilities.

These days, the memory of Jase brought a flood of warmth instead of their old stab of pain. In many ways, Talon too was able to see again. Meeting with Jase one last time had given him a chance to do what had been impossible before, to really say good-bye.

ABOUT THE AUTHOR

The Burning Time is Steve Kenson's fourth novel
set in the Shadowrun® universe. He is also known
to fans of Shadowrun® as the author of numerous
game books like *Portfolio of a Dragon, New Seattle,* and *Underworld.* He's been involved with
Shadowrun® since the game first appeared in
1989, and the character of Talon was created
shortly thereafter. Steve lives in New Hampshire,
and readers and fans of Shadowrun® can reach
him via e-mail at *talonmail@aol.com.*